The Pastor

The Pastor

Ed Treat

Library of Congress Control Number:		2018900655
ISBN:	Hardcover	978-1-5434-7905-8
	Softcover	978-1-5434-7904-1
	eBook	978-1-5434-7903-4

Print information available on the last page.

Rev. date: 02/22/2018

To order additional copies of this book, contact:
Xlibris
1-888-795-4274
www.Xlibris.com
Orders@Xlibris.com
766271

ACKNOWLEDGEMENTS

IT'S AMAZING HOW many people it takes to write a book. First my wife, Karen, and family, Jo, Grette, Charlie, Jasper—and Clara our dog, who support me and love me always and keep me going. I owe an enormous debt of gratitude to Rev. Al and Hildred Dungan who made it possible for me to get away long enough to begin this project. Thank you to the members of Transfiguration Lutheran Church in Bloomington, Minnesota, whom I serve and who allow this to be a part of my ministry. To Louise and Jerry Olson who provided such careful and capable copy editing for free. Great thanks to the best editor in the world, Maria D'Marco at Reedsy for her amazing eyeballs and brains and her willingness to call me an idiot, in the nicest way of course. She pulled my story out of the crapper. Mostly to the Maker of this universe who loves us all so much. I don't know why that is, but I sure am glad for it.

To my love, The Rev. Karen.

PROLOGUE

CANDY VINTER SPENT that whole day in her bedroom closet. Her head was completely bald. She never wore the itchy wig at home even though she hated looking at her shiny white scalp. *Cue ball, alien, devil* is what she thought whenever she looked in the mirror, razor in hand.

Everyone loved Candy Vinter. Everyone, that is, except her husband and two children who knew her too well. She couldn't hide from them and despised them for knowing who she really was.

Her husband and two children wouldn't be home until much later though, so she would be alone in her closet for many hours yet.

Her pretty blue eyes were wide open, blank and staring straight ahead, as they had been since late the night before. The rope tied around the metal wall hook, meant for her robe, was also around her neck. Hours ago, it had squeezed the breath from her, leaving her hanging lifeless, slumped against the closet door, her bottom hovering just inches above the floor.

CHAPTER 1

PASTOR BRIAN MATTERSON was lost in thought as he sat in his weekly Alcoholics Anonymous meeting. The topic was "gratitude," but he wasn't feeling grateful at the moment. As members took turns droning on, he half-listened while staring out the window at the Caribou Coffee Café across the street. His gaze drifted to the leafless, lifeless trees lining the boulevard and thought of the tree across the street from his office, where a shredded plastic Target bag had been snared in its branches. Lately, he had taken to watching the tattered thing as incessant gusty winds tugged and jerked at it, trying to rip it loose.

The bag, what was left of it, refused to let go.

I know what that's like, he often thought to himself.

Winter should have been gone long ago. Cars zipping by the meeting hall all wore the same coating of dirty gray salt. It was five below zero and wind was whipping up fragments of dry broken leaves and bits of garbage. Everywhere he looked it was bleak, which was exactly how he felt. He was aching for spring to come. He believed in the hope of springtime. He clung to it like the bag in a tree.

Words of grateful alcoholics buzzed around him, but Pastor Brian was oblivious, deep in his existential funk. Ensnared in his reflections, he thought about life, as he too often did—what did it all mean? *I know I should be grateful right now*, he thought, *but why don't I feel grateful?* For Brian, gratitude was a fleeting thing, something he had to continually strive for through his program of recovery from alcoholism.

Had he been paying closer attention to his life patterns he would have recognized that whenever he fell into this type of funk, interesting things happened.

It never failed.

On this day, though, "interesting things" would prove to be an understatement.

When the meeting concluded, it occurred to him he actually felt grateful he didn't have to share about gratitude at the meeting and a wry grin crept across his face.

Driving back to his church and parsonage in Martin Valley his mind turned, as always, to all the problems facing him. Martin Valley, a mature second-ring Minneapolis suburb, was slowly transitioning from aging single-home residences to starter homes and lower-income families. His congregation was aging too and generally the very few new families joining the church did not tend to be people with great means to support the church. Consequently, the congregation was fighting a long, slow battle of attrition. It was a common inner-ring suburb church issue and generally the story of too many mainline congregations in recent years.

His church, All Saints Lutheran, was declining physically too and there was little money to fix it. Worship attendance was fading, slowly but surely. While most mainline churches faced this problem, it was still hard not to take it personally. Vocal groups of churlish people, people who don't like their pastor, would amplify every little negative issue, laying them at the pastor's feet, making the issues feel very personal. These groups exist in every church, and even the best pastors can be vulnerable to them given the right circumstances.

How many stories had he heard of good pastors harassed out of their church? He figured his turn was bound to come along eventually.

He thought about the bag in the tree.

Suddenly, a song blasted through the car audio system.

I'm gonna pop some tags
Only got twenty dollars in my pocket
I-I-I'm hunting, looking for a come-up . . .

It was his phone. His eldest son, Robert, took great pleasure in nabbing his phone whenever he could and changing his ringtone. Young Robert relished hearing about the awkward situations this created for his pastor father.

Pushing the telephone icon button on his steering wheel, he said, "Hello, this is Pastor Matterson."

"Hi, Pastor Matterson, this is Andy Mosely, do you remember me?" The voice came through in stereo.

"Yes, of course. Hi, Andy, how are you?" His mind scrambled. *Andy Mosely, Andy Mosely, how do I know that name?*

"I was wondering when my fiancée and I could come in for a visit, um, to talk about our wedding. Would you have time in the next week or so?"

Oh, yes, that Andy Mosely.

He hated that he couldn't always keep track of all his people, but in this case at least, Andy wasn't technically one of his flock. He and his fiancée were just looking to get married at Brian's church.

"Yes, I would be glad to meet with you, but I'm in my car right now and I can't check my calendar. Could you email me with the times and dates that would work best for you and then we can go from there?"

"Yes, I can do that today. I have your email."

"I'll look for it. See you soon."

"Thank you, Pastor," Andy said and hung up.

Marriage counseling was just one of many mundane things in the life of a pastor and definitely not what would make this particular day "interesting."

As Brian pulled into the church parking lot, Aksel Erickson, the church maintenance volunteer, was waiting for him. Aksel was a retired, stoic Swede, and a widower, who had spent his life as a contractor in home construction. Tall, lanky, and made of solid muscle from a life of hard labor, Erickson was a precious asset. The church thrived on volunteers like Erickson, who give so much of their time and expertise to keep the church running without expecting anything in return.

Erickson approached the car, nodding, a shoulder turned to the wind, much like a hawk effortlessly stabilizing his flight.

"Well, good morning, Aksel. How are you today?" Brian stepped from his aging Honda Civic into the freezing wind. "What are you up to?"

"Well, I'm looking at the roof, Pastor, and it seems we have a leak."

"I had heard about that. You're talking about in the nursery, right?"

Another brutal, frigid gust buffeted them. Erickson, in a jacket but no hat or gloves, seemed completely unfazed by the conditions. *He could stand there all day I bet.*

Brian's eyes watered from the cold air as he hunched over, his back to the wind to ward off the biting cold. He just wanted to get inside.

"Yep, for starters," Aksel said. "The rubber membrane has a crack and is letting water down into the nursery. Jennifer complained about it this morning after yesterday's brief snowmelt. It's a pretty good leak. We are going to have to fix it right away."

"Okay . . .," Brian said. "What's a rubber membrane again?"

Erickson smiled. "That's that solid rubber coating on the roof that keeps water out of the church, Pastor. If it cracks or tears, water comes in."

Brian could tell by Aksel's expression and response that he enjoyed "educating" the pastor.

"Okay. What's that going to take?" Brian wished Aksel would wait for him outside his office like normal people and not ambush him in the parking lot all the time.

"Well, I'm not sure. We will have to get someone out to look at it. Should I call someone?"

"Do we have a choice?"

"Well, no, not really."

"So, yes, call someone and find out what it will take. Any idea what we are looking at?"

Brian started to make his move for the protection of the church, but Aksel seemed to sense his retreat and edged over to cut him off.

"Well, if it's just a crack in one place, then they can patch it and that wouldn't be so bad. But if there are lots of other cracks, we could be looking at a whole roofing project. That could get pretty expensive. It's going to be hard to assess with snow still up there, but if I had to guess, I would say that's probably what we're going to end up having to do."

Brian didn't want to hear this. He already had too many other pressing issues and didn't need a huge financial challenge on top of everything else.

It just never seemed to end.

"What's the worst-case scenario?"

"Well, if they have to put a whole new roof on the church that could run up to twenty thousand, or even more."

Brian cringed. "Let's hope we can get away with the patches. How much for a patch?"

"A whole lot less, but I'm betting it's going to be the whole roof," Aksel said, then turned into the wind and trudged away.

Brian lurched toward the church. As he neared the door, a church member stepped out of the church and approached him.

"Morning, Pastor."

Arvid Jesperssen was all smiles, bundled in a heavy winter coat, hat, and gloves.

Brian was envious. Even after twenty years in Minnesota, he still hadn't learned how to dress for winter and always underestimated the cold. He assumed it was some kind of denial.

At this moment, he realized he could no longer feel his toes.

"We had such a good Bible study this morning, Pastor. There were six of us. We talked about Paul and his conversion. Did you know Paul used to be a Pharisee before he became a Christian?"

"Yes, I was aware of that . . ."

"Ya, it was his job to get rid of the Christians. That was his job. He was throwing them in prison and everything. Then, he was going off to some city to get rid of some more Christians when Jesus spoke to him and made him blind and knocked him off his horse and made him a Christian. It's a great story."

"Yes, it's quite a story." Brian nodded, eyeing the church door. So close . . . "I really need to get inside, Arvid."

"How come you never preach about that, Pastor? Only a few of us had ever heard that story before. Everyone should hear that story, don't you think?"

"Well, yes," Brian said, marveling at how little people knew about the Bible. It continually surprised him.

"Maybe I'll preach on that this Sunday," he added. "I've really got to get inside now, Arvid. I'm freezing out here." His ears were starting to burn.

"Oh, sorry, Pastor. Just one more thing. We didn't know if Paul was married or not. Do you know if he was married or not? Did he have a wife?"

Flustered, Brian said, "Nobody knows for sure, Arvid. It doesn't really say, but Pharisees were usually expected to be married, so a lot of people think he probably either was or had been. Now, can I go please?" He pulled away from Arvid and made for the door, desperate now. However, as he did so, three men from Arvid's study group came out and approached Brian, cutting off his retreat.

"Good morning, Pastor," they said in near unison, standing between the pastor and the warm church inside.

"Good morning, guys," Brian said, intending to squeeze through them, but they closed ranks and blocked his way.

"We have some questions about the Bible lesson we studied today," said one of the men.

"That's fine, guys, but can we just step inside, please?"

"It'll just take a sec," one said. "Why was Paul struck blind by the Lord? We argued about that for a long time this morning. Did God blind him to teach him a lesson or was it to punish him for the way he was treating Christians? Or maybe it was just to get his attention?"

Brian looked up at the men and he immediately knew by the looks on their faces they were up to something.

"What's going on here, guys?" Brian said, noting that the men wore Cheshire cat grins on their faces. He turned and saw Arvid and Aksel both looking on with great mirth.

They were trying to freeze him to death.

"Okay, guys, very funny," he said, pushing through the men as they broke out in laughter. "You realize that you can end up in hell for torturing a pastor, don't you?"

"But, Pastor, you taught us we just have to say we're sorry . . . and we're sorry," one of the men replied.

"You're sorry all right," Brian said, almost inside. "You're going to be sorry too. I have some connections in high places and I'm going to call in a few favors just for you guys." He squeezed through the church door into safety, then looked back at the men, all of them yucking it up.

Brian smiled, grateful for the men of his church who loved him enough to want to kill him and then laugh when they came close.

Brian had been the victim of these kinds of pranks his whole career, his whole life in fact. He loved playfully teasing people and got it back as much as he gave. As a boy his friends called him "Brain Matter," a play on his name, because he was such an exceptional student. He had one teacher who loved to say, "What's the *matter, son?*" whenever he got something wrong, which was seldom.

Now here he was, a fifty-year-old man married with two kids, slightly balding, and a growing midsection he fought constantly with little success. He had three post-graduate degrees; he was a parish pastor of a midsized congregation, and he was still getting hazed regularly.

The church secretary, Maureen, was there to greet him as he came in.

Maureen, in her mid-sixties was the iconic church lady. Frumpy, hairstyle stuck in the fifties, horn-rimmed glasses, floral print dresses, and an ample bosom. She had been at the church her whole life and knew more about it than anyone. If she was for or against something, she would pull all the right levers to get what she wanted. She was not to be trifled with.

There were plenty of times Brian fantasized about ways to move her out of the job or get her to retire, but that was a political hot potato that could end up in a church schism if it went sideways. Truth be told, he would be lost without her. Despite his many frustrations with her, he was grateful for how hard she worked and how much she cared. He did his best to work around Maureen.

"Did you know anything about what just happened out there?" he asked, wondering just how far the plot freeze him to death extended.

"What are you talking about? What happened out there?" she said, seemingly genuinely perplexed.

"Nothing, never mind. Good morning, Maureen."

"Good morning," she said. "I have some messages for you. And also, the women's group was in this morning wondering why you don't ever have coffee with them. I said I would suggest it to you. Also, Heather called this morning and said the sound system is still shutting down whenever she practices. She is worried it's going to happen during a service and she really needs to be sure that won't happen. She wants you to call her."

Brian sighed. *Okay, Lord, keep piling on; I'm just a bag in the wind.* "I thought that was fixed already?"

"It was, twice. It's still happening."

"How much have we paid to have that thing fixed so far?" he asked, trying not to sound overly annoyed.

"I don't know. You can ask Beki."

Beki was the financial manager for the church. Every dime of the church's money was kept under her watchful eye and tight fist. She was also a lifelong member of the church.

"Would you call her and ask her? Is there someone who can follow up and find out why their repairs aren't fixing the problem? This is crazy. We shouldn't have to keep paying for this." He had lost his struggle with exasperation and now sounded thoroughly annoyed.

"You don't have to tell me," Maureen said, "but I can't call them. I've got bulletins to get done today and I haven't even finished the newsletter. I'm still waiting for your article, by the way."

Brian groaned inwardly and made his way back to his office. He had other plans for the day, but as usual those were going out the window. He wondered how it ever became his responsibility to make sure the sound system was working.

Agitated, Brian took off his jacket and flung in over a chair instead of hanging it as he normally would. He hurried to the heat register in the corner of his office and cranked it to full blast. He stood there with his toes and ears burning, rubbing his hands together over the warm air pouring out, grateful the boilers were still working, though not for long he was warned.

Brian's office was tucked into the corner of the education wing of the church building off the main entrance. His office sat immediately behind the reception area and Maureen's office. His was the only office with a window. Congregations tend to cut corners on comfort and quality, especially when it comes to the administrative areas of the church, areas where the members seldom ever figure to go.

The room was a twelve-by-fifteen-foot space filled with office basics. His extensive education made his wall-to-wall, floor-to-ceiling bookshelves hang heavy with reading materials ranging from history, theology, and doctrine, to sermon resources and books on Christian practice, leadership, youth ministry, and church growth. Brian's small desk, buried under stacks of books and piles of project papers, was tucked under the single north-facing window from where he could see out to his home and lawn connecting the church with his house, a lawn he shared with the church and his family. Then there was the full-grown pear tree he had planted years ago (because he had always wanted a parsonage and a pear tree). Across the street was the tree with the plastic bag caught in its branches.

Once sufficiently warmed and he could feel his fingers again Brian sat his desk and began shoveling the pile. He thumbed through his cell phone directory looking for the repair service number and called. He listened to the phone ring several times before going to voice mail. In times like this, he wanted to rant, rave, and let off some steam. However, he was a pastor, and pastors aren't supposed to get angry, so he left a polite but urgent message regarding the repairs that didn't work, again!

He then began listing calls from his voicemail and comparing them to the notes Maureen had given him and prioritized them. There were always calls he wouldn't return, like calls from salespeople and other solicitors. Then there was the constant barrage of people scamming churches with their sob stories. It was hard to know who was genuine and who was not. Early in his ministry he responded to all these calls and found most of them were people working every church and charity in town trying to scheme as much money as they could. After a while, Brian decided he didn't have the time or energy to keep up and so didn't try anymore, although not without some guilt for those with a genuine need.

His first callback was to a distraught mother whose son didn't want to have his faith confirmed in the upcoming confirmation service.

"Hi, Connie and Del, this is Pastor Matterson. I got your message and I share your concern. However, Jeffrey's hesitation to be confirmed is not unusual. Students who have doubts almost always keep it to themselves until the last minute. I'm hopeful Jeffrey and I can have a conversation about this. Please let me know when he can meet. In the meantime, have Jeffrey write down two or three things that bother him the most. I look forward to meeting with him. I will be praying for you."

A leaking roof, members who try to freeze you do death, no money, a difficult secretary, constant repairs, a rebellious youth–typical daily challenges for any pastor, not things that would make this an "interesting" day.

CHAPTER 2

BRIAN WAS ABOUT to make his next call when someone rapidly knocked on his door.

"Come in!" he yelled, barely keeping the irritation from his voice.

Sue Solberg, the parish worker, entered. She was pale and appeared to have been crying, her eyes looking puffy and red.

Brian began to rise from his chair, but she waved him down as she sat in the chair in front of his desk.

"Sue! My goodness . . . what's got you so upset?"

"I'm really sorry to bother you, Pastor, but something's happened."

He noticed then that she was shaking, her hands trembling as she straightened her skirt.

"Please, tell me, Sue, I've never seen you like this–"

She stood suddenly, wavering a bit and touching the desktop with her fingertips.

"I don't think I can sit right now, I'm just too upset."

Brian left his chair and circled the desk, saying, "What *is* it, Sue . . . please, tell me."

"Well . . .," she whispered, but tears welled in her eyes. She folded her arms and shook.

He stepped to her side and gave her a reassuring hug. Sue folded her arms to her chest, sobbing, and leaned into him like a woeful child.

Then she choked out the words, "Candy Vinter has committed suicide."

An enormous silence followed, and then Sue expelled the breath she had been holding and her quiet weeping filled the room.

Brian stood there, his body rigid with the news. He couldn't quite comprehend it.

Candy Vinter? Candy *Vinter*? It just wasn't possible. Candy wouldn't commit suicide. Candy Vinter was one of the most beloved members of the church and the community. She was known by everyone and loved by everyone. She was involved in every kind of service, was at church every week, and always had a smile and a spirit of joy about her. How was it possible that she would take her own life?

Brian's mind reeled. "Are you sure?" was all he could think to say, as Sue's tears soaked his shoulder.

She nodded, but was still crying too hard to say anything. Brian held her, let her cry, soothed her as if she was a baby.

"It's okay, don't hold it back, let it out . . ."

He felt he should be crying too, but knew he would later. Right now, he was too stunned to react with grief, too unbelieving to allow tears.

This can't be true.

As Sue cried herself out he held her awkwardly until she suddenly felt self-conscious and pulled away, embarrassed by her uncontrolled emotion and the imposition of what her weeping had done to the pastor's shirt. He guided her into one of two comfortable visitor chairs across from his desk and he sat in the other one, their knees touching.

"Tell me what you know," Brian said gently as he handed her a box of Kleenex

"I don't know much. Just that one of the neighbors called Jonelle when they saw the paramedics and the police there. When they saw the county coroner's car, they asked one of the medics what was happening. He told her the mother took her own life, but didn't say anything else. I wondered if they meant Candy's mom, or Mick's, but Jonelle said no, they were sure it was Candy they were talking about. This person called some friends, including Jonelle, so she called me right away to tell me to put the Vinters on the prayer chain." Sue's words had tumbled out, rapid-fire, as she wiped her eyes and nose, and when finished, she started crying again.

Brian suddenly felt light-headed and his gut churned. His world had just been transformed. He had been through suicide more than once. As a pastor, he knew he would need to deal with his own emotions, but also would bear the emotions of the whole community as they went through this together. People would look to him to make sense of a senseless loss. Yet it was something he could make very little sense of. He would feel pressure to have answers, when he would have just as many questions.

He again prayed for help and strength.

Sue had wiped her eyes and regained something close to her usual composure.

Brian said, "Well, first things first. Let's pray."

He took Sue's hands and, bowing their heads, they shared a prayer.

"Dear Lord, we are overwhelmed by this news. How can it be true? We don't know what's going on here, but if Candy did take her life, forgive us for not knowing she was in pain and for not knowing how to intercede before this. We lament this loss so deeply that there are no words. How, Lord, how could this be?

"Now, Lord, guide us as we attend to the family and the community and our congregation. They will want to know what this means and we don't know what to tell them. We need your help. Please be with us as you promised you would. Give us the firm and bold confidence to know that Candy is with you now and will be forever, and that she is free from whatever terrible pain drove her to this desperate act. We know we shall see her again with you. But in the meantime, her husband . . ."

Brian went silent as he wracked his brain for Candy's husband's name.

Sue came to his rescue. "Mickey . . ."

"Mickey. Mickey needs your extra help. Both he and the children need you. Give them comfort. Help them believe in you and your promises. Help all of us to make peace with this, to heal, and give us always the appropriate words to share with them."

He was silent for a moment, searching his soul for any other thoughts, listening to anything God might have to say. Sue took the silence as an invitation that the pastor expected her to say a few words.

Sue prayed with people every day all day long and was very good at it, but she always felt self-conscious praying with the pastor.

"Gracious God," she began tentatively, "give us your strength and peace. Bless Mickey, Kyle, and Hannah as they go through this difficult time. Help us as we minister to them with your love."

She paused, not knowing what else to say but feeling that wasn't enough. Before she could add any more, Brian concluded the prayer.

"Lord, without your promise of hope and life after death, something like this would leave us in a pit of despair, but even in these darkest moments we can know that something good will come from this. Help us to carry forth with confidence and trust, in Jesus's name we pray. Amen."

Brian let go of Sue's hands.

"Well, I need to get over there," Brian said as he grabbed his jacket and headed for the door. "Please, Sue, send out a prayer chain request for the Vinter family . . ." He paused. "But don't give any details until we know for sure what's going on." A false report about something like this would be bad.

As he went out the door, he said, "I will call you when I am on my way back. I need you to pull everyone together for a meeting. We need to think through all the ways we will need to deal with this."

CHAPTER 3

AFTER GETTING THE Vinters' address from his phone, along with directions, Brian took off, trying to recall all he knew about the family. Candy was a longtime member of the church. Brian had baptized her children, Kyle and Hannah, now fourteen and eleven. Her husband, Mickey, was a blue-collar guy, who didn't seem to have much love for the church. He came once in a while with his family, and would show up for those things like baptismal instruction, confirmation service, Christmas, and Easter, but Pastor Brian could always tell that it was painful to Mickey to have to be there. He seemed to simply endure it.

He remembered Candy worked for the Martin Valley Police Department, in accounting. Over the years, she had suffered with one health issue after another. She seemed to be one of those poor unfortunates afflicted with far more than her share of challenges.

Brian often wondered why some people seemed to be given far more than others. He didn't think God dished these things out, which would be repugnant. Who in their right mind could believe in a God who would micromanage such things? Chance was the culprit, more than anything else. He believed life wasn't about what happened to you, but how you responded to the things that happened.

Candy was one who responded with grace, who seemed to take her health issues in stride. Over the years, she was diagnosed with diabetes, kidney disease, asthma, arthritis, and other things Brian couldn't remember or pronounce. Her latest challenge with breast cancer put her through chemo and radiation. She had lost all her hair, and the scarves she wore to church were striking reminders of her plight.

Perhaps this drove her to take her own life. That would make some sense at least.

Despite all her terrible challenges, she had always maintained a happy demeanor, not accepting sympathy or pity. Brian had marveled at her ability to bear such difficult burdens while working full-time, being a wife and mother, and giving of her time and energy in a hundred different ways.

How she coped did not seem humanly possible, which is why the thought of her taking her own life seemed so incongruous. But then again, it might also be part of the explanation.

Brian turned into the Vinters' neighborhood, a lower middle-class neighborhood with decent but aging homes. Most were small and simple in design, harkening back to the bygone era of the fifties and sixties, when new neighborhoods popped up like mushrooms, with streets full of playing children. It had transitioned into a lower-income-area as growing families moved to larger homes in outlying suburbs. Older residents eventually passed away or moved to care centers, and lower-income families bought their homes.

Brian expected to spot the Vinters' house by all the cars that should be there. He had been to enough death scenes to know when someone dies, especially someone too young and well liked, people came in droves to bring food and support, and to remind the survivors, the family, that they were not alone.

However, as he rolled down the street, he saw no obvious collection of cars. Double-checking the address, he confirmed that he was indeed in the right place.

Moments later, he pulled up in front of the Vinter home, a basic one-story rambler. The yard was tidy and well groomed. All the shades were drawn, making the house look vacant. Only the two cars in the driveway, a sedan and a van that looked like a work vehicle, hinted that someone might be home. Brian remembered that Mickey was an HVAC specialist, heating and air conditioning, and did freelance and subcontracting work.

Brian stepped from the car, surveying the house and street again. Where was everyone? A suicide, especially involving a young woman like Candy, should have sparked a steady stream of well-wishers. Could his information about her death be wrong?

Hunkering over against the wind, he walked up the narrow concrete pathway to the door. Bracing himself with a quick prayer, "Help me, Lord," he pushed the doorbell.

He knew how important this moment was, since he was the pastor and the pastor represented God and the church—and if pastors didn't comport themselves properly, it could have negative consequences for years to come.

Brian's sister died when he was only fourteen, and even though his family was active and gave regularly to the church, the priest did not bother to come to the house. It was a source of resentment for Brian's mother, and the reason she and all his siblings left the church for good. They all scattered and continued for years to retell the story of the awfulness of the church. Brian didn't want anyone telling a story like that about him.

He pushed the doorbell again, and waited.

Nothing happened.

He didn't hear anyone moving about inside and wondered if they were all at a relative's house, or perhaps already at the funeral home, but that was unlikely. Then it occurred to him that the doorbell might be broken, so he knocked on the aluminum screen door. Shortly, he heard the lock turn and the door slowly opened.

It was Mickey. He peered at the pastor from behind the barely open door.

"Hi, Mickey. It's Pastor Matterson from All Saints. I just heard about what happened and I came right over. You all must be overwhelmed right now. May I come in?"

Mickey seemed to debate a moment about what to do, then reluctantly opened the door and let the pastor in.

This too was strange. In the more than one hundred death visits during his ministry, he had never encountered anything like this. Even the most antichurch people threw open their doors to the pastor when someone died. Deep grief usually knocked down normal walls of resistance, as people became engulfed in their pain.

Mickey opened the door, and as Brian stepped in Mickey backed away, positioning his body as if to block Brian from coming too far into the house. The apparently distraught young husband had a harrowed, haunted look about him. It was not grief as much as devastation. He said nothing and refused to meet Brian's eyes as they stood there.

Brian spoke first, filling the silence. "Can you tell me what happened, Mickey?"

"Would call me Mick, Pastor Matterson?"

"Yes, of course. I'm sorry."

"That's okay." Mick looked at the floor, and the awkward silence returned.

Brian repeated his question, his voice quiet, but firm. "Can you tell me what happened, Mick?"

Mick shifted from foot to foot, then shoved his hands into his pockets.

Brian took the opportunity of Mick's delaying to look around the house from where they stood in the foyer. He could see the kitchen through an opening on his left. To the right was the family room with fireplace, sofa, recliner, and large-screen television. No, not large, it was mammoth—way too big for the room. He could see gaming system controllers littering the floor in front of it.

Mick began slowly. "Well . . . yesterday . . . Kyle came home from school . . . and he found Candy. She had hung herself in her closet. He called 911. They came and took her down. Then they called me. I was at work."

Brian was astounded that Kyle, their fourteen-year-old son, had found his own mother dead.

"My God, how is Kyle doing? He must be devastated."

"Yeah, he was pretty shook up."

"And you, Mick, how are *you* doing?" Brian asked, leaning slightly toward Mick.

"Well, I'm trying to be strong for the kids," Mick said. "But it's hard."

"Of course, it is. I can't imagine anything harder. I feel so bad for you . . . everybody does," Brian said. "We are all just sick about it. You have many people who love you and care for you." Brian paused as Mick nodded blankly, then added, "Did you see this coming? Did she leave a note or anything?"

"Well, no. She didn't leave no note. I know she was having a hard time with her cancer and all. She was in a lot of pain, all the time—couldn't sleep. But I didn't see nothing like this coming. She never really talked to nobody about it. If it was this bad, she never said. I think she just kept it all inside her, didn't want nobody to worry about her."

Well, they are worrying now. "Do you have friends or family that can be with you?"

"Our family is kind of spread out all over the country. I've been calling them to let them know." Mick kept nodding, as though agreeing with himself, then continued, "They'll be here for the funeral."

Mick was fidgeting. His arms were crossed, he wouldn't meet Brian's eye, and he kept edging toward the door as if he was trying to herd Brian out. Mick took a half step toward the door and put his hand on the knob, and Brian got the hint that he wanted to wrap this up and let Brian be on his way. Normally, Brian would have expected to be there for a much longer conversation, usually after being ushered into the kitchen or living room, where family and friends surrounded the bereaved. There would be coffee and food, and everyone would look to him to provide comforting words that gave meaning to their loss.

Wondering aloud and ignoring Mick's body language, Brian asked, "Where is everybody?"

"What do you mean? The kids are in their rooms."

"I mean family, friends . . . neighbors? They usually come by . . . I know Candy knew a lot of people. Have they been supportive?"

"We've had a lot of people stop by, a whole lot . . ." As he spoke the doorbell rang. Stepping around the pastor, he looked through the peephole and then opened the door slightly. "Yeah?"

"Hi, my name is Dee." Brian could hear the visitor clearly. "I work with Candy. I heard the terrible news and just stopped by to tell you how sorry I am to hear about what happened."

"Thank you," Mick said. "I appreciate it." He made no move to open the door any further, and following an awkward silence, Dee said, "I brought you some brownies. I thought the kids might like them."

Mick again thanked her, and after another long pause the screen door squeaked. Brian assumed a pan of brownies was being conferred.

Again, Mick thanked her.

After another awkward pause, Dee got the message and said, "We will be praying for you."

Brian heard quick footsteps moving away as Mick slowly closed the door. He was mystified, but clearly understood that Mick wanted to be left alone, which left him thinking about his own exit. He didn't want to push himself on Mick, but was deeply concerned about how Mick and his family were coping with this loss. What he'd seen so far wasn't normal, or healthy.

Brian debated about what he should do, feeling like he had done all he could at this point.

Mick turned back to him, finally looking him in the eyes. Brian's visit was over.

Acquiescing, Brian said, "Mick, I won't stay if you don't want me to, but may we at least share a word of prayer?"

Mick hesitated, but then nodded.

Brian quietly asked, "Could we include the kids?"

Mick paused, then seemed to realize he had to give in.

"I'll go get them."

Brian expected Mick to at least usher him into the living room for the prayer, but he didn't. Instead, he simply said, "I'll be right back."

Mick dropped the brownies off in the kitchen, then went off to gather the kids.

When he returned with Kyle and Hannah, Brian saw that Kyle had the same hollow, haunted look as his father. Hannah's face was blotchy, and her eyes were red and swollen and yet had managed to put on the happy-go-lucky charming smile she always seemed to wear. She was clearly the only sunshine in this home. They gathered around the pastor, but only Hannah would meet his gaze.

"I just came to let you all know how sorry I am for your loss," he started. "I don't know why things like this have to happen, I just know they do. Terrible things happen in life and sometimes they don't make sense. This makes no sense. All I know is that your mother was in a lot more pain than any of us knew. I am guessing that she was so caring and loving that she didn't want her pain to be a burden for anyone."

Whatever pain she had just got multiplied and magnified tenfold and placed on these poor souls to bear for the rest of their lives.

"Are you guys going to be okay?" he asked them. They nodded, but Brian thought that they wouldn't be okay. Something was going on here. They weren't talking; they weren't looking at each other. It wasn't natural. The grief was real, but when someone dies the living come together and cling to each other. These people were withdrawing, pulling apart.

He was suddenly very sad for them, but also felt like crying or screaming at them. "I was fourteen when my sister died," he told them. "It was the hardest thing I ever experienced in life. Our family fell apart after that because we did not support each other. Don't let this pull you apart. You need each other." He looked at their faces for any sign of reaction, unsure that they were hearing him. "May I say a prayer?" he asked.

They all nodded and Brian reached out to hold hands. They formed a small circle there in the foyer. He began, "Dear Lord, a terrible thing has happened. The mother of this family has been suddenly and painfully ripped away from them. We don't know what she was going through but it must have been worse than any of us ever knew. We thank you that whatever pain she was feeling is now over. Her pain is gone, but she has left behind more pain than these whose hands I hold now have to share. Help them now and in the days ahead to endure the hardship that this is for them. Help them in the midst of this terrible darkness and pain so they can get through it and they can heal from it. Comfort them with the sure knowledge that Candy is now with you and free from any more pain. Comfort us all with the knowledge that when this life is over we will see her again and we will spend eternity in your presence experiencing joy and wonders beyond imagination. We know this is true because you have promised it through your Son, Jesus Christ, in whose name we pray, Amen."

Brian open his eyes and saw that Hannah had tears streaming down her face. Mick's face hadn't changed. His distant, haunted look was still locked in place. Kyle looked angry. His mouth was turned down and he looked like someone about to explode. He had already pulled his hands away, crossed his arms, and turned his body away from the circle. He seemed to be a boiling cauldron of emotion.

"It's important that you hold on to each other in the days ahead. Stay close and keep talking. Tell stories. Talk about Candy. It's important for the healing process. If you don't do it now, it will haunt you for years to come. Believe me, I speak from experience," Brian said.

They all nodded, seeming ready to pull away, anxious to get away from this uncomfortable situation despite the advice they had just agreed to.

Brian released their hands, which he had held through the prayer, and gave them a small smile. "I'll keep you in my prayers," he said, turning to Mick, which signaled that the kids could leave, and they did.

"Mick," Brian said, "you are the father and the leader of this family. You need to keep your family together. I am worried about what I see here. Your family will come apart if you don't help them get through this. Kyle is really having a hard time and needs help. Are you up for that?"

Mick nodded but would not look Brian in the eye, which to Brian meant Mick was not up for it. *What is going on with this guy?* He had never seen a man so disconnected.

"I want you to know that I will do anything I can to help you. If you need to see someone, a family therapist, or there is grief counseling available through the church. Whatever you need, okay?"

Mick nodded again and edged toward the door, seeming to want this visit to end.

Brian was overstaying his welcome, but he didn't care. This was an extreme situation and he needed to be pushy, but thought he had done all he could at this point.

"Mick," he said, "I will be in touch with you tomorrow and we can talk about funeral plans, okay?" Mick nodded. "In the meantime, get your kids together. Force them to talk about this. It's not good to close down. You need to talk. If you need me to help with that, I will. Okay, Mick?"

"I will, Pastor, I appreciate your help," he said as he pulled the door open.

CHAPTER 4

DRIVING BACK TO the church, Brian wondered what kinds of secrets were happening in that family. There was something not good going on there, a heavy darkness beyond the suicide; he could sense it. He also feared for what they might go through in the days, weeks, and even years to come if the grief they faced wasn't well handled. Unresolved grief didn't just go away. It festers and grows more powerful and comes out in all manners of unhealthy behavior. He didn't want that for this family, or anyone for that matter. He had come from a family of secrets and he recognized the signs. When Brian's own sister died, his family did not ever talk about it. Rather than deal with the pain, they all pulled apart. Brian eventually gravitated toward alcohol and drug-using friends, where his pain was medicated and personal feelings avoided—a place where his friends too came from families of hurt that did not talk. It took fifteen years of strife and substance abuse treatment before he properly addressed his grief over his sister's death and slowly got his life back.

Once back at the church the staff was anxious to hear details. They wanted to know what happened, how the family was, what they could tell people. They wanted to know when the funeral would be and how it would affect each of their schedules. Brian knew they wanted all this information, but he had little to give them. He was only able to tell them that yes, it was true, she had killed herself, that Kyle had found her and that they were all in a state of shock. They were nowhere ready to talk about funeral arrangements yet. This would be a big one. The whole community would be there. Up to 1,000 would come for visitation and another 500 for the funeral, Brian guessed. Lunch would be 300 or more.

Of all the things Brian did, helping people when someone dies was what he felt most called for and capable to do. That clarity of his calling came to him during his internship as a pastor at seminary. He had been serving a local parish and got asked to perform his first funeral ever. He had been very nervous and afraid. What an awesome and frightening thing to do, walk into the worst moment of someone's life and try to help them make sense of their loss and say something that will somehow make it better.

The service was beautiful and he gave a thoughtful, sincere, and meaningful sermon. After lunch, there was a procession to the graveyard for the burial. Brian rode in the hearse with the casket and was the first to arrive at the gravesite. As the funeral director waited by the back of the hearse for the family to arrive, Brian made his way down to the gravesite to pray and prepare his thoughts for the committal service. He would never forget that day.

It was freezing cold. A path cleared through the snow led to an area large enough for a small crowd around the grave. Six green velvet chairs sat in a neat row for the immediate family. A carpet of Astroturf covered the area next to the hole and over the fresh mound of dirt. The sky was cloudless and deep blue. There was no wind and his breath created billows of frosty clouds. He wore his black wool London Fog coat, gloves, earmuffs, and wool cap, and still was too cold. From where he stood by the open grave, he had a spectacular panorama of the Minneapolis skyline against the bright blue sky. At his feet was the raw, gaping grave.

As he stood praying, staring into the dark hole, Brian had a sudden and profound spiritual experience. It was an epiphany, a moment of surreal intensity. One moment he was staring into this grave, then suddenly saw it wasn't a grave at all. With a clarity that was as real as the day, he saw not a grave, but a doorway. On the other side of the passageway was eternal life, heaven, a place filled with light and wonder and awe.

Brian was both deeply shaken and overjoyed in that moment, which was gone as fast as it came, but he understood it was an incredible gift. God had given him a glimpse of . . . of what? What was it? A flashing glimpse of a hidden reality? He couldn't say, exactly, but his faith never wavered from that moment forward. It was real and he had seen it with his own eyes even if for the briefest moment. The miraculous image so clear and meaningful he could recall it in detail even all these years later. In that moment, he clearly understood his calling—to be God's doorman, to stand in the gap of that thin place between this world and the next.

Since that time, Brian clearly understood the good news of the Gospel. There is a God. God is real. Heaven is real. Life is short, beautiful, difficult, ugly, hard, but also wonderful, - and then, we die. However, that's not the end of the story. In some mysterious way, far beyond comprehending, there will be more.

In between funerals, Brian would fix plumbing and roof leaks and sound systems, try to figure out how to pay for things, baptize babies, teach adolescents the most important tenets of faith at a time in their lives when they were least interested, counsel couples and marry them, preach and lead worship, and do his best to keep his flock from turning on him and running him out of business.

It was a strange calling.

CHAPTER 5

B RIAN GOT TO his office and closed the door. He needed a minute to breathe. Hanging his jacket on the hook behind his door, he headed for his desk and got his laptop powered up. As he waited for the computer to boot up, he leaned back in his chair, put his feet on the desk, closed his eyes, and repeated the prayer that always helped him when things seemed the most impossible. "Let go and let God. Let go and let God. You can do all things through Christ who strengthens you."

When he opened his eyes, the first thing he noticed was the little red light flashing on his desk phone, which meant voicemail messages were waiting. Each flash was a message. He counted twelve. His eyes swiveled to the computer screen. Fifty-seven emails were waiting for him. Many of the fifty-seven would be junk, but beyond those, he would still have twenty to thirty left to read and respond to.

He wondered what people did before email. His congregation loved having direct access to him, and now with cell phones, emails, and texting they could reach him 24/7. Sighing, Brian briefly lamented the time he would spend responding to everyone, time he needed to complete the many other projects he had underway.

With a quick shake of his head, he smiled a bit ruefully and reached for the phone, preparing to dig in, when he heard someone try to open his door, followed by a knock.

"Come in," he said, forgetting the door was locked. "Hang on," he called out, and went to unlock the door.

Phil Barney, the building custodian, greeted Brian with a smile as the door swung open. Barney, as everyone called him, was in charge of the building. He was hardworking, efficient, and knew how to get things done. A twenty-year employee of the church, Barney was appreciated, but not loved by everyone. He didn't like to waste time and could be short-tempered and a little abrasive, especially if he thought someone was disrespecting the church. More than once the pastor had to talk with him about his behavior, especially toward the younger church members.

He also had the irritating habit of bringing way too many things to Brian's attention, a habit that seemed to hinge on him expecting things should be the way they were when he was young. He had a certain conviction that if we could just travel back in time fifty years and live like they did back then, the world would be the utopia that it had once been. Brian always marveled at how often people wanted to preserve a certain time in history and hold on to an idealized version of it.

Barney started to enter the room, but Brian moved in front of him, making it clear that he wasn't invited in.

Caught up short, Barney said, "I need to talk with you. Have you got a minute?"

"I am pretty buried right now, can it wait?" Brian asked, standing firm.

"Well, I don't think so. We have a problem with the coffeemaker in the kitchen," Barney said, clearly annoyed that Brian wasn't letting him come in.

"What's the problem?" Brian asked.

"Well, I think it's broke," Barney said.

"I assumed that's what you meant. What's wrong with it?" Brian said, inwardly sighing.

"Well, it looks like somebody poured water into it last night and it seems to be shorting out."

"What do you mean it seems to be shorting out? What's it doing, or not doing?" Brian said, and then added, "And why would somebody pour water into it? That's not how it works, right? It's already hooked up to water, isn't it?"

What next? I ask you, Lord, to take these burdens from me and you give more? What are you trying to do to me?

"They must not have known that. They must have thought it was one of those you have to pour water into it to make coffee. They lifted the lid right up and poured in a whole carafe of water right into the electronics. You're not supposed to do that. I don't know how they got that lid up either because it don't come up that easy."

So, what does this mean? Can we wait for the water to drain out, let it dry out, and see if it works again?"

"I suppose we could wait, but we have the kids doing a pancake feed this Sunday and they are gonna need coffee."

"What do you want to do? Is this something you can fix? What do you suggest we do?"

"Well, I could probably try, but it would take me a while. I would have to unhook it and take it apart and then get the manual and see if I can figure it out. It will probably need some parts and that could take a while to order."

Brian could tell Barney didn't want to do this and he knew if Barney didn't want to do something he would be very passive-aggressive. Brian could order him to try, but he knew Barney would elevate things to the point that he would get his way anyway. He would break something else in the coffeemaker, or find any number of ways to make the problem ten times bigger. He always had to pick his battles with Barney.

"What do you suggest we do?" Brian asked, which is where he should have started in the first place.

"I think we might need to call the service people and get this fixed right away," Barney said. For such an old-fashioned guy, Barney wasn't always so conservative when it came to spending the church's money, especially when it got him out of a job he didn't want to do.

"Any idea what this might cost?"

"No idea. We could get an estimate."

"I would expect an estimate. Call and find out what they think it will cost. Tell them what happened and see what they would charge to fix it. Compare that estimate with what a new one costs, and if it's close, we should consider getting a new one. Then maybe you could fix and sell the old one in your downtime to help pay for it."

Barney had not considered this option and Brian could tell he didn't like it. Barney was sure he had just gotten out of having to fix it and now it looked like that might still happen. Brian was kicking himself for telling Barney this option. He should have just told him to get the estimate. By revealing the possibility of Barney still fixing it, he allowed Barney to sabotage his efforts to find the most cost-effective solution. It looked like there would be no avoiding another costly expense to the church.

At every church Brian had served, finances were always at issue. Every congregation ran behind and every congregation wrung their hands with every monthly report and wondered if the sky would be falling soon. Every month Brian would have to calm everybody down and remind them to trust in God, remind them that this happens every month to every single congregation no matter how big or small. Finances were always the friction point.

"I will let you know what they say," Barney said, turning away and heading down the hall toward his office.

Brian had some hard choices to make. The plan for the day had been to focus on the Scripture for the coming week so that he could begin the process of formulating a sermon. He also needed to prepare the worship service so Maureen would have everything she needed for the bulletin. If he didn't do that, she would make him pay. So that's what he did.

He was about to start in on his sermon preparation, which involved looking up the Bible passages assigned for the coming Sunday, when Barney was at his door again.

"Pastor, you got a minute?" Barney said, opening the door without knocking.

"Barney, you have to knock. I might have been counseling someone. You just can't come in without knocking, okay?"

"I was on the phone in the front office and never saw anyone come in here, so I knew you were alone."

"That's beside the point, Barney. I could have been on the phone. Please, just knock before you come in. It's common courtesy." Brian tried not to be too harsh but wondered what it would finally take to get through to Barney.

"You want me to go out and knock?" Barney asked. He was serious.

"No, Barney. Next time. Every time. Knock before you go into someone's office, anyone's office. It's what people do. Now, what's up?"

"Well, I called the coffeemaker repair place and they said they wouldn't know what it would cost to fix until they come out and look at it. They charge $80 for trip charge and then $45 per hour for labor plus parts. We might have to wait for parts to be shipped and that could be another trip charge."

"Couldn't we just take it to them and save the trip charges?"

"Yeah, I asked them about that. They said because it's a built-in unit they wouldn't recommend that."

Brian thought about the giant funeral he had coming up and the youth breakfast, and realized they had little choice. They needed coffee. What is church without coffee?

"What's a new one cost?"

"Brand new, they're about eleven hundred," Barney said. "But we might find a used one on eBay."

"We don't want to deal with used. You never know what you are getting. We either fix this one or buy a new one. I'm only worried that if we pay for repairs and trip charges they will tell us we need a new one and we end up paying for trip charges, repair, and a new coffeemaker. But I can't believe the repair would cost eleven hundred, so I think we should just get it fixed."

"That seems right, Pastor. Should I call them?"

"Yes, Barney, please do, and let them know we need it done as soon as possible."

They might have to come up with a plan B for the funeral and fundraiser if they had to wait for parts. You can't gather Lutherans without coffee. At All Saints, coffee was considered a third sacrament.

CHAPTER 6

BARNEY LEFT AND Brian went back to studying the Scripture for the coming week, which included an exchange between Jesus and the Sadducees, who were confronting Jesus about life after death. The Sadducees didn't believe in life after death and presented Jesus with a scenario about a man who dies and leaves a wife behind. She ends up marrying his brother, who also dies, and she marries the next brother, and then the next, until she finally marries all seven brothers. They question Jesus about whose wife she will be in the afterlife, proposing this scenario as a way of mocking the whole concept of life after death and of heaven.

Jesus's response is a rebuke of their understanding of the afterlife and essentially affirms that heaven is indeed real. The flaw in their thinking, according to Jesus, is assuming heaven will be anything like life on earth. Marriage is not even a category to be concerned with in the life to come.

Brian thought this was an interesting passage, considering the suicide of Candy Vinter. Not about divorce and marriage, but of the certainty of heaven.

His thoughts once again drifted to Candy and the disturbing visit to Mick and the kids.

What was going on in that house?

The last time he dealt with a suicide was in his previous church, when a young high school boy hung himself in his room. In that case, he'd had to park nearly a block away because so many people showed up to support the family. Once at the door, he could barely get through the house. Those crowds remained for days.

He recalled the scene when the father of the boy showed up after returning from a flight. The crowd was already present when he arrived and had been anticipating his arrival. Brian watched as the father drove into the driveway packed full of people anxiously awaiting his arrival. The father got out of his car and everyone went quiet. The wife heard he was finally there and the crowd parted as she ran out of the house to embrace him. It was as though he had been holding it all in until that moment. With the crowd around them the husband and wife embraced in terrible tears and they melted to the ground holding each other. The crowd closed in around them, laying soothing hands on them and comforting them with their own tears and support. It was a profoundly moving moment, and so different from what he had seen at the Vinter home.

Many questions turned in Pastor Brian's mind. Why was there no note? What wife and mother of two known for her self-giving love would not leave a note of some kind? Why would she hang herself? She was being treated for cancer; she had access to all kinds of lethal medications. Surely, there was a far less violent and painful way to take her own life than hanging. Why would a mother leave herself in a place that one of her own kids could find her that way? Hadn't she thought of that? What mother wouldn't think of that no matter what her pain?

He tried to clear his mind of these thoughts and doubts, but they kept creeping back. Something was terribly off.

His intercom buzzed, jerking him out of these thoughts and back to the fact that he had calls and emails to return.

It was Maureen informing him Phil Mason was calling to ask him about the Vinters. She said they were starting to get calls about the tragedy, and so wanted to know what she should tell people.

"Tell Phil I can't talk right now and just tell him what I told you. Candy took her own life. We don't know anything beyond that and the funeral plans are pending. It's too soon. Please hold these calls. I don't have time for them right now. Just say we will announce details of the service when we have them. In the meantime, tell them to pray for the family."

"Okay, but I don't have time for 'these calls' either. I'm trying to finish the Sunday bulletins and newsletter and now it looks like I have a funeral bulletin to make and volunteers to get," she said.

"I know, Maureen. Just do the best you can. If it gets to be too much let the phone go to voice mail."

"I would never hear the end of that . . ."

"I know, just do what you can. That's all any of us can do. Thanks, Maureen, I really appreciate all you do."

"Okay, Pastor, thank you," she said and hung up, mollified for now.

Brian knew it was no good trying to focus on his sermon now, but was glad to know the topic was eternal life, life after death. He knew that under these circumstances this Sunday's message would be just as much a funeral message as the funeral would be. Candy's suicide would be on everyone's hearts and minds, and he would need to remind them of the hope we always have even when the unthinkable happens.

Brian's cell phone chirped to remind him he had an upcoming meeting. Checking his calendar, he realized his ministerial conference started in thirty minutes. Where was the day going? He was getting nowhere fast.

He listened to his voicemails, jotting down notes, then scanned his emails for any pressing emergencies and prepared to leave for the conference. The ministerial conference was a monthly gathering of local pastors from area congregations of many denominations. They gathered to talk about ministry in the area and explore ways to work together. It was a good thing, but everyone had their hands so full with their own congregations that actually doing something jointly was rarely possible. Nevertheless, it was good to stay connected with his colleagues and keep the relationships strong. He knew these relationships were important and needed the investment.

He grabbed his coat and let Maureen know he was out for a bit. She waved her hand without looking up from her computer screen, making it clear she was the busiest person in the world, and without a doubt, among the greatest martyrs who ever lived.

CHAPTER 7

BRIAN MADE HIS way once again out into the cold and blustery Minnesota afternoon and drove to the Presbyterian Church where the meeting was being held. He remembered his first meeting when he was new to the community. Walking in, many pastors had greeted him with the comment, "A Lutheran! We never get Lutherans!"

"Why is that?" he asked, but nobody could answer.

"Who knows? But we're glad you're here," one of them said.

The meeting, as usual, did not produce much of practical value, but sharing their mutual struggles, challenges, and prayers was always uplifting and powerful in its own way. When it was Brian's turn to share, he told about the suicide that had just occurred. Most of them understood this particular challenge and that he would not only be tending to the family and friends, but the whole community. The sermon for a suicide also needed to be crafted with special care. It was delicate work and everyone in the room commiserated with the challenge facing Pastor Matterson.

Brian asked the group what they thought of the circumstances of Candy's death, wondering if any of them had experienced anything like it. None of them had, but they were also puzzled by the description of the scene at the Vinters' home, and supported his feelings that, yes, it did seem strange. Pastor Beth Shermer, from United Church of Christ said, "I find it strange that she hung herself. Hanging is usually how men kill themselves. Women will normally cut their wrists or take pills. That seems very abnormal to me."

"I didn't think of that," Brian said. "Although I did wonder why, if she was being treated for cancer and had plenty of access to lethal doses of pills, she didn't go that route. It would have been simple and less violent and even could have been accidental. Hanging takes thought and intent and figuring out how to do it." He paused, then went on. "I don't understand anyone who hangs himself. It would be so violent and painful, almost vengeful."

Heads around the room nodded.

Brian appreciated their input, but more than that, just being able to share his concerns with people who understood these situations was especially helpful. He knew that only those in the ministry could fully appreciate the unique challenges he faced.

CHAPTER 8

BACK AT HIS office, Brian found more emails and phone calls waiting, many related to the Vinter family. People were concerned and wanted to know details. However, his highest priority was to get everything Maureen needed to her to keep her from falling into a martyrdom tailspin. This would include announcements and bulletin details regarding worship, including Scripture, prayers, liturgy, and hymns.

His day was passing too quickly. He still had so much to do, plus two more meetings to attend before the end of the day. The stewardship team meeting was at 6:00 p.m. and the foundation meeting at 7:30. These late meetings made him constantly lament not being home more. It felt like he was cheating himself and his kids out of a normal family routine. As much as he tried to make his family a priority, the demands of ministry were always squeezing him. He pushed back, but it was a relentless battle.

He understood this was the battle every parent faced in today's busy world, but also knew it should not be surrendered to under any circumstance. Brian believed that if your family wasn't the top priority in life, then you really didn't understand God's will. Martin Luther once said, "There is no greater calling in life than for a parent to raise their child well," or something to that effect. He couldn't recall the exact wording of the quote, but understood it and believed it. He did what he could to be the best husband and father he could be, but felt that too often he fell woefully short on that account.

* * *

Brian fell into bed exhausted that night but unable to sleep. His brain was racing over the details of Candy Vinter's suicide. *What was she thinking? What is going on in that family? How are they going to get through this?* From what Brian could see so far, they were heading for the rocks. They needed help and Brian knew he had the best chance to provide that, as it appeared there weren't many with access to the family.

He often found himself drawn by forces beyond his control into difficult situations. Candy Vinter's suicide was certainly one of them.

After his brain raced for far too long, Brian finally began praying. His mind became still, and before long he was sleeping peacefully. Brian loved to sleep, loved laying his head down at the end of the day. He would fall into bed as though he was falling into God's hands. He talked with God and felt especially close in those precious moments before sleep. He believed when he dreamed that he was as close to the heavenly presence as we get in this life. Sleep and dreams were his alone time with God.

Brian met his wife at seminary where she was a year ahead of him studying for the ministry. Brian spotted Donna his first day there, this cute, short, Norwegian blonde with a lovely figure. He was behind her in the communion line during chapel and couldn't take his eyes off her backside, which was not what a seminary student should be doing while taking Holy Communion, but he couldn't help it. She was like an angel. She later told him he had caught her eye as well. She noticed him requesting grape juice instead of wine for communion and wondered what was wrong with him and was drawn to the opportunity to fix something.

After they married and had children, Donna left parish ministry. She decided she did like fixing things, just not people. Her father had taught her a great deal about auto mechanics, so she started her own little home business repairing cars of friends, changing oil and transmission fluid, brake jobs, and tune-ups. She did a little writing on the side. It allowed her to stay home and still earn some money, and best of all, not have to deal with the messy, never-ending, and seemingly irreparable human problems.

Brian found the change difficult financially but much better for the family. Two pastors in one home made for very little sanity. Then there was the smell of gasoline and motor oil in his bed at night, which took some getting used to.

At breakfast the next morning Brian sat at the kitchen counter eating his raisin bran and staring out the kitchen window at the church beyond, deep in thought. Donna, having gotten the kids off to school, was cleaning the small galley kitchen and noticed his pensive mood.

"Okay, what's up?" she said.

He told her everything going on with the Vinters. Donna was his sounding board, the person who kept him grounded in reality. Growing up in a highly dysfunctional, chaotic family and being a recovering alcoholic, Brian often sought Donna's guidance when it came to understanding what constituted "normal." Not coming from "normal" himself often left him with little frame of reference when it came to family dynamics. Donna, who was raised in an extranormal environment, a grounded, stable, Scandinavian Lutheran home, was always glad to provide a balancing view on "normalcy." Brian felt certain she had been sent by God to guide him on his path to sanity, or at least, toward normalcy.

After relating his thoughts, he asked what her take was on the situation.

"I agree, it makes no sense," Donna said. "None of it does. I don't understand a mother committing suicide, no matter how bad she got. I would want to be around as long as possible, no matter what I was going through. If a mother did take her life, she would absolutely leave a note. It would be a long and loving letter, with some careful explanations of her love and why she needed to take her own life. No note makes no sense."

She drummed her fingers on the kitchen counter for a moment, then continued, "And I also don't see why she would hang herself. She had pills. And the real kicker in all this is doing it so that one of the kids would find her. That's not the actions of a normal mom. Not even a crazy mom would do that." She paused. "I think you're right, something's fishy."

"Well, I meet with them today, so maybe I will get some more answers," Brian said with a sigh.

"Good luck with that," she said. "I don't envy you. By the way, what are you going to preach on for the funeral?"

"I haven't even thought about it," Brian said. "I won't either until I meet with them to plan the service. That's when I usually get the inspiration I need. The text for this Sunday is about life after death, which seems fitting." He hesitated, then added, "But it's also about divorce, so I don't think that will work."

"No, that's probably not what you should be preaching. I will pray for you, as I always do." She smiled as she said this, and he knew the truth of it. She hugged him and he could smell what must have been . . . was that brake fluid?

CHAPTER 9

BRIAN WALKED ACROSS the parsonage lawn to the church, noticing as always the stark and frozen winter landscape. Suddenly, "Gangnam Style" erupted from his phone, "*Eh, sexy lady,* 오-오-오-오 오빤 강남스타일. *Eh, sexy lady,* 오-오-오-오."

He glanced at the caller ID, and then wondered when his son could have gotten to his phone since last night.

"Pastor, it's Maureen. Are you on the way in yet?"

"Yes, I am, almost there, what's up?"

"Well, Shirley Klein is here to see you and insisted on waiting out in the narthex until you get here . . ."

Oh crap. Shirley Klein was one of those chronically dissatisfied people who felt it was her official duty to inform the pastor of everything that created her dissatisfaction. She too frequently expressed her opinions and liked to imagine that she represented "many people who feel the same way." Since Lutherans in general, and Minnesotans more specifically, were extra nice people, nobody ever called her on her attitude or constant complaining. Instead, they would politely nod, apparently in agreement, when she went off. These were nice people who didn't like to disagree. That would be unchristian. And all those polite nodding heads added up in Shirley's mind to "many people who feel the same way." Therefore, it was her self-appointed calling in life to represent what she perceived as the disgruntled masses.

Today, all Brian knew was that whatever she had to say he was in no mood to hear it. He knew that because he was never in the mood to hear what she had to say because it was never anything positive. Despite his understanding that she was not a well person and that he should try to be understanding and gentle with her, she still managed to get under his skin.

"Do you know what she wants?" Brian finally asked.

"She didn't say, but if I had to guess I would say it's probably about the marriage equality conversations we've been having all year. From what I hear, that's all she goes on about anymore."

Brian thought about all that was on his plate and really didn't want to deal with Shirley, but he also knew she would become more relentless if she was put off. He'd better get this over with.

"Can you tell her I'm busy with the Vinter tragedy and the large funeral coming up? Let her know I will be there shortly and can give her just a few minutes, okay?"

"I will tell her. Thank you, Pastor. And while I have you on the line, Aksel Erickson called to say the roofing company confirmed a whole new rubber roof would likely cost more than he told you, like between thirty and forty thousand dollars, but they wouldn't know for sure until they come out and look at it." Maureen took a breath, then asked, "How are we going to pay for that?"

Brian could hardly bear to hear the news.

"Don't worry about it, Maureen. When you see Aksel, please let him know that we are not looking for a bid on a new roof. We are looking for the cost just to fix the leak we have now. I don't even want to think about a new roof right now. Don't let him go there, okay, Maureen? He'll listen to you."

"Don't worry, Pastor, I'll set him straight."

"Thanks, Maureen, you're the best."

"Yeah, right . . ." And the call clicked off.

In 2008, the Lutheran church (Evangelical Lutheran Church in American or ELCA), wrestling with the question of homosexuality, voted to allow individual congregations to decide for themselves whether to allow homosexuals in same-sex committed relationships to serve as pastors. The ELCA voted it would no longer sanction congregations for having homosexual pastors. If a congregation wanted to hire a gay or lesbian pastor, even if they were in a committed monogamous relationship with a same-sex partner, that congregation was free to do so without fear of reprisal from the greater church. A few years later, the state of Minnesota voted to allow gay and lesbian partners to be legally married. Pastor Brian, who had managed to avoid this divisive issue to that point in his career, realized it was time for a serious conversation. Therefore, he had set up a yearlong process by which the congregation would engage the topic and come to a thoughtful and faithful conclusion. He was not a top-down leader and didn't think most Lutherans responded well to that kind of leadership. He had always felt Lutherans liked democracy and that the people need to have a voice in matters that affected their community. Therefore, in his leadership, he sought to discern what the will of this congregation was, but only after they had done some serious study, conversation, and prayerful consideration. His egalitarian leadership style was a constant source of tension from middle and upper-management types, who believed he needed to be more authoritative. He had dealt with these types his whole career and knew they looked upon him as a weak leader, and given the chance, they could do a much better job whipping the church into shape than Brian.

Throughout the yearlong conversation discerning human sexuality, Shirley did not say a word or attend any discussion. It wasn't until the decision was made to move ahead with a statement of welcome that Shirley invaded his office many times, convinced the church would be torn apart and that the majority of people were opposed. "Why are we wasting our energy on this?" was her constant refrain.

Brian was aware of several gay and lesbian couples in the congregation. Most were not open about their status, but had let Brian know in their own way. There were also a number of parents with gay, lesbian, and transgender children that Brian knew had been through some terrible heartache and challenges. They longed for the church to take a leadership role on this issue and give voice to their ongoing suffering. When Brian began the process, without having examined the issue very closely to that point, his position was: *perhaps homosexuality is a sin, but there are worse things out there to worry about.* The Bible had very little to say about homosexuality but much to say about divorce and injustice and caring for the poor and the marginalized.

Why people spent energy on this particular, seemingly harmless issue made little sense to him. He thought people were overly focused on homosexuality; perhaps because it affected such a small percentage of the population, and by scapegoating a small group you don't have to look so hard at yourself. He knew sometimes it was easier to be concerned with the sins of others rather than our own.

However, as he dug into the topic, his eyes were opened in new ways. He listened to many people in his own congregation tell of their own terrible struggles in coming to terms with their sexual orientation. He listened to the anguish of parents struggling with their own feelings and having to watch their children suffer at the hands of bullies and a society that didn't care, a society that was complicit in their persecution by looking the other way.

Brian realized that he had also been complicit by looking the other way. He had been negligent in his understanding of the magnitude of human suffering right under his nose. He was convicted by his own ignorance and unwillingness to learn and understand. The more he learned, studied, and prayed, the more disturbed he was with himself for not caring about this sooner.

When Brian told the congregation of this important community conversation, he promised he would respect and abide by the conclusion they reached together. However, as he learned more, he realized he could not in good conscience serve a congregation that didn't welcome and support gay, lesbian, and transgender people. He came to see that they were some of the most persecuted people in society and always had been. He finally appreciated the injustice of it and concluded that not only was homosexuality not a sin, but it was part of the created order designed by God. He believed homosexuality was not a choice, but if people were born that way then God made them that way. And if made that way by God, then not only were they not sinful people, but rather they were special people who should be respected and honored for the special way God made them.

The six Scripture references in the Bible regarding homosexuality have been ruthlessly reviewed and discussed. How one interprets the Bible and understands God dictates what will be heard in these passages. To Brian, they each spoke of sexual immorality in all its forms, ultimately taking issue with any form of physical intimacy outside of a loving, committed, healthy, mutual, monogamous, and honorable relationship. They speak of using the body in ways for which it was not intended and of terrible physical violence, but not necessarily particularly of homosexuality per se. Brian had written about his position on the matter and had posted it publicly. He was surprised to find that his views were well supported. The church was moving ahead with a statement supporting the consecration of gay and lesbian couples in marriage.

Brian was strongly in favor of this and had formulated the statement. It was simple and straightforward, stating: *All Saints Lutheran Church will adopt the following policy of practice regarding marriage equality. The pastor of All Saints Lutheran will welcome, officiate, and bless marriages for all who seek to be legally married according to our current standard practices and procedures.*

The past year had been impressive with the depth and quality of discourse around this important topic. People really cared about it and wanted to do the right thing. They also wanted to be certain what was the right thing. Changing 4,000 years of religious practice should not be done lightly.

Brian grit his teeth, certain that this statement was the reason Shirley was waiting for him. She would be determined to try to head it off, because in her mind it spelled doom for the church, - just as she had been saying all along.

CHAPTER 10

BRIAN WENT TO his office through a side door to avoid Shirley. Before he was settled, Maureen was at his door.

"Are you ready to see her yet?" she asked. "She's just sitting out there, tapping her foot."

Brian knew better. She wasn't just sitting there. Shirley was dumping her litany of complaints on Maureen, who had been nodding to appear "nice" while trying to get her work done.

"Just give me a couple minutes to get settled," he said. "I need to check email and schedule an appointment with the Vinters first. I'll let you know when I'm ready, okay? Thanks . . ."

"Well, I would appreciate it if you would hurry," Maureen said. "I have a lot of work and she's talking nonstop."

Moments later, relieved and sitting at his computer, he checked his emails and voice mails and then dialed Mickey Vinter to set a time to visit, hopefully sometime yet today.

Mick answered the phone.

"Hi, Mick, it's Pastor Matterson. How are you feeling today?" he asked. It always felt like the wrong question to ask after someone died. How are you supposed to feel? Like hell, or worse, that's how.

"I'm okay, I guess. Hanging in there," Mick replied.

"I would like to stop by sometime today and talk about funeral plans. I've done this a lot and I can make it easy for you. Would you be up for that?"

"Uh, yeah, I guess so. We are supposed to meet with the funeral home later this morning. They came and took the body yesterday and want to talk about the funeral today. Who are we supposed to talk to first?"

"That's fine. You should visit with them first. They will help you through this too. They are very good and they think of everything."

"Okay, that sound's good."

"The funeral home will help you through many things and then when you are done with them we can go over the service." Brian paused, and then went on when Mick stayed silent. "If you find you're not ready after meeting with them, just let me know and we can give you a break and do it another time. Otherwise, I can plan to stop by sometime after lunch. Would that be okay?"

"Sure, Pastor, that's fine."

"Okay, Mick. Just know there are a lot of people who love you and care about you. There are many people praying for you. God bless you, and I will see you this afternoon."

Mick thanked him and hung up the phone.

Brian took a deep breath and then said a little prayer before going out to confront Shirley: "God, grant me the serenity to accept the things I cannot change, the courage to change the things I can, and the wisdom to know the difference." It was a time-honored favorite from his recovery meetings. He walked out to the front office to face the music.

"Hi, Shirley," he said with a cheery sincerity, despite his personal feelings. Sorry to keep you waiting. Lots going on this week."

Shirley silently rose from her seat and strode toward his office, her face frozen in a tight, pursed-lipped expression. Brian walked behind her, meeting Maureen's gaze, and noting her big smile. *She's enjoying this.* He followed her to his office noticing her perfectly coifed blue hair with not a single strand out of place. Shutting the door behind him, he was about to invite her to sit, but found she had already done so.

"So, what can I do for you today, Shirley?"

"Pastor, it's very hard for me to come in here to talk about this, but my husband and I are just so concerned about the direction this church is taking that we feel we have to do something."

"Oh my goodness, Shirley. This sounds serious. What on earth is going on?" Brian wondered where the distraught husband might be. Hiding from her most likely.

"Pastor, I think you know what I'm talking about. It's this decision you've made to hold gay weddings at the church. That's just not how I was brought up to believe," she said, then tilting her nose up, she added, "and we think it's against the Bible."

"Well, Shirley, I understand your concern. I really do. We did not enter into this conversation lightly. It wasn't a decision I made, the congregation decided it. It was a decision made after more than a year of discernment and discussions. This was the congregation's decision, and I fully support it. I think it's right. I do know that some, like you, don't agree, and I understand that too. I'm hoping we can continue the conversation."

"Pastor, there a lot of people who don't think it's right. I've talked to many of them and people are thinking about going to another church. I think it's going to ruin this church." She leaned forward and pointed a curled finger at Pastor Brian.

"Well, we did say at the beginning we might arrive at a place not everyone would like. It doesn't matter where we ended up, someone was bound to be unhappy, Shirley. I've had people threaten to leave if it *didn't* go the way it's going. What we committed to was a process that was honored by everyone, as it should be. I mostly heard support, so I'm not sure there is the uproar you describe."

"That's because people are being nice to your face, but they really are upset. I know many people who think this is just awful." Her nose rose again as she crossed her arms across her ample bosom.

"Well, I don't like to hear that, of course. We did try to figure out ways for everyone to voice their opinions, through surveys and even anonymously, but I only recall a few dissenting voices, and even some of those were still pretty gracious."

"Well, that's not what I hear. I hear lots of angry people who feel like their church is being taken down the wrong road."

Brian leaned forward with a gentle smile and spoke in a confiding tone. "Would you be able to tell me who they are, Shirley? Maybe I could talk to them and keep them from leaving."

"I'm not going to tell you their names. They wouldn't appreciate that."

Brian maintained his stance, softening his expression even further. "So . . . Shirley . . . you are here. What would *you* like to do about this? Are you thinking about leaving All Saints?"

"I can't leave this church, Pastor. This is my church. I was baptized here and have been here my whole life. I just don't want to see it changed."

Brian relaxed back into his seat, spreading his hands before her in a gesture of generosity. "What do you want, Shirley? We took a survey. Support for marriage equality was 5 to 1 in favor. Many of those opposed indicated they weren't strongly opposed but were actually still struggling with their decision. Only a small handful voted 'no' outright. That seems like pretty strong support to me."

"That vote didn't represent the congregation, Pastor. Only 250 people were at that meeting. There were many people who weren't even there, and many of them are those families I'm talking about. They didn't get their voices heard."

"Well, actually, Shirley, 250 members at a special congregational meeting is a pretty good turnout. It's a lot more than needed for a significantly accurate statistical representation of the congregation." Brian leaned forward again, clasping his hands together on the desktop, and added, "It's a very reliable number, I believe."

"I don't think so. You didn't hear from people I've been speaking to, and these are longtime members. I think we are going to lose them." Shirley stated defiantly, her dyed blue hair sitting as high and as perfect and rigid as she was.

"Well, that will make me sad, Shirley, but I have to honor the will of the congregation and their careful, faithful discernment on the matter. I'm really sorry this upsets you so much," Brian said, but then decided to add, "you know, I don't remember you attending any of the conversations we had, or sharing your opinion on this through all the ways we canvassed church members over the past year. Why did you wait until now to express such a strong opinion?"

"I have been telling people all along how wrong this whole thing is, you just didn't listen."

"Shirley, I never once heard from you in this process. You never wrote. You came in here and told me how you felt personally late in the process, but you were only one of two people who did that. You never spoke at any of the meetings. This makes it hard to respond to your concerns after the fact, after a congregational agreement has been made."

"Well," she said. "I'm saying something now. My husband and I have decided we are not going to give our offering anymore until this is changed. We are doing that and telling other people do to the same. I hate to do that, Pastor, but we have to do something."

Brian was doing pretty well up to this point, but blackmail was something he wouldn't tolerate. He could handle differences of opinion, anger, could even handle people leaving the church if that's what they had to do. But he couldn't handle threats and coercion.

"So, you are going to withhold your money until you get your way? Is that right?" Brian asked quietly, his hands now gripped the edge of the desktop.

"Well now, that's not what I'm saying. I'm just saying we don't agree with this decision and we can't support it."

"But you're not leaving the church?"

"No, we are not."

Brian stood and moved around the desk, headed for the door, as he said, "I'm sorry you feel this way. I don't think the actions you are taking are healthy for the church. You might want to reconsider, and I hope you will." He reached the door, knowing he wasn't being very pastoral at the moment, but he had lost his patience and needed to end the conversation before he said something he would regret.

Shirley seemed surprised by his dismissive action and didn't seem ready to be done talking, but with Brian standing at the door, holding it open, she realized they were done and reluctantly got up to leave.

Brian held his smile as he wondered what she was thinking when she came in. Did she really expect her threat to work? Was he supposed to overturn the work and will of the congregation because she insisted on it? For what seemed the millionth time, he marveled at what some people were capable of.

"Have a nice day, Shirley," he said firmly as she passed by wordlessly.

He knew this was not over for her, but he wished it was. He knew these little battles were part of every pastor's job and a cross they had to bear.

CHAPTER 11

B RIAN WAS DIALING the number to his next phone call when someone knocked at the door. Before he could respond, the door opened and Barney stuck his head inside.

"Pastor, I really hate to bother you, but we've got a problem."

Hanging up the phone, Brian put his face in his hands and took a deep breath. "Barney, please. I just told you about the door. You just can't come barging in here."

"I'm just sticking my head in," Barney protested. "I thought you needed to know this."

"Barney, I need to you to close the door and knock," Brian said.

"But I did knock already, Pastor."

"I know you knocked," Brian said, "but the way it works is that you knock and then you wait for the person behind the door to acknowledge the knock. Even if it's urgent, you wait for an answer. The only time you *don't* wait for an answer is if the building is on fire."

"Okay, okay, Pastor, geez. I just thought you would want to know about this."

"Out!"

"You're kidding, right?"

"Nope, not kidding. You have to start over." Brian's tone was calm, almost breezy, but he sat with one hand grasping the other, which was fisted.

"Okay, but it seems kind of silly now that we are already talking."

"But I am trying to get you to learn, Barney," Brian said. "You will never learn if I don't make you learn."

"Okay, okay, I get it. I will knock next time." Barney's head was still sticking through the door, as though that was somehow respecting Brian's boundary.

"No, Barney, you don't understand. Not next time, this time. You have to go out, knock, and wait for an answer."

"You're kidding, right?"

"Nope, still not kidding. You have to start over."

"But I'm already here. Can't I just tell you what it is?"

"Not until you go out and knock."

"Well, that just seems silly . . ."

"But if I don't make you do this, Barney, the next time you won't knock again and won't wait for an answer. I'm trying to make a point."

"But–"

"Out! Close the door!" Brian commanded.

"Holy cow, Pastor, what's the big deal? It will just take a second . . ."

Brian put his face in his hands again, took a breath, and heaved out a plea: "Help me, God . . ." Then, he quietly stated, "I'm not listening to a word you have to say until you close that door and knock."

"Okay, okay, Pastor," Barney said. "I just don't get what the big deal is."

Brian didn't answer. He just stared at Barney. Barney stared back, but his brows began to furrow and a rueful frown pushed his lips downward. It was a stare-off.

Finally, Barney said, "So, should I just tell you?"

Brian shook his head, both in answer to Barney and as a reaction of amazement at what he was dealing with, and then pointed at Barney, flicking his finger outward. The signal was clear. He was not going to say another word.

"So, I just go out and knock again? I feel like a little kid."

When Brian didn't respond or lower his finger, Barney slowly pulled back and then closed the door.

Brian waited for the knock, but when it didn't come, he wondered if Barney had just left.

Finally, a timid knock sounded.

Brian didn't say anything and waited, knowing there was no way Barney was going to walk away. He would never give up, it wasn't in him.

The knock came again a little stronger this time. Brian thought about not answering to see what Barney would do, but he did want to know what the issue was. "Who is it?" Brian finally said.

"Pastor, you know who it is. It's me, Phil Barney, the janitor. Can I come in?"

"I'm very busy right now, Phil Barney, can you come back later?"

"It's kind of important . . ."

"Well . . . what is it?"

"Can I come in?"

"No, just tell me what it is," Brian said, feeling a little guilty he was pushing Barney so hard.

"I really should come in to tell you."

"No, just tell me what it is. If it's important, I'll let you in."

Silence followed. Brian figured Barney was considering his next move.

Finally, Barney spoke. "Well, it's just that I was downstairs cleaning and I found a pair of boy's underwear on the bathroom floor. They were wet and the smelled. They smelled, you know . . ." Barney lowered his voice to a loud whisper. "They smell like . . . pee."

Brian wasn't sure if he should laugh or scream. "What? I can't hear you . . ."

Barney whispered, "Pee . . ."

"What, Barney? I can't hear what you are saying. You have to speak up."

There was another silence, then Barney said, "Can I just come in and tell you, Pastor? I really don't want to say it out loud."

"Just say it, Barney, what's the big deal?"

"Pee!" Barney said loudly, then whispering again. "It smelled like pee, Pastor."

"What do you think happened, Barney?"

"I think someone wet their pants and left their underwear on the floor after cleaning themselves up."

"I think that's a pretty good guess," Brian said. "What do you think we should do about it?"

After considering the question, Barney said, "I guess we should just throw them away and clean the bathroom really good."

"That sounds like a plan, Barney. I think you are right. Is there anything else?"

Silence reigned for a long moment. "I just thought you would want to know," Barney said, his voice plaintive. Then he added, "I guess I'll go do that."

Brian resisted the temptation to speak. He knew Barney was still standing there, waiting for some final word from him.

After a long moment, the conclusion to the conversation arrived. "Okay, Pastor. I will take care of it. Thank you."

Brian heard Barney's footsteps finally moving away from the door. He leaned back in his chair and expelled a huge rush of air, the breath he hadn't realized he'd been holding.

CHAPTER 12

SINCE BRIAN DIDN'T get all his calls and emails responded to from the day before, he added them to the new pile from this morning. He felt the urgency to stay on top of them because if he didn't he would fall hopelessly behind and he hated that feeling. He did have, however, more pressing commitments. For one, he had his Sunday sermon to prepare, and if he didn't take care of that properly he was neglecting the most important part of his job. He knew preaching was the centerpiece of every pastor's ministry, and if he did not take it seriously and do it well everything else would suffer. Along with the sacraments, preaching the Word of God was foundational to the faith and needed his careful attention.

Brian prayed and read the text and was making notes when the door was knocked upon. Brian didn't want to be disturbed, so he quickly went to the door and opened it a few inches. Sue Solberg, the parish worker, stood before him. Brian had tremendous respect and regard for Sue. She was the most dedicated disciple of Jesus he had ever known. Her life had been shaped most profoundly by one major event. Her husband, a pilot, had taken her three kids up for a flight one day. She didn't like flying, so stayed home. Then that fateful moment arrived that is seared in her heart forever. It arrived with a police officer at the door along with her pastor at the time. In a single moment, everything that meant anything in her life was ripped away from her in one plane crash.

Following years of dark depression and debilitating grief, she emerged to become one of the most beautiful and caring people Brian had ever known. Her own faith and commitment to Christ put his own to shame. He would do anything for her and she would do anything for anyone who needed help. There were very few in the congregation who had not been touched by her love.

"Pastor, I know you are busy, but there is something you should know."

Brian let her in, knowing it must be important for Sue to interrupt him. He closed the door and gestured to the open chair in front of his desk.

"I just heard that Patty Seversen was taken to the ER earlier this morning. When she didn't get up this morning, her daughter went to check on her and found her lying beside her bed on the floor. She couldn't get up. Her left arm and leg didn't work properly, the left side of her face was drooping and she wasn't making any sense. They're sure she had a stroke. Anyway, the family is all headed to the hospital. The daughter called me from the emergency room."

Brian asked Sue for a few more details, and after sharing a prayer with Sue, prepared to head out to the hospital. He told Maureen to cancel his next appointment and that he would probably head over to the Vinters' after the hospital call. He added to expect him back well after lunch.

Patty Severson's confirmed stroke was relieved by clot-busting drugs in the ER. Their quick response and the luck of her daughter finding her shortly after the stroke hit gave her an excellent chance for a good recovery. Brian was with the gathered family members in the ER waiting room when the doctor relayed this good news.

He shared a prayer with the family then excused himself amid their thanks for his coming.

When he got to his car, he checked his phone. He had a voicemail from Mick Vinter. "Oh, hi, Pastor. This is Mick Vinter. I was just calling . . ." There was a long pause and then Mick continued, "I guess I will just try calling you at the church. Thank you."

Brian called the church and Maureen answered, not sounding very pleased to be answering the phone.

"Hi, Maureen, it's Pastor. You don't sound so good. You doing okay?"

"No, I'm not. I have a lot to do and people just keep calling and stopping by. They want to know all about the Vinters and now they are asking about Patty Severson. You promised to get me some help." Her tone was accusatory.

"I'm working on it, but you're going to have to be patient. You know how it works. But you have to try to be nice on the phone. That's important. We've talked about this before."

"I know, I know. I'm sorry. I'm just a little stressed right now."

"I'll see if I can get Jerry Meyers to come in this afternoon and help with the phones, okay?"

"NO, thank you. He is more work than help."

Brian knew this would be her response, but he also knew that she always turned down his offers of help because she didn't really want help, she wanted pity. She complained so the person she was complaining to would know how hard she worked and how unappreciated she was.

"Okay," Brian said.

"It's fine. I can handle it. I've been through this drill more than a few times. I'll just get it done. I always do."

Brian smiled to himself, relieved to have gotten through yet another exchange with Maureen. "Do I have any messages?"

"You always have messages."

"I'm sorry. Anything from Mick Vinter? Did he call?"

"Yes, he did call. I wanted to put him through to voicemail, but he insisted I just give you this message. I don't think he really wanted to talk to you. It looks like they don't want to have a service at the church."

Brian was taken aback. "Why . . . what? What did he say?"

"He just said he had been to the funeral home and they decided they just wanted to keep it small and private. The funeral home would handle everything and he said to say thank you for stopping by the other day."

Brian was baffled. "I don't understand. They don't want the funeral here? That's just crazy."

"I know, that's what I thought. They must be taking it hard. People are not going to be happy about this."

"No kidding. I'm going over there and see if I can talk some sense into him. I'll keep you posted."

"I know you will. You always do." Maureen's tone made it clear that she wanted to get back to her work.

"Thank you, Maureen."

She hung up without responding.

He hated that.

CHAPTER 13

B RIAN TURNED UP the Vinters' street and again was amazed to see there were still no cars lining the streets and this time not even the car and van in the driveway. He could see no lights on in the house. With the shades pulled, the house looked vacant.

He parked in the driveway and walked up to the door. He knew nobody was home, but thought he should at least try the doorbell. One of the kids might be there and they might know something. There were several cards tucked into the screen door and even a plant sitting on the porch outside the door, wrapped in colorful plastic but now certainly frozen solid. Otherwise, the place seemed deserted. Brian rang twice before remembering the bell was broken. He knocked. He waited, but as he suspected, nobody came to the door.

Brian wondered what to do next. He really felt he needed to know what was going on with the Vinter family. He decided to stop by the funeral home to see if they could tell him anything before realizing he didn't know which one it was. He had all the local ones on his phone, and after the third try he found the right one. Walton-Garrison Funeral Home was a small family-owned operation that was slowly going out of business.

Brian knew all the funeral home directors in the area, had worked with them for more than twenty years. He had ridden with many of them in the hearse with the caskets or in a town car leading the way to the graveyard for the committal service following a funeral. He found them to be an unusually humorous group of people for the most part, likely because their work was so morbid. When they had the chance to lighten up with a pastor who was easygoing they took advantage. Brian figured being a funeral director must be a little like being a pastor. He assumed they must appreciate opportunities to be around someone who understands what it's like to be in a profession that limits your social life. The director at Walton-Garrison was Tom Fullery. Yes, that was really his name and he'd heard all the jokes.

Brian drove to the funeral home to try to get a few minutes with Tom. As he walked in, he could feel the years of sorrow spent in this place. Heaviness and grief seemed to seep from the walls and furniture. It was an outdated building showing years of wear. It even smelled sad. Fullery had bought the business from Walton-Garrison years before, when the business was still strong and just before it went south. He kept the name because it had been long established in the community and had a good reputation.

Fullery lamented the state of his vocation every chance he got. He originally went into the business because he truly believed it was a dignified profession and a sacred calling. He wanted to serve people in their moment of greatest need and enjoyed giving comfort to loved ones and providing a smooth transition through their grief. Now he felt the squeeze of all the McFuneral homes of the world that, it seemed, wanted to grab as much business as they could. It was all about numbers for them. They didn't care about people like he did, he would tell you.

The receptionist waved Brian through and he found Tom in his office.

"Hi, Tom, how are you?" Brian said, standing in the doorway.

"Well, if it isn't the right Reverend Matterson. Bless my soul. What brings you in here, Pastor?" Tom said.

"Well, I am wondering if I can ask you about one of my families."

"Let me guess, the Vinters?"

"That's right. How did you know?"

"Well, I knew she was yours and I just spent the morning with Mick planning the funeral. Very unusual fellow that guy."

"Yes, I know," Brian said, "I was just over at the house and there's nobody there. There never is. It's very strange. Then I got a message from him that they didn't want the funeral at the church. I wanted to check with you before I go over there again. What can you tell me? Do they really want the funeral here?"

"That's right. I tried to convince him that our place wouldn't be big enough, but he was very adamant that he didn't want a big funeral. He just wanted his own family and close friends and nobody else. He wanted it to be low-key and as quiet as possible."

"Does he know that there are a lot of people who want to come to the funeral? I don't understand this at all. Usually people need as many people as possible around them at times like this. Don't you think this is strange?"

"It is. I don't know what to think about it. He came alone, and that's unusual too. Usually there are at least a few close family or friends to help with making plans, especially in situations like this. He just wants this over with, doesn't want anyone else involved. I've never seen anything like it."

"Well, I need to talk to him some more. I don't think he realizes that he's not the only one impacted by this. There are many people who need comfort and help. I don't know how we do that without some kind of memorial service. I just need to make him see that."

Fullery agreed. "If there's anything I can do to help with that let me know." As Brian turned to leave, Fullery asked, "Say, Pastor, did you know that they are changing some of the rules for burials?"

"What?" Brian said. "What do you mean?"

"They are always making new rules for us to follow. There's a new one now where they want us to tie the shoelaces together of everyone we bury."

Brian was lost. "What do you mean, Tom? Are you serious? Are you really supposed to tie people's shoelaces together? Why on earth would they want you to do that?"

"Well, apparently, they are thinking that if a zombie apocalypse happens it will make it harder for them to walk." Fullery let out a hearty laugh at his own humor.

Brian groaned at the joke and rolled his eyes. "You are one sick puppy. You know that, don't you?"

"It takes one to know one," Fullery shot back. "They also want us to start burying German people with their heads out of the ground now."

Brian bit. "Really, why is that?"

"Because their heads are so hard they last longer than tombstones," Fullery said, laughing again at his own joke.

Both men chuckled as Brian walked out. "I will pray for you, but I don't think it's going to help," Brian said as he continued out. Fullery guffawed as Brian shook his head. "How do you work with that guy?" Brian asked the receptionist as he passed by.

She smiled. "Somebody has to, I guess."

"I will pray for you, too."

"Have a nice day, Pastor," she said primly as he walked out the door.

CHAPTER 14

BRIAN DECIDED TO try the Vinter home again but didn't expect to find Mick there. He really needed to help Mick see the importance of a service the community could attend. He drove by the Vinter home, but it looked as abandoned as ever. Shades down and no cars in the driveway.

As he was about to drive on, something caught his eye. He had just glanced at the front door and noticed the cards in the door were gone, and just as he had done so, he saw a curtain move slightly. He realized with a start that someone was there and watching. He backed into the driveway and strode to the door. He knocked and waited. He knocked again and waited some more, determined to talk to whoever was in the house. He suspected it was Mick. Brian knocked a third time and spoke loudly enough so that anyone on the other side of the door could hear him.

"Mick, is that you? I saw the curtains move, so I know you are in there. I need to talk to you. Mick, is it you? Kyle? Hannah? Please open the door. I really need to talk with you!" Brian shouted.

He waited for a response and then knocked again, more firmly than before. "I'm not leaving, so you might as well let me in," he said.

Finally, after another pause, Mick's voice came through the door. "I don't want to talk you to you, Pastor. I just want to be left alone. Please just go," he said.

"Mick," Pastor Brian said through the door, "I know you are going through a tough time right now. There is nothing in life tougher than what you are dealing with. If I know anything at all it's how important it is at times like these to not shut everyone out. We are human and we need each other, especially at times like this. Please, just give me a few minutes of your time and I will leave you alone."

There was a long pause of silence. Apparently, Mick was debating in his mind about what to do. Finally, he spoke. "Will you promise to go when I ask you to go?"

"Yes, Mick, I promise."

Again, silence, and then Brian heard the click of the deadbolt and saw the door handle turn. The door opened a few inches and Brian could see Mick, who appeared to have not showered or shaved recently. His rumpled clothes looked slept in and dark rings lined his eyes. He had either been crying or not sleeping, or more likely both. He looked like hell. Brian realized then that Mick had no intention of letting him inside. He spoke through the narrowly opened door.

"Okay, Pastor, what?"

"Come on, Mick, let me come in for a minute. Let's sit down and talk. Just give me a few minutes, but not at the door like this."

Mick really didn't want to comply, Brian could see, but he was also weary and confused and didn't seem to know how to respond.

Brian pressed. "Mick, it's vital that we talk. Please let me in. Give me a few minutes, and if you don't like what I have to say you can ask me to leave and I will go, I promise."

Mick reluctantly let the door come open a little more and Brian pushed his way in before Mick could change his mind. "Have you eaten anything lately?" Brian asked as he crossed the threshold. He knew the best thing right now was to get some nutrition into Mick. "Let me make you something to eat."

"No," Mick said. "I'm not hungry."

"How about just some coffee then?" Brian countered and made his way to the kitchen, not waiting for a response.

Mick, a little exasperated, followed. "You can make some coffee for yourself. I don't want anything," he said, following Brian into the kitchen.

The kitchen was a mess. The sink stacked with dirty dishes, the counters cluttered and dirty. Most of the counter space had food dishes given by friends and neighbors and placed on the counter. They were mostly unopened. A few opened ones had small amounts dished out and left uncovered. Most of the food should be in the refrigerator. An odor emanated from the sink area, probably from a garbage bin underneath.

On seeing the state of the kitchen, Brian decided to pass on the coffee and momentarily considered cleaning it all up, as Mick was clearly unable to function.

"Let's just go in the living room and talk," he said. "I don't need coffee." He grabbed a plate of cookies to take with him in hopes of getting Mick to eat something.

Mick followed, with a look of dread on his face. They sat in the living room—also a mess, but not nearly as bad as the kitchen. Brian marveled again at the size of the TV. "That's quite the television you have there. The kids must love it."

Mick nodded numbly as Brian sat down on the sofa and Mick sat across from him on a recliner.

"Where *are* the kids, by the way?"

"They are with Candy's mother," Mick said.

"So, you are really all alone here?" Brian asked.

"Yep," Mick said.

Brian looked at Mick, who was avoiding his gaze. "I got your message that you don't want the funeral at the church, Mick, and I need to tell you that you really need to reconsider that. When someone like your wife dies, it affects the whole community. Your loss is the greatest of course, but the fact is we have all experienced a loss when she died and a funeral helps us all to get over this. I respect your desire to keep things private, but this is important, Mick, that we allow people to be a part of this. I really need you to reconsider that."

"I appreciate your concern, Pastor," Mick began, "but I've thought about this and I just want a small, private service. We just want to be left alone," Mick said, seeming to hope this would end the conversation.

Brian wasn't sure what to say. He could see that Mick was dug into his position and wasn't about to budge. He asked God for help for the words he needed. He had never seen anyone respond to death like this and he knew it was important that he not let Mick go it alone. He could sense Mick was in a dark and terrible place, and he felt like it was up to him to pull him out—he couldn't see anyone else there for him.

"Well, Mick," he began, "When Candy died, you lost a wife and the mother of your children. Your loss is the most devastating. However, the rest of us lost something too. We lost a member of our church, a member of our family, a member of our community. We need the chance to deal with that. If you just want a private service, I understand and support that. But would you mind if we were to have a funeral for her too? There are so many people who need to grieve and I would like to offer a time and a place for that to happen. But I won't do that if you don't want me to. Would you be okay with that?"

Mick pondered this for a moment and said, "I don't know, I guess I will have to think about it."

An awkward silence hung between them. Mick sat with his legs and arms crossing his heavy frame his body language as closed as it could get. His dark eyes were perpetually downcast, rarely looking up and never making contact. His wide brow was deeply furrowed beneath his receding black hairline. Matterson's heart went out to him.

"I don't know, Mick," he said. "I believe in God and I've committed my life to serving God. I don't always know what that means all the time. It takes me to some strange and difficult places, like this. I am deeply concerned for you and for your kids. Something like this is devastating and it takes a lot to heal. You and the kids need things to get better now, not worse. I also know for that to happen you will need some help. I see something happening with you that terrifies me and I don't want to see you go there. I feel like your life is at stake. I want to make sure this doesn't take you down with it."

"I will be fine, Pastor. I just need everyone to just leave me alone. That's what I need."

"I don't mean to be pushy, Mick, but I do have a lot of experience with these things and I'm worried you don't recognize the magnitude of this. This is serious stuff. I see people go through grief and loss on a daily basis, but what I see here has me seriously concerned. What you are doing is not normal, healthy, or good. I am in your face about this because I care and I want to see you come through this without losing everything else you love."

"People are different. They handle things their own way. We'll be just fine. We don't need anyone's help," Mick insisted.

"You are wrong," Brian said. "You are in deep trouble and you don't even know it. If you don't accept some help, things will get even worse than this. I have never been more certain about anything before, Mick. You need help with this. This is too big. Let me help you."

They sat in silence for a few moments before Mick finally spoke.

"There isn't anything more to say, Pastor. I guess it would be good if you left now."

"Okay, I'll go, but can I ask you one more thing, Mick? Can you tell me exactly what happened?" Brian asked. Brian knew the basic details but he asked because he knew how important it was to keep Mick talking about it.

Mick hesitated and Brian could tell this was torture for him. This was hard for Brian too because it wasn't in his nature to make people so uncomfortable. He just knew how important it was to get Mick to talk about it and that this might be his only chance to try to help.

"Well," Mick began, "as I told you before, Kyle came home and found Candy in her closet where she hung herself. He called 911 and the police came. Kyle called me and I came right home. The police asked a bunch of questions and then the coroner came and they took the body down after the police was done taking pictures. That's about it."

"Did you have any idea this was coming? Did she give any indication this was something she was thinking about?"

"No. Well, she was fighting cancer and everything, so I guess that's what might have been it."

"How are the kids doing? How are they managing?"

"They will stay with Candy's mom for a while until I figure this out."

"They doing okay you think?"

"The kids? They are sad, but Candy's mom is taking good care of them. They are better off there than here."

They sat for a moment in the darkening living room, shadows growing longer. The silence was heavy. The grandfather clock from the front hallway was ticking away the seconds, the sound hollow and sad.

Brian was struggling. He'd never experienced anything like this before. Mostly people open up at times like this but Mick was shut down tight and would not budge. Brian decided he had no choice but to let it go for now.

"Well, Mick, I would really like you to reconsider having the funeral at the church. If you do go ahead with a private service we would really like your permission to do a community memorial service for her. You wouldn't have to attend, but there are many people who need to have some closure. I am hoping and praying that you will be a part of that. I think it will help you and the kids to be around other people who will give you support. I will call again and let you know what we are planning to see what you think, okay? Please think about it and pray about it. I know it's the right thing to do," Brian said.

Mick sat, apparently agonizing. Brian could see he realized that he was in a bind, that if the church held a service for Candy he would have to attend. How would it look if he didn't? Brian could also sense Mick's growing annoyance at him for being so pushy.

"I will think about it," he said with a dark expression. Then the uncomfortable silence again.

Brian finally spoke. "Okay, Mick, you seem to want to be alone. I don't think that's a good thing right now, but I will go. Okay if I say a prayer with you first?"

"Fine," Mick said.

Brian bowed his head and took a deep breath. These were the hardest prayers to say. What do you ask for in this situation? He began, "Dear Lord, we are at a loss here. Someone we love has left us in a surprising and sudden way. We don't know how to respond. We have so many feelings. We need your help. Help us please. Help Mick and his children come to terms with this terrible new reality. Help them, Lord, in the days ahead to bear the weight and darkness of all this. Help too all of us who are reminded that there is pain and suffering among us and that sometimes it's way worse than we know. We pray for all those who are struggling or wanting to die. Mostly, Lord, help us to have confidence that while Candy is gone from us, she is not gone from you, that she lives with you now, and that when our turn comes, we will cross over to wherever you are, and we will join you and all the saints in the glory that we call eternal life. We ask all these things in Jesus's name. Amen."

Brian hated the feeling of leaving a situation he did not feel he was able to help. But he also knew that's not how it worked, that God was doing things he could know nothing about. Still, that didn't keep him from feeling incompetent at times.

"Okay, Mick. Sorry I'm so pushy. It's because I do care and I am worried about you. I want to make sure that you don't let this destroy your life. Will you promise me that you will reach out when you are ready? I will do everything I can to help you and your family."

"I will, Pastor. Thank you," Mick said, getting up eagerly to move toward the door.

"And will you also think about having the service at the church?" Brian added, rising and making his way to the door.

"Well, I think it's already set up at the funeral home."

"I've spoken to them and they agree this would be better at the church. They would be glad to change it. That's not hard to do."

Mick didn't seem sure how to respond to that. He finally blurted out, "I'll think about it, I guess."

"Okay, Mick, that's all I ask. I appreciate it. I will be praying for you and you need to know there are a whole lot of people praying for you and your family right now. You are loved."

Mick was holding the door open now and Brian made his way past and through.

Brian could see a dark seething anguish in Mick as he passed. It occurred to him he might have another suicide on his hands before long. *This is a man about to implode.*

Before Brian could say goodbye Mick had closed the door, and that was that.

As he walked back to the car, he wondered if he really would actually hold a funeral for Candy if Mick didn't agree to have the funeral at the church. He would have to do something. Probably not a full-blown funeral service, but some kind of vigil that would allow people to say a few words, light some candles, sing some hymns, and say a few prayers. People needed rituals to get them through difficult times. After all his years in the ministry, Brian had come to truly appreciate the great value in the rituals that accompany death. Rituals are a lifeline to hold onto when uncertainty threatens something that holds people together. It keeps people grounded and secure until the storm has passed.

Driving back to the church Brian recalled one of the first times he went on a death call and how meaningful and healing rituals can be. It was one of the worst imaginable situations. A young couple had been expecting their first child. It was near their delivery when their baby's heart stopped beating. It was determined the child was no longer alive and the mother was in the hospital waiting to deliver her dead baby. Having been through childbirth with his wife two times, Brian couldn't think of many scenarios more depressingly devastating than having to go through full labor and delivery for nothing. The only thing worse would be to go through all that pain only to be handed your dead child.

At that time Brian was still in seminary doing his clinical pastoral education, a formative time where students work at a hospital for a semester and learn to minister as chaplains wherever they are needed. It was Brian's turn for being on-call for the night, and when the fellow student handed off the beeper she explained the situation with the mother.

"She is in labor and delivery. They think she will deliver tonight. The parents have already told them when the baby comes they would like a chaplain to be there. I just thought you should be prepared," said Lynn, a Presbyterian student chaplain.

Brian was shaken by this information. He dreaded getting that call. What could he possibly say to them? What words were there? He racked his brain but he could think of nothing. He was terrified of this situation and prayed that he wouldn't be called.

That night a storm blew in, a big electric storm with high winds, thunder, lightning, and torrential rains. They say women tend to deliver when there is a low-pressure system. Brian consulted his wife, Donna, that night before going to bed about what to do if they called. They talked and prayed about it.

"The words will be there when you need them," she told him.

He knew she was right, but still he wouldn't mind the chance to review them and rehearse them a little, or at least know what they might be. It was so scary to trust God that much. Donna's words were comforting nonetheless.

Sure enough, just after 3:00 a.m. the phone rang. Brian answered and a nurse informed him the couple had delivered, their child was not alive, and they want to see the chaplain. Brian told her he was on his way.

He dressed, kissed his wife, and made his way out into the wild storm, a knot in his stomach, still having no idea what to say. On the freeway, he could drive only 35 mph even though the freeway was empty, because the rain was falling so hard his wipers could not keep up. Visibility was so bad he was afraid he would miss his exit. He prayed desperately for God's help as he fought through the downpour.

He made it to the hospital and entered through the ER, cleared security, and made his way to labor and delivery. The nurse at the desk advised him of the situation.

"It was a hard delivery. Jennifer is exhausted. She and Jim are very distraught and sad, as you would expect. We offered to call a chaplain and they immediately agreed. They're in room 308," the charge nurse told him.

Brian thanked the nurse and walked reluctantly to the room. Pausing to pray once again, he knocked lightly and then pushed the door open. Jenny lay in her hospital gown with her eyes closed. Her eyelids were red and puffy and her hair was a sweaty, tangled mess. Her husband sat next to her bed holding her hand, staring blankly at the floor, hardly acknowledging Brian was there.

"Hello," Brian began tentatively, "I'm Chaplain Matterson," he said, entering the room.

Along with the typical hospital room accoutrements the room also held a number of their personal items strewn around, food, clothing, bags, books, an iPad, a boom box. It was clear they had been camped here for days.

Jenny opened her eyes a little, saw him, and then closed them again. Jim made no response, didn't even look up. This was about what he expected. He had imagined this numbness and detachment with him standing there like a bumbling fool trying to make meaningless conversation. Words feel like an annoyance at times like this.

"I am so sorry for your loss," Brian managed. "Since hearing of your situation last night, I have been praying for you. I can't even begin to imagine what you have been going through and feeling right now."

Jenny's mouth tightened and turned down as though she was going to cry again, but she didn't. Jim continued to stare numbly down at the floor and nodded his head ever so slightly.

Knowing he had to say more yet feeling like whatever he could think to say felt so hollow and weak at this moment, he ventured on. "There are no words I can say that will change how you are feeling right now. You are in a dark place, and you will be for a while yet. It's just such a terrible blow that there is nothing you can do right now but feel it. I just want you to hang on through the days ahead. It's not going to be easy. Nothing will feel right to you for a long time to come. You need to be prepared for that. But I want you to know it won't stay this way forever. You will come out of this and you will find life again. You will. And as strange and out of place as it sounds right now, I know in the future this terrible pain you feel now will even turn out to be a gift. That sounds crazy right now, but this will make sense to you one day. I have no idea how, but I know it's true. We don't understand why things happen or what they mean, but they always eventually make sense one day, either in this life or in the next."

Brian paused, but felt okay about his words and could feel the Spirit speaking through him. He went on. "I believe your baby is with God right now and that you will see your child one day and you will understand everything."

They seemed to be listening, but their body language did not change, so Brian wasn't certain how they were hearing what he had to say or what they thought of it. Who could really know what anyone could hear or understand in such a dark moment? And then there was the question of their theological background.

Were they fundamentalists? What exactly did they believe and how could he speak to it?

Brian was not sure where to go from there. They weren't talking or even looking at him, and for him to keep talking seemed like an intrusion. He didn't want to make their lives worse, so he wondered what to do next. It was too soon to leave, but there was nothing more to say. He stood struggling with himself when Jenny spoke without opening her eyes.

"Pastor, would you say a prayer for us?"

Of course, duh? Why didn't he think of that?

"Yes, I would be glad to." He moved closer to the bed. "Could we all hold hands?"

Jenny opened her bloodshot, swollen eyes and offered her hands to Brian and her husband Jim stood and closed the circle of hands.

Brian's mind reeled. *What would be the right prayer? God? A little help here?*

Trusting that it would come to him, he began softly. "Dear God . . . we are not very happy right now . . . a terrible thing has happened and we would like to complain about it. It doesn't seem fair that Jim and Jenny had to come all this way for nothing. Why did it have to happen this way? Why was so much time and hope invested in this child only to have it ripped away from them so far along the way? Father, that's not right and that's not fair and it shouldn't be this way!"

Brian paused, thinking these were good words to express about how they were feeling, but what now? Anything else he could think of seemed inadequate. *Am I supposed to say your baby is in heaven with you now?* He sincerely believed that was true, but those words felt so trite in that moment. They would need to be heard in the days ahead, but right now, who cares about that? The wounds were too fresh and too deep and too painful for that to be of much help right now. Brian thought if he were to say "Your baby is in heaven" in that moment, it would make them angry with God.

He struggled and the silence grew longer and then grew awkward. He had to say something, but what? His mind was blank. "God," he finally managed, "we are just so very sad, won't you help us?"

With that sentence, the thought of losing one of his own children suddenly entered his mind and he was overcome with powerful emotion. His chest constricted and he lost control. His throat tightened and he couldn't breathe until suddenly he began weeping uncontrollably. He was mortified by this loss of control. He tried but couldn't stop himself. There he was, holding hands with a bereaved young couple, tears streaming down his face, snot running out of his nose, cries of anguish whimpering from his throat. In the back of his mind a voice was screaming, *What are you doing you idiot? This isn't about you.* Try as he might he could not stanch the flow.

Jenny quickly joined him, then so did Jim. All three of them holding hands in a hospital room with a storm raging outside crying their eyes out. Like the storm outside, their grief grew in intensity. What started as quiet weeping built into a full-on gale of deep, mournful wails from all three of them. A passing nurse heard the anguished lament and put her head in the door. She saw the three holding hands and balling their eyes out and ducked out again shaken by the force of their immense grief.

Eventually they wound down as their grief was spent. The room grew quiet except for the low grumbling of fading thunder outside. Brian took a deep shuddering breath, and still holding hands, concluded, "So, we obviously need your help, Lord, and we ask it in Jesus's name . . . Amen."

Brian turned away, embarrassed, and looked for Kleenex. They cleaned themselves up, blew their noses and dried their eyes. Brian, feeling self-conscious by his unprofessional behavior, was preparing to excuse himself. He was thinking about how to graciously depart, but a sudden thought hit him and he asked them, "Would you like me to baptize your baby?" He knew this was not something practiced or sanctioned in the church–Christians don't baptize the dead–but he didn't care. This was a baptism ritual not for the child but to benefit the parents in this instance. This was to help Jim and Jenny find peace, and so he offered it.

For the first time since his arrival, they actually brightened. Jenny said, "You could do that?"

"Yes, of course," Brian said and went out and asked the nurse for a bowl and to have the baby brought in. The nurse brought a stainless-steel bowl he filled halfway with water. Brian cleared the rolling patient tray table where meals are served and set the bowl on it. The nurse brought their baby bundled in blankets and asked if she could stay for the baptism, to which the Jim and Jenny gladly assented.

Their tiny baby was a lifeless thing that didn't really look like baby anymore. It was a dark purplish blue and had long ceased to have any life in it. There was little consolation in looking at it, as it barely resembled a human. But for these parents it didn't matter. All they knew is they had spent the last year of their lives investing all their hopes and dreams in this baby and it all came down to this small bundle of lifeless flesh that was hard to look at. So sad and so wrong.

"Do you have a name picked out for your baby? Do you have a name you want me to use to baptize him?" Brian asked.

Jim and Jenny looked at each other and weren't sure what to say. Jim finally said, "We were going to name him Phillip, after his grandfather, but I don't know now. Do we save that name for later?" They looked at each other some more and Jenny finally said, "No, this is Phillip. We have to let Phillip go."

Brian talked about the promise and hope we have in baptism, a hope that never ends, not even in death. He then had Jenny hold Phillip over the bowl. Three times he scooped water from the bowl and ladled it with his hand over the baby's head, saying, "Phillip Larson, I baptize you in the name of the Father, the Son, and the Holy Spirit." He anointed little Phillip's tiny head with the sign of the cross, saying, "Phillip, you have been sealed by the Holy Spirit and marked with the cross of Christ forever." Then he commended him into God's hands. It was a strange baptism and was more for the living than the dead–a poignant reminder of the reality of death and the very promise and hope we hang on to no matter what may happen to any of us, what *will* happen to every one of us.

To Brian it felt right. As a young pastor in training, he felt as though he was providing real pastoral care and was even grateful he had the chance to experience this terrible moment. He believed God brings some of the best things out of the worst things. Unlike many prosperity preachers who will say with the right faith, things will always break your way, Brian knew the truth. The cross is a symbol of torture and death, something awful and terrible, and yet it symbolizes God's love and our greatest hope. The message is God is especially present when things *don't* break your way. That's the big paradox of our faith–hope and salvation from suffering. Death turned into life!

Brian said a final brief prayer and there was a little more weeping, but nothing like before. Jenny held her baby and closed her eyes and Jim moved away and looked out the window into the dark night. Jenny extended little Phillip to the nurse, who took the baby and bowl away.

As Brian was planning his exit, the couple had become quiet and disconnected again and he wondered what they were thinking. He held her hand, said goodbye to Jenny, and then went over to say goodbye to Jim. Brian said, "So, Jim, where do you see God in this? How is this impacting your faith? Are you angry at God?"

Jim was quiet and thoughtful for a long moment then said something that Brian would never forget. Still staring out the window into the dark storm he said, "Well, at first I was mad at God. I just couldn't understand this at all. Then you came and I was sure I didn't want to hear anything you had to say. Then you started crying so hard and then we all cried together. It really surprised me. I didn't expect that. Now as I look out at the storm and I hear the thunder and I think 'God must be sad about this too.'"

Brian was thunderstruck at this observation. It would change forever how he understood God. Of course, God was sad about this and Brian understood the amazing truth of it in that moment. This wasn't what God wanted. This wasn't something God caused. The human body is complex and sometimes things go wrong and life does not come forth. It's not part of the plan, but in a way it is. Who knows what broke down in the process, but something wasn't right and so the body was wise enough to terminate the process. It's not what God wants, but it is what can happen quite naturally. When things don't go as designed and life does not come forth, creation laments. Brian would never forget that awful night or the powerful lesson in theology: "God is sad about this too!"

CHAPTER 15

AS USUAL BRIAN'S brain was making mental lists of what still needed to be addressed that day. With everything on his plate at the moment he felt a distinct loss of control, more so than usual. He needed to make an actual list. That usually helped when things seemed to be spinning out of control.

Back at his office, Brian got out pen and paper, old technology, and began. After writing two-dozen tasks he stopped. There were about ten other things Brian could think to put on the list but gave up because it wasn't helping. Already overwhelmed, making the list just made him want to cry.

He felt like a drowning man.

This feeling reminded him of why he had become an alcoholic in the first place. When things got like this, he wanted to run away, and alcohol had been his escape in the past. He had been here plenty of times before in his recovery and he knew what he needed to do. His recovery had taught him well. First things first–get to a meeting! Brian pulled out the AA directory, found a meeting nearby starting in a few hours, and determined to go. He took a deep, cleansing breath, and then he prayed the Serenity Prayer. He thought about calling his sponsor, but as he too often did, told himself it wasn't that bad yet.

He looked at the list and said, "Lord, can you take some of this from me please?" Then he took the list and threw it in the garbage, saying, "Thy will be done, not mine." He knew from experience that the most important tasks he should be concerned with were "people" not "things."

He turned to his computer and wrote an email to the church staff, calling a brief meeting for that afternoon. He knew Maureen would put up a fuss because she was so busy, but he didn't care. He knew there were others who couldn't be there as not all staff were full-time, but they knew the drill. When there was a death, it was first priority. Everything else is put on hold. The email advised they would only meet briefly to discuss the Candy Vinter situation.

He then emailed Sue Solberg and asked her to follow up on Patty Severson. He asked if she would see her in the hospital, take her a prayer shawl, find out what will be happening to her next, then send out an update on the prayer chain. He emailed Andy Mosely with some possible dates to meet for marriage counseling. He emailed the Stephens with some possible meeting times for Jeffrey and to remind them he needed Jeffrey to list his top issues with the faith before they met. He set the alarm on his phone to go off three times, the day before the next meeting of the women's group, then an hour before, then ten minutes before. He wrote the appointment in his calendar so he didn't schedule anything on top of it, being the world's worst scheduler.

He reviewed all his messages, emails, mail, and phone calls to double check for anything urgent, then made the executive decision to leave so he could focus on his sermon for Sunday. He knew the only way he could make any progress on it was if he left.

Since he was putting people first, Brian felt that if he neglected his sermon he was neglecting the highest number of people, and he owed it to them to give them his best effort. As he thought this, the phone rang. He let it go to voice mail and felt a small victory won as he walked out with his computer.

CHAPTER 16

B RIAN TOLD MAUREEN he was off to an appointment, which wasn't true technically. If he said he was going to a coffee shop to work on his sermon without distraction he would never hear the end of it. He could hear the litany, "I would love to work without distraction too, but I don't have that luxury." "Oh fine, I will just take care of everything here, Pastor, you just go and enjoy some peace and quiet. Don't mind me . . ." And so on.

She wasn't happy, but she waved him off with a flip of her hand, her trademark martyr's salute that said, "Fine, save yourself, I'll go down with the ship."

Soon, he was comfortably ensconced in a quiet corner of *Oly and Lena's*, a restaurant in the middle of a nearby strip mall that boasted a first-rate bakery and unique menu of Scandinavian dishes. The homey place had introduced Brian to an entirely new way to appreciate Scandinavian food, and also taught him that Scandinavian cuisine really was more complex than he originally thought. He learned to love many of the dishes offered on the menu, his favorite being the *lefse* melt. He had weekly lunches here with local colleagues from other Lutheran churches. Pastor schedules can be incredibly unpredictable but a few of them would make it each week.

He ordered coffee and began working on his sermon tucked away in the corner booth. With the death of Candy Vinter fresh on everyone's mind, he wanted his sermon to deal with life and death issues. Brian was certain of life after death. He knew it was real, but had no idea how to think about what it might be like. It was a complete mystery, one that he knew was far beyond anything mere mortals could even begin to imagine. Yet he knew that the best way to describe it was to use positive human experiences and project them as similes.

Brian was fascinated by people who report having an NDE, a near-death experience. The multitude of stories and testimonies he had read described similar experiences of what it's like on the other side. Those who experience death and come back often talk about how frustrating it is to describe where they were. There are no words, descriptions, or human experiences that come anywhere close to conveying the joy, peace, and wonder they encounter in heaven.

Focusing on this great promise of life after death would be fitting with the nearness of Candy Vinter's death. What he wasn't sure about, however, was how or even whether to address the matter of suicide. That wasn't in the text and he wasn't sure if he even needed to go there. But without a funeral planned for Candy to address it, then maybe he should try to work it into his sermon. People will want to know.

He knew God would never forsake any of his children for any reason. Brian was a theological universalist in this regard. He believed everyone had attained heaven because of Jesus Christ, whether they knew it or not, or whether they believed it or not. He knew that his more conservative Christian brothers and sisters go ballistic over this. They insist a person needs to confess faith in the name of Jesus to be saved for the afterlife. Pastor Brian, however, believed that even if there was a hell it was empty because of

Jesus. What kind of God of love would create a place of flame and eternal torture as a way to threaten the children he loves? That makes no sense at all. What Jesus did on the cross was for the whole world, for all sinners for all time—without condition. Unfortunately, so much of Christian theology focuses on being moral enough or believing exactly the right thing to get into heaven, which did not fit in Brian's mind with a God of love revealed in Jesus Christ. Jesus loved sinners, plain and simple, and he challenged anyone who tried to exclude them for any reason. Jesus never condemned sinners, but he most often condemned self-righteous and religious people. Given that fact, who would ever want to be a self-righteous Christian?

Brian was just beginning to get his focus when someone approached his table.

"Hello, I'm sorry to interrupt you, but are you a minister?" the woman said.

Brian looked up from his laptop and saw a middle-aged woman wearing dark slacks and beige jacket, a professional of some kind. She had medium-length dark hair with an outdated haircut and too much makeup. He stood and greeted her with a forced smile as he endured yet another interruption.

People first, he reminded himself.

"Yes, I am. I am Pastor Brian Matterson from All Saints Lutheran church, and you are?"

"My name is Susan Grant. I was at the funeral for Nate Morley a few weeks ago. I just had to tell you that was one of the most meaningful funerals I have ever been to. Your message was so perfect. I had never heard things put the way you did. It just made so much sense."

"I'm sorry," Brian said. "I didn't hear you. Could you repeat that?"

She started to say it again when Brian cut her off. "I am kidding. I just wanted to hear it again. Those are very kind words. Thank you."

"Well, I do mean it. It was just wonderful. I had thought I wanted to track you down someday and talk some more. I have a lot of questions that I feel like I could trust you with, and well, here you are."

"I would be glad to meet with you. Any time," he said and began digging for his card before realizing he didn't have one.

"Are you busy now?" she asked and then said, "well of course you are. I can see that." Seeing him unable to locate a card, she said, "How about you text me your number and I can call and make an appointment?" handing him her card.

"That would be fine."

"Well, I don't think now would work for me anyway. I have a busy schedule today. I better get moving. I will call you and we can talk. I would really appreciate that."

"Of course, I would too. I really would. It's what I do," he said. He typed her number into his phone and she let it ring once so she would have it in her contact list.

The problem Brian had with interruptions is that it took him so long to get back mentally to where he was, particularly when it comes to writing. He sat back down and tried to zero in on his thought process once again. Just as soon as he got back into the zone, his phone went off. "*Eh, sexy lady,* 오-오-오-오 *오빠 강남스타일, Eh, sexy lady,* 오-오-오-오."

He should have ignored it, but by habit he looked and saw that it was the church's phone number. He knew that Maureen didn't bother him when he was away unless it was important, so he reluctantly answered. "This is Pastor Matterson."

"Oh, hello, Pastor. I thought I would get your voicemail since you were at an appointment," Maureen said with a slightly sarcastic tone.

"What is it, Maureen?"

"I thought you should know that Officer Mike Hemsley from the Martin Valley Police Department came in looking for you. He wants you to call him."

"Did he say what it was about?"

"No, he didn't, but he said it was important that he talk to you as soon as possible. He left me his cell phone," she said, and gave Brian the number. "Are you coming back soon?" she asked. "I can't get anything done with the phone and people coming by. They all want to know about the Candy Vinter and Patty Severson."

"Just tell them we don't know anything yet about Candy's funeral. I will go over that at staff later. Patty is going to be just fine. Check with Sue about Patty. She will know more when she gets back."

"Okay, but we may not have bulletins for Sunday."

"We'll live."

"You might, but I won't."

"Maybe if we didn't have bulletins we could convince everyone we need more help."

"It wouldn't work," she said. "They would just wonder what we do all day."

"Well, Maureen, as always, do the best you can. That's all any of us can do."

"I know, I know," and she clicked off without saying goodbye.

He hated that. She knew he hated that.

CHAPTER 17

B RIAN KNEW OFFICER Mike
Hemsley. He was a longtime
member of the church. His family was there every Sunday, his
wife and three children. They were active members and Mike was
forever apologizing for not being there for worship as his schedule
did not allow it. Brian constantly told him not to worry about it,
joking that as long as his offering made it each week he was happy.

Hemsley would attend worship occasionally in his uniform,
but he didn't like being in church with his uniform, badge, gun,
handcuffs, stun gun all hanging off his belt. It didn't seem right for
church, but Brian told him he loved it. "Your uniform is a reminder
of the blessing we have in the heroes of our community. Having
you here makes us thankful, not uncomfortable," he would tell
him. Hemsley tried a few times, but told Brian he could never get
over feeling like a pariah in the church. He would rather be there
as a civilian.

Brian called and Hemsley answered on the first ring. "Officer
Hemsley," he said curtly.

"Hello, Mike, this is Pastor Matterson. I heard you were looking for me. Is there a warrant for me?"

"Thank you for calling, Pastor. I need to talk to you as soon as possible. I can't talk about it over the phone. Any chance you would be available now?"

Brian rolled his eyes and surrendered once again. "Yes, Mike, of course. I could talk to you now. I'm sitting over at *Oly and Lena's* working on my sermon. Could you talk here?"

"Is it private? Could we talk without being overheard?"

"Yes, it's very slow right now and I am in a corner booth and there isn't anyone closer than two tables away."

"That should be fine. I will be right there."

"Can you tell me what this is regarding?" Brian asked, but Hemsley was already off the line.

What the hell is with everyone today? Brian wondered. He couldn't remember the last time he had been hung up on two times in a row . . . or even once, if you didn't count Maureen.

Brian turned his attention back to his sermon, but it wasn't long before he knew that was pointless now. He had too many distractions in his head, and knowing Hemsley would arrive any moment made the effort to zero in not worth it. Instead, he did email. He had knocked off about six responses when Mike Hemsley arrived in his full uniform, gun and all. Even though he had told Mike his full uniform was a visible blessing, Brian still felt uneasy in the presence of all that power and authority. He wondered if other people felt the same way and assumed they did. He was sure the men in blue gave everyone some kind of emotional response. That was probably part of the point of wearing it, wasn't it? He thought about his own uniform, his Roman clerical collar, and was sure his collar was off-putting for many. It was obvious at times.

Brian stood and greeted Mike and invited him to sit down.

"Thanks for making time for me."

"No problem, Mike. I'm pretty curious. This isn't anything serious, is it?" Brian said after they sat.

"Well, yes, it is serious. It's also very delicate. I need you to keep our conversation very much to yourself."

"Of course, Mike. I always do. What's going on?"

He was about to begin but the server came with a menu. They ordered a coffee for Hemsley, and when she walked away he began. "You are aware of the situation at the Vinter home?"

"Well, yes of course. I have been in touch with the family; I know what's going on. Candy hung herself, right?"

"Well, it would appear that way," Hemsley said, "but . . ."

The server returned and put down the coffee. Brian watched Hemsley pour cream into his coffee. "I thought cops took coffee black."

"We do, Pastor, but not when there is real cream sitting on the table," Hemsley said.

Cream is another thing Scandinavians liked a lot, real cream. It keeps you warm. It was just another form of butter, which Scandinavians can't get enough of.

Hemsley waited again until the server was well out of range. "We are looking into things and we think there might be something more going on."

"Something more going on, like what? What do you mean?" Brian asked, confused and surprised.

"Well, certain things don't add up. I can't tell you what those things are, but I can tell you we are thinking she didn't take her own life."

Brian was stunned and speechless. His brain was computing this new information. Would this explain Mick's behavior and some of the inconsistencies around the how and why of Candy's death?

But Mick? No way, couldn't be. "Who is the suspect, Mike? Who would want to kill Candy Vinter? And why are you telling me this?"

Hemsley stirred his coffee and thought for a minute before he answered. "You cannot share this with anyone," Hemsley said, "I could lose my job."

"Mike, I'm your pastor. I can't even share what you tell me in court. I could lose my job too. My lips are sealed."

"I guess I'm telling you because I need to tell someone. I've been going to church with the Vinters for the last twelve years. Our kids go to Sunday school together. I'm just having a hard time with this . . . no matter how it turns out it's disturbing," Hemsley said. "As a cop, you see a lot of things, but when it hits close to home it's hard to stay objective."

"I understand how you feel. I'm feeling some of it too. When someone close dies like this, everyone feels it personally. People think, 'Why couldn't she have come to me?' That's what I keep asking myself. I could have done something, should have done something," Brian said. "But you really don't think it was suicide?"

"Well, we're not sure, Pastor. Like I said, there are some things that don't add up and some forensics that make us wonder pretty hard. We are looking at her husband for this. They are not going to do anything just yet but they are starting to dig. That's another reason I thought you should know. You will be working with the family and preaching at her funeral, so I figured it might make a difference on what you might say. And if this turns out to be true, the kids are going to need all the help they can get. That's probably my biggest reason for wanting you to know. I need your prayers for me and for them."

Brian's head was spinning. He tried to imagine a scenario where Mick could do something like this. It just didn't seem like him at all. He was so withdrawn and passive. Brian had been a judge of people as part of his daily ministry and he could not see Mick as a murderer under any circumstances. He also thought about Mick's behavior and how desperately reclusive he was acting and wondered if that made him seem guilty. His gut had been telling him something strange was going on with Mick. Was this what he was feeling? Still, Mick killing Candy?

"I just don't see it, Mike. I can't see Mickey Vinter hurting anyone. Just doesn't make sense."

"I agree. He doesn't seem like the type, but you never know what people can do given the right circumstances. We are moving slowly on this, so they won't do anything until they feel like they have a solid case. It would be terrible to falsely accuse someone of something like this, but they will be looking for any evidence, particularly motive. You don't know anything going on with the family that would give him a motive, do you, Pastor?"

Brian looked Hemsley in the eye and said, "You know I can't answer that, Mike. They are my parishioners just as much as you are and my job is to care for them. I can't be used to incriminate anyone."

"Yes, yes, of course. I know that. Old habit. I'm sorry, I didn't mean to cross any lines."

"Don't worry about it, Mike. I know you have a job to do and sometimes that job is pretty unpleasant. I don't envy you on this one."

"Well, it isn't really my job," Hemsley said, "it belongs to the detectives, but they are so short staffed we get sent out to help tie up loose ends. I will be asked to do some of the legwork on this, but I won't be the one to take any action. Besides, it's all up to the DA to pull any trigger."

"Well, you've certainly given me some things to think about . . . and pray about. I appreciate you sharing this with me. I will pray for you for sure. Please come and see me any time you need to talk, okay?"

"I will, Pastor. Thank you. I really appreciate you seeing me on such short notice, but this is really helpful. And I appreciate the prayers." With that, Mike Hemsley tipped back the rest of his coffee and got up to leave.

"God bless you, Officer Hemsley. Thank you for the all the ways you give your life in service," Brian said as Hemsley was walking away.

"Same goes for you, Pastor," Hemsley said without looking back.

At the register, Officer Mike took care of both cups of coffee before leaving.

CHAPTER 18

B RIAN KNOCKED OFF a few more emails, jotted down some notes for his sermon, and packed it up. He knew he couldn't concentrate now with the information Hemsley just dumped on him.

As he drove back to the office, he reflected on their conversation. *Mickey Vinter killed his wife? Is that possible?* Brian tried to figure out how he could have done it. *How do you hang someone against their will? Is that possible? She would have to be knocked out at least.*

From what he knew of Candy and Mickey he could not envision any way Mick could get her to do anything she didn't want to do. It was clear who was in charge in that relationship. Mickey was an obedient husband and let his wife take the lead. No, he wouldn't be able to hang her if she didn't want him to.

Hemsley had mentioned forensics. *Maybe he knocked her out? Maybe there were drugs involved.* That's the only way it made sense. He could have drugged her and then hung her, but he must have known they would check her for drugs?

And what about motive? What reason would Mickey have to kill his wife? Yes, she was the domineering one, but not overly much from what he had seen. He was quiet and retreating, letting her do all the talking. Maybe he snapped, just couldn't take it anymore. Still, it didn't ring true for Brian. He needed to know a lot more before he could believe it.

Back at the office, as Maureen handed him three new messages, he asked how she was doing, knowing full well the answer already, and then just for fun, added, "I could still get Jerry Meyers to come in and help out if you want. I don't mind."

"You wouldn't dare. I will walk right out that door. I mean it," she said.

Brian chuckled to himself all the way to his office.

* * *

Brian met in the church boardroom for the special staff meeting that afternoon. Gathered around the large folding tables and chairs they discussed what to tell people who asked about Candy Vinter. It was important they all say the same thing to limit any rumors. Rumors would fly regardless, but Brian felt it was imperative the church staff not be a part of the rumor mill. Brian reminded them all how vital it was not to speculate or be drawn into conversations based on speculations. They talked it over and agreed that all they could say was what they knew. As of then, they only knew Candy had taken her own life; the family was doing as well as could be expected and were asking for privacy; the funeral at this time would be a private family memorial service at the funeral home for the coming Saturday afternoon. If people pushed for any details beyond those, they needed to contact the pastor.

Thinking of his conversation with Mike Hemsley, he asked the staff if they had picked up on anything from the Vinter family that would give any indication things were this bad for Candy. The Sunday school superintendent, Robin Rawley, said the kids have seemed the same as ever, but that didn't mean she didn't have concern for them. It was clear there was something unhealthy happening in the home, but that's the case with so many families. The Vinters were not much different from anyone else in that regard.

Candy's death was of course a huge shock to all of them and Brian wondered how much shock there would be if the news about Mick being a murderer turned out to be true.

The staff discussed how to bring healing to the church if the family did not want a public service. It was decided they needed to do something, and agreed that if Brian couldn't convince Mick to hold a service at All Saints, they would offer a candlelight vigil for the community with music, hymns, readings, and maybe a short message. It would be a time for people to share, and would end with lit candles, a prayer, and a hymn. They would have it Sunday evening, if necessary. Brian would invite the Vinter family and hoped they would come.

The staff prayed together as they always did and each went back to their duties. Brian returned to his office and decided he would need to take his sermon home to work on that evening. He hated bringing work home, but sometimes it got like this and he had no choice.

Just as he made this decision, a text came from his wife reminding him he was to pick up Dougie from band practice at 5:15, feed him dinner, and then get him to soccer practice by 6:00. After that he was to be at a swim meet for Robert as fast as he can get there because Donna had signed him up to be a timer. "Don't forget, they want the timers there a half hour early," her text reminded him.

Brian was the worst scheduler in the world. He could not manage a calendar to save his life. Beyond his inability to manage his own work schedule, he didn't even attempt to keep up with the home schedule. He relied entirely on prompts from his wife to keep him on track.

Jesus . . . he thought to himself and instantly heard a voice in his head shaming him for taking the Lord's name in vain, to which he replied, "It isn't in vain. I was serious! It was a cry for help, so shut up."

So much for his sermon. It would have to wait. His children took precedence.

CHAPTER 19

BRIAN SAW HIS time drawing short. He needed to get a few urgent matters done before he could get away. He got the rest of what Maureen needed for the bulletin put together: the announcements, the prayer list, the order of service, the readings, the litany, the prayer of the day, post communion prayer, and the benediction.

He was updating the website, a job he detested, but he was the only one on staff who had the technical ability to do it. He knew he could teach someone else, but just couldn't seem to find the time to do it. Every time he updated the website, he berated himself for not handing this off to someone else already.

As he was updating the weekly calendar, the door of his office popped open and Barney came through. Just as suddenly as he came through he said, "Oops, almost forgot," and he backed out, shut the door, and knocked, calling out, "Pastor, are you in there?"

Brian couldn't believe it. He decided not to answer. He waited. The knock came again, along with, "Pastor, are you in there?"

Brian still didn't respond.

It was quiet for a moment and then finally Barney said, "Pastor, I know you are in there, I just saw you. Can I come in?"

Brian remained quiet.

Some more time passed and then Barney said, "Pastor, I don't have time to play games. I need to talk to you."

Brian went over to the door, opened it a crack, and said, "Barney, you know I care about you, don't you?"

"Well, yes, I guess so. Yes."

"Well, I'm not playing games. You really need to learn you cannot come barging in here like you do. It's important. Please don't do it again, okay? Will you promise me?"

"Well, yes, of course, Pastor, but it's hard to remember. Pastor Nelson never minded when I came in here. His door was always open, even when he had people in here."

Brian took a deep breath. *He had been here for how long already and still lived under the shadow of the previous pastor?* "Okay, Barney. But I am not Pastor Nelson and I like to work with my door closed. And I like people to knock before they come in," Brian didn't have time for this. "What do you need, Barney?"

"They can fix the coffee machine and they can have it ready by Friday. It's going to cost between six and seven hundred."

"Six or seven hundred?" Brian exclaimed. "A new one is eleven hundred. What could be so wrong that we have to spend more than half the cost of a new one?"

"I don't know. They didn't say. What do you want me to do?"

"Get it fixed. Tell them to go ahead. What else can we do?"

"That's what I thought too."

"Okay, Barney, thank you," Brian said, shutting the door. He opened it again quickly and shouted down the hall, "Tell them to hurry!"

"Okay," Barney waved without looking back.

Time was up. He needed to pick up his son.

*　　*　　*

When Brian arrived at his office the next morning Sue Solberg was waiting to talk to him and so was Aksel Erickson. Brian asked who was first, knowing Aksel was always first but usually ambushed him in the parking so he could be sure to have first access. Brian knew this is what Erickson did, and whenever he saw him waiting and he wasn't in the mood he would pull out his phone and pretend to be in a conversation so he could get into the building unmolested. He hated getting piled on the minute he pulled in. He liked to have a few minutes to get settled, boot up his computer, use the restroom, say a prayer, and take a breath. Like it or not, most days he hit the ground running.

Sue indicated she could wait, which was just like her and Erickson came into his office as Brian settled in. "Okay, Aksel, what's the bad news?" he began. He knew Erickson was there to talk about the roof leak.

"Well, they came out yesterday and were looking around. They can see several other places that look like they could go any time, but with snow up there it's hard to be sure. Probably worse than what they could see. The roof is in pretty rough shape and they say it's time to replace the membrane."

"Of course, they do. And how much?"

"They are sending me a bid later today, but they estimate around $35,000 to replace the whole thing."

"Holy cow, Aksel! You said twenty to thirty before. That's a lot more!" Brian exclaimed.

"I know, I know, but prices keep rising. I was surprised too."

"What about just patching the bad spots for now?"

"Well, they don't really recommend that. They've already done some patching and we are well beyond the original warranty."

"I know that," Brian said, "we all know that. But can we buy a little more time with some patching until we can figure out how to pay for it?"

"Well, yes, they can. They don't recommend it, but they can."

"Did they say how much that would cost?"

"Probably about $10,000," Erickson said. "They are sending a bid for that too."

"Ten thousand. That's a third of what it cost to replace the whole thing. I don't understand these things. The coffee machine was $700 to fix and $1100 to replace . . . it's crazy, it makes no sense."

"I know. It's all in the labor, I guess. People are expensive."

Brian sat for a minute wondering how they would possibly pay for this. He certainly couldn't authorize any of this without going to the council. They would probably have to do another fundraiser. He could hear the people groaning already. If he had to do fundraising he would prefer to do it for sending missionaries out, or help the local food shelf, or a million other good causes, but who can get excited about replacing a rubber gasket on the roof? That just wasn't very sexy. Could he use that word? It was just so darn frustrating trying to do great things for God when coffee machines and building repairs cause so much distraction and suck up all the money.

"This will have go to the council, Aksel, and you know what they are going to say, don't you?"

"No, I don't know, Pastor. What will they say?"

"They will ask if we got any other bids or opinions," Brian said. "Can you get at least one other person here to make a bid?"

"Pastor, I know these guys. We are not going to find anyone better."

"I know, I know," Brian said. "But the council always wants to know that we did our homework. If we don't come with at least two bids, they are going to table this until we get another bid to compare. I just know that's what they'll do. We might as well save ourselves the time. Can you get one other bid on this?"

Erickson appeared annoyed. He was a volunteer and already gave a great deal of time and energy to the problems of the building. Brian could understand his frustration. He sensed on a number of occasions that dealing with the bureaucracy of the church made Aksel want to throw in the towel.

Erickson seemed to suppress his feelings and said, "Okay, Pastor. We won't get a better person or price, but I will get another bid. I supposed that's the right thing to do."

"Thanks, Aksel. What you do is such a gift and hardly anybody appreciates the extent of how lucky we are to have you. I sure do and I thank you. I would be lost here without your help."

Aksel nodded his thanks to the pastor and got up to leave. "Thanks, Pastor. I will try to get that by the end of the week. Let's hope the snow doesn't melt too fast before then," he said as he walked out.

"I will pray and do a dance," Brian said and Erickson smiled a little.

Sue Solberg came in right after Erickson left and asked if she could close the door, signaling an important discussion.

She moved quickly to sit down and began speaking straight off. "I'm so sorry, I know you have your hands full, but I heard something I think you should know."

"Okay, Sue, go right ahead."

"Well, it's about Candy Vinter," she said, looking anxious.

Brian nodded and leaned forward in his seat behind his desk.

"Well, I don't like gossip and I make it a point to never repeat it, but this isn't gossip. I have it through a very reliable source."

"Sue, you are the most caring person I know and you are also one of the most professional church workers I have ever worked with. You are discreet and trustworthy. And if you think this is something I need to know, then it must be important."

"Well, I can't tell you how I know this, but a family member confided to me that Candy Vinter was a serious hypochondriac. She has been sick with all those things through the years but they were all fake. She was never really sick, she never went to the doctor. It was all made up." Sue's words came out in a rush, with a strained look on her face. "I would never repeat something like this, especially when it was about someone who just died, but I also couldn't bear to have you stand up and go on at her funeral about all her challenges and pain and suffering when none of it was true."

"None of it!" Brian was flabbergasted. *She was never sick?* "What about the fundraisers we did to help her and her family?"

"I know . . . that's what makes this so terrible. She was taking advantage of people, church people and people from work. Maybe that's why she killed herself. Maybe she couldn't bear it anymore or maybe she was afraid of getting caught."

On the other hand, maybe Mickey couldn't bear it anymore. "But, Sue, she had cancer. She lost her hair. She was wearing scarves to cover her bald head," Brian said. "Are you telling me she didn't have cancer? She wasn't having chemotherapy?"

"No, Pastor. It was all a lie. I don't know how a person does that, but it wasn't true."

Brian's mind was reeling. He couldn't imagine a person going through life playing that kind of game. *What must that be like?* He couldn't fathom such a thing. "You are sure about this, Sue? You know this for a fact?"

"I do, Pastor, and the person who told me wanted you to know and asked me to tell you. They didn't want you to make her out to be somebody she wasn't."

"Do you have any idea how many people know this?"

"Very few, Pastor. It's been a well-kept secret and part of the reason the Vinter family is so troubled, I think. I have always felt there was something going on with those kids and this explains a lot. What must it have been like to have her as a mother? It must have been just awful."

"No kidding."

He thought about Mick's behavior, the house so quiet and deserted, the kids in their rooms, how Mick treated visitors, how he wanted the funeral to be private. It all fit. Whether she took her own life or whether Mick took it, it did help explain some of the oddities around this death and this family.

"Well, Sue," Brian said, "thank you for telling me. This explains a lot of what I'm seeing too. It must have been hard for you to hear this and to have to tell me."

"You have no idea, Pastor."

"Right now, I don't even know what to think about this. This is so crazy. All I can think about is her shaving her head and telling people she has cancer . . . how does somebody do that? She was really sick, wasn't she? But not in the ways we thought. It's so sad. And none of us knew it. And what about that poor family having to live with these terrible lies and secrets? How will they ever adjust? And if this gets out . . . even worse. They will have to move for the shame of it. What a mess. I'm going to have to talk to Mickey and see how he's doing. He needs to know I know so he can talk about it. He needs to talk," Brian said, thinking out loud.

"No, Pastor, you can't say anything, not even to Mickey. I swore and guaranteed them you would keep it a secret. If you say anything to Mickey he will know who told or he will figure it out. You can't say anything."

Brian was at a loss. He had never encountered anything like this before. "Okay, Sue, I won't then. I won't do that to you. But would you do me a favor?"

"Yes, of course, Pastor, anything."

"Will you ask this person if I could talk with them? I need to talk about this and so do they. It's really important. Can you do that?"

Sue was hesitant but then said, "I will try, Pastor. I don't think he will want to talk to you. He's very afraid, but I will see what I can do."

Brian suddenly knew she was talking about Kyle. He wasn't sure how he knew but he felt very certain. This made him even more determined. "You need to try and be as persuasive as you can, Sue. It's really important. Try not to take no for an answer. If no is all you get, then negotiate, say at least think about it. I really must talk to this person. Let them know I am easy to talk to and it's because I care, and that I will keep their secret, I swear. Please do your best."

"Okay, Pastor, I will," she said with conviction, appearing emboldened by Brian's passion.

"Then let us pray," he said and they bowed their heads together and asked God to help them through this to bring healing, peace, and hope.

CHAPTER 20

$\mathbf{B}$RIAN LISTENED TO a phone message from Connie Stephens that her son, Jeffrey, would like to meet with him after school today at 3:45 and would he have time to meet. Brian picked up the phone and called to confirm. Connie did not answer but he left a message and hoped she would get it. You never knew these days. He asked her to text his phone or send an email to confirm that he was planning to meet them.

He dreaded matching wits with a fifteen-year-old because as he had learned over the years, fifteen-year-olds pretty much have everything figured out already and are pretty sure if you are over thirty, you are old school and unenlightened. Brian believed it was God's sense of humor that pastors are expected to teach youth the most important thing they will ever learn at a time in their lives when they least care about it. Teaching confirmation to seventh, eighth, and ninth graders is like trying to give answers to questions they aren't asking and could care less about. It was a cruel irony and a large challenge. Any other age would be better than those three years.

Brian decided he needed to talk to Mick again to see about having the service at the church and get his blessing to hold a memorial vigil for Candy. He also wanted to feel Mick out for the possibility of his involvement in Candy's demise. With the new information he had from Sue Solberg, he was beginning to imagine a possible motive. If he knew Candy was faking all these diseases was he threatening to expose her? Was that why she threatened him when he left the house? Was that enough to make him want to kill her, perhaps before she could kill him? Was he that afraid of her? He still didn't think so and couldn't imagine how he would he have done it. If Mick was guilty of this thing, he surely was going to need a friend more than ever.

Brian was not giving up.

He headed over to drop in on Mickey Vinter once again.

Arriving midmorning, about 10:00 a.m., the house looked as strangely alone as always. This time, however, there was a different car, a tan Nissan, in the driveway. Brian parked next to it and made his way to the door. He knocked and waited. This time he heard stirring in the house right away and wondered who was here with Mick. A woman opened the door. She had graying dark hair, blue eyes, and fair skin. She was wearing a dark button-down blouse and black slacks. He knew she must be a relative of Candy's as he could see something of her in this woman—Candy's pretty blue eyes, he realized suddenly.

"Can I help you?" the woman said through the screen door.

"Yes, hello," Brian said, "I'm Brian Matterson and I am the pastor to the Vinter family. I came by to see Mick."

"Mickey isn't here right now and won't be back until later. I can tell him you stopped by."

"Are you related to Candy by any chance?" Brian ventured.

"Yes, I am her mother. I met you once at a Christmas program my grandchildren were in. I wouldn't expect you to remember me."

"You're Candy's mother . . . I'm so sorry for your loss. I can't imagine how this must be for you. I can't imagine a worse pain for a mother to experience."

The woman hesitated, seeming to be fighting back her emotions. Finally, she said, "Yes, it's been very hard."

"The experts say there is nothing on earth more painful than a mother losing her child," Brian said, immediately feeling stupid for saying it.

"I would say that was true," she said. "I don't know how I'm ever going to get over this."

"Well, I don't think you ever will," Brian said. "I think it will always hurt, but I do believe you will eventually make peace with it . . . but not for a long time, I'm sorry to say," he added.

The woman seemed to appreciate Brian's brutal honesty and nodded her head in agreement.

"I've been concerned about the kids. They have been at the church their whole lives and so many people, including myself, are concerned for them. Are they doing okay?"

The woman looked off to the side, seeming to consider her response. As she did so, she reached up and tucked her short brown hair behind her ear. The motion reminded him so much of Candy. Looking at her profile—the long narrow nose, the abbreviated chin, and the way she held her head—he could see she was an older version of Candy. She looked back at him with Candy's blue eyes and he could see the worry and pain in her gaze.

"Well, Hannah is a mess. She can't stop crying. She tries to be the happy little girl she always is, but suddenly she loses it and it just breaks my heart."

"I figured Hannah would have the hardest time with this. I'm glad she's got you to be there for her."

Candy's mom cast her eyes down. What did Brian see in her expression? Was that guilt and shame?

"And Kyle? How is he?"

"Kyle?" she scoffed. "He's just like his father. Angry, sullen, quiet, brooding. Won't say a word. I can't get anything out of him. He's locked up tight. I can barely handle his moods and his temper."

"I figured that too. I worry for them and I want to try and help as much as I can. They are going to need a lot of help. I tried to tell that to Mick, but I don't think he appreciates how serious this is. Please know that I and the church will do whatever we can to help you through this. I hope you will let us."

She smiled a vague smile but didn't say anything, avoiding his eyes.

Brian paused for a moment then said, "I realize this is not the best time, but could I ask you some questions?" Brian said, deciding to pry a little. "I tried talking to Mick, but as you know he's pretty devastated and not a real talkative guy to begin with. I'm worried about him, and there a lot of things I don't understand. People are asking questions and everyone is mystified by this. Would you mind talking about what happened?"

She seemed to ponder this for a moment and then said, "Well, I'm just as mystified as you, but I can tell you what I know. Would you like to come in?" she said, opening the door to let Brian enter.

As he was moving through the door she said, "I really don't know why I'm doing this. I really don't like ministers," she said. "Nothing personal, but I just don't believe in church. I don't see anything good from it."

"I understand," he said. "You aren't the only one that feels that way and I can sure understand why people feel like you do," he said. "You might be surprised to know I probably agree with you on a lot of things about what's wrong with the church."

She seemed taken aback by his response. Brian thought she must have expected him to be defensive, but he'd had this conversation many times. "Well, a lot of good religion did for Candy," she said, then immediately apologized. "I'm sorry; I don't mean to be rude. I just don't understand what happened. I'm just so angry and confused and sad."

As she said this, her face grew red and Brian could see she was about to cry. Then she did start crying. Her face constricted severely and what started as weeping erupted suddenly into anguish from deep within, almost an animal sound. Brian was overwhelmed by the suddenness and strength of her grief and he was deeply moved. He stepped toward her and she let him hold her as she cried so powerfully in his arms, letting loose what felt like a lifetime of stored grief. He felt the enormous weight of her pain and tears of his own began to flow from his eyes.

They stood like that in the foyer for several minutes, Brian holding her as she wept and wailed. Then, just as suddenly as it began, she came to herself and seemed embarrassed. She pulled back from him quickly and hurried away.

"I'm so sorry," she said, returning with a box of Kleenex. "I don't know what happened. I've never cried like that before . . . I don't know where that came from. I'm so embarrassed," she said, wiping her nose and eyes, her face still bright red.

"Please don't apologize; it's good to cry, and you have every good reason," Brian said, wiping his own eyes. "It's healing."

She invited him into the living room and said, "Please sit down. Would you like some coffee? I could make some coffee," she said.

"Yes, I would love some coffee, if you wouldn't mind." He had already had his double latte that morning, but was hoping for a longer visit. It wasn't really a lie, and even if it was, the right reason was behind it. This was a very Lutheran thing. Martin Luther had instructed his followers to "Sin boldly!"

Instead of sitting, Brian followed her into the kitchen and was happy to see it was in order and assumed she had cleaned it. He said, "I don't even know your name."

"I'm Diane Gunderson," she said, moving through the kitchen looking for what she needed. "I don't know where anything is in this house."

"Diane, did you have any idea Candy was in so much pain? Did you see this coming at all?"

"Oh god, she was always in pain. I've never known her not to be. With her, it was always something. Even as a little girl, she was such a hypochondriac. I think she did it for the attention most the time, so I never knew when it was real," Diane said, opening and closing cupboards and drawers.

"But did you ever think she was on the verge of killing herself? Had she ever talked about it or tried anything like this before?" Brian asked.

"No. No way. Not Candy. She never talked about it or threatened it or anything like that. I would say that if she ever did try, she wasn't really trying to kill herself but trying to get attention. That would be more like her. I think that may be what happened. She was trying to get attention but she just went too far. She would never have done this for real, I don't think."

"But she was sick a lot. I've never known anyone who has had so many challenges with her health."

"Well, she was a drama queen. I don't know if all of that was as bad as she made it out."

"What do you mean?"

"Well, I never knew what to believe with her," Diane said. "She always had a complaint, and sometimes it was legitimate but most times it wasn't. It used to drive me crazy. I never knew what to believe, so I just stopped listening. I know that sounds terrible, doesn't it? But like I said, I thought she did it for attention and I just didn't want her to keep doing it. I thought if I stopped giving her so much attention when she complained that maybe she would find a better way."

"She was being treated for cancer, wasn't she? I mean I assumed the pain of the cancer is what drove her to kill herself?"

Diane stood over the coffee machine and was spooning coffee into the filter. She paused there and didn't move for several seconds. "I don't know. I just don't know," she finally said.

"What do you mean? You don't know if that's why she took her life?"

"I'm really not comfortable talking about this."

"Yes, of course. I'm so sorry. I don't mean to be pushy."

Silence hung in the room mixed with the smell of ground coffee.

"So where is Mick?" Brian asked as Diane poured the carafe of water into the back of the coffee machine.

"Mickey? I asked him if I could have the place to myself for a few hours to go through her things. I am putting some things together for the memorial service."

"How do you think he's doing?" Brian asked. "I'm a little worried about him."

"I never know how Mickey is doing. He keeps his distance. Always has. I see him at holidays, but that's about it. Whenever they would come over, he would sit there and you could tell he was just waiting for the time to leave. Whenever I came here, he would make himself scarce. I don't think he liked me, but Candy said he was just shy," she said. "He does seem particularly lost right now. I offered to take the kids and he quickly accepted. I don't think he knows what to do."

"Should I be worried about him?" Brian asked. "Because I am."

"I suppose," she said, "I just don't know him well enough to even know."

"Does he have family?" Brian asked. "I haven't seen anyone around and I worry that he has no support."

"His family is all out of state and not very close, from what I understand. His mother passed away years ago from something and he and his father rarely even talk, let alone see each other. I don't think there's a lot of love there."

"Are you okay with the private service at the funeral home?" Brian asked. "She was a member of our church and there are a lot of people who knew her and would like to be a part of saying goodbye." He paused, then said softly, "A private funeral makes it hard for her church family to grieve this."

"Well, I'm fine with it. It's what I would prefer. As I said, I don't have a lot of love for the church, and so this works just fine for me."

"Did you have a bad experience with the church?"

"You could say that," she said and Brian could tell that's all she wanted to say on the subject.

Diane slid the filter holder and grounds into the drip coffeemaker and switched it on. The two sat at the kitchen table while the maker began to immediately hiss and gurgle.

"Well, Candy was a member of this church and her kids were very involved. There are many people who want to pay their respects and grieve her loss. I honor Mick's and your desire to have a private funeral, but I would like you to know that we are talking about some kind of gathering to honor her memory and give thanks for her. It would be great to have you, the kids, and Mick there. Right now, it's planned for Sunday night. I was hoping to talk to Mick again about having the service at the church."

"I don't know," she said. She was staring off over Brian's shoulder and apparently debating something in her mind. "I'm afraid it would just make me angry."

"Angry? Really?" Brian asked. "What would make you angry?"

"The whole church thing," she said. "I don't want to offend you, you seem like a nice person, but I just don't believe any of that stuff. I think it's all crap and I think the church makes the world worse, not better. I just think sitting there and listening to all that would be just too much for me."

"Can I ask you what your background is, with the church I mean?"

"My parents were strict Christians," she said. "They made us dress up and go to church every week. They had rules about everything and how we should be. We were always in trouble. I watched my brothers get beatings for the simplest things, like just for swearing. My parents were fanatics, and irony was, they were hypocrites. They were judgmental and hateful toward people and they were in a loveless marriage. They would fight constantly, and if they weren't fighting with each other they were punishing us for the simplest infraction.

"I used to believe. When I was a little girl, I would pray and pray that God would help my parents and our family. My father drank and pretended he didn't; my mother nagged him constantly. It was pure hell. All my prayers went unanswered. My brother left home as soon as he could and I was stuck there with them. It was awful. I spent my high school years walking on eggshells and was grounded more times than not. Where was God? I begged and begged, but nothing happened. No, it actually got worse. I left home as soon as I could too and by then I swore I would never set foot in a church again. Like I say, Pastor, I don't mean any disrespect, I really don't, but I don't believe there is any God and I think the church does more a lot more harm than good."

CHAPTER 21

B RIAN HAD HEARD these stories before. In fact, as an ex-Catholic he could relate to some degree to Diane's experience. There were many stories like hers and he knew there were countless examples of how the church had done more to hurt the cause of Christianity than help it.

Brian too at one point had walked away from the church for many of these same reasons. Early in his recovery from alcoholism, he was confused by the fact that he had found the healing he prayed for in Alcoholics Anonymous and not in the church. He had been a faithful churchgoer and prayed fervently that God would rescue him. He prayed fervently for deliverance, but instead of getting better, his life only grew worse.

When he finally hit bottom, crashed and burned, he ended up in treatment and required AA meetings. He sat through his first meeting terrified because the people he saw in the room were awfully beat up. He was sure he didn't belong there. He believed his faith in God would provide him an easier, softer way than having to go through the humiliation of belonging to AA.

Through those early years of recovery, he often wondered why God had not rescued him in the church and grew to resent the church for failing him. Sitting in meetings in those early years he would often think if Jesus were alive today he would more likely be at 12-step meetings than at church. Because from what Brian could see, the 12-step meetings were where he saw lives healed and saved. Meanwhile, the church seemed to resemble more the religious institution Jesus was constantly challenging. Eventually Brian gave up on the church and made 12-step groups his spiritual home. He involved himself in service and chairing meetings and spreading the message of recovery to those who still suffer.

Now here he was, a pastor, a representative of the very church of which he was so critical. He marveled at the journey that had brought him here after all. He eventually made peace with his feelings about the church after sorting through his theology and coming to a fuller understanding of the unique role of the church. He understood clearly now how both the church and AA had essential but separate and unique roles to play and that both were life-giving gifts of love from God. He was deeply grateful that he was one of the very few who had the privilege of experiencing both blessings in his life. It was his mission in life to help other people realize these blessings in their lives too.

Brian looked at Diane with compassion and understanding. "I can understand why you would feel that way after what you experienced. I've had some of the same struggles with God and the church and with my family, but nothing like yours. I'm so sorry that happened to you."

She simply nodded her head.

"So, have you given completely up on God?" he said matter-of-factly. "I understand giving up on the church, but you really don't believe in God?" His experience had taught him that when people say they have given up on God what they really mean is they are pissed at God.

"Well, I didn't make Candy go to church or teach her any of that stuff. She went on her own. I don't see it did her much good.

No, Pastor, I don't think I do. I can't believe there is a God, and if there is one, he doesn't really care about us. Maybe there is something out there, I don't know, but all the talking and prayers don't do a bit of good. So maybe I believe there is something, but it isn't something that cares or gives a damn about us."

Brian understood that too. He had struggled mightily with the idea of God being personal. Why would God or whatever power it was that brought the universe into existence and ordered things so marvelously care personally about us and our individual needs and wants? When the God he earlier in life believed in, the one he was taught about growing up, did not act as he wished or expected, it was endlessly discouraging. He had countless times come to point of feeling there was nobody there, that it was all just imagined wishful thinking. Yet he could never let go of believing. What he believed about God had changed dramatically through his recovery and working the twelve steps. He was now far more certain of a loving, caring, personal God, but it was a far different understanding of God than he had before his alcoholism recovery. He still had his questions and doubts, but his belief was stronger than ever. He certainly could, however, understand why someone could not believe.

"Have you lost all your faith in God? You don't believe there is anything out there?" he asked her.

Diane paused and didn't seem to know how to answer. "I guess I don't know. I just stopped thinking about it because it just makes me too angry when I do . . . so I don't."

"Do you wonder at all where Candy might be now? Do you think she still exists or is she just gone now?"

At that, Diane's cheeks colored and she grew tearful. "I don't know," she said. "I want to believe she's not just gone, but I don't think . . . don't know what to think . . . I just don't know."

"Well, you're not alone. Nobody knows for sure. If anyone says they do they are lying. We have no proof at all if or how life might carry on beyond the grave. I can tell you what I think—no, what I believe, with every bit of my being," Brian said. "Do you want to know where I think she is right now?"

Diane glanced up at Brian with a flare of anger in her eyes as she looked through her tears, and then she quickly looked away. "I'm not sure I want to know what a preacher thinks. I know what my parents would say, or their pastor. Anyone who commits suicide is surely going to hell."

"Shit," Brian said under his breath but loud enough for her to hear. It seemed to startle her and she looked at him surprised. "I'm sorry," he said. "That just slipped out. That's the kind of thinking that makes it very hard for me to be a pastor. There is so much crap out there being taught about God that who can ever know what's really true. Anyone who says Candy is doomed to hell doesn't know what they are talking about."

Diane's brows furrowed. "That's not what you believe?" she said.

"Of course not," Brian said. "Candy was a child of God. What kind of God would condemn any of their children to hell? That's pure bullshit. I'm a father myself, and I can tell you that I would send myself to hell before I would send either of my children there no matter what they did. And if I am that way, how could I be more merciful and gracious than God?"

"You don't believe in hell?" she asked, looking at him, astonished. "What kind of preacher are you?"

Brian smiled and said, "Well, I do believe in hell, because I've already been there. Hell is on earth and it's what we create for ourselves when we live apart from God. But no, I don't believe a loving God would create a place to punish his children forever for being naughty. Isn't that just a crazy notion? It's nuts."

Diane was looking carefully at Brian, seeming to listen warily to what he was saying. Her brow was furrowed and her expression was one of bewilderment. Brian knew then she had never heard any other interpretation of Christianity than the fundamentalist crap she grew up with. Her head was slightly cocked as she appeared to be listing and computing his words. He was sure she had not heard the Gospel before, but only the law. He was excited at the opportunity to present Jesus in a new way to someone who had only felt judged and excluded her whole life.

"I think Candy was already experiencing some form of hell here on earth. Anyone who takes their own life is incredible pain. You have to be in tremendous pain to do something this radical and desperate. She needed to be free from the hell she was already in. Who knows the extent of hell she was dealing with, but she obviously could see no other way out of her pain. I am quite certain, though, that right now she is with God. I believe she has been set free from her pain and that she is in a place that is beyond human description, a place of immense joy and peace and wonder. She is there now and she will be there when you get there when your turn comes. She is alive and you will see her again."

Diane's body relaxed visibly as though an enormous weight suddenly lifted. Her furrowed brow went smooth. She sat and her tears continued to flow. She reached for a Kleenex and wiped her face as though she was trying to stop the flow but with little success.

When she had regained herself, she blew her nose and said, "Well, I hope you are right."

CHAPTER 22

DIANE GOT UP and filled two cups with fresh coffee. "Do you take cream or sugar?"

"Black is fine. Should we go sit in the living room?" he suggested.

"That's fine," she said, "but I told Mickey I would only need a couple of hours. I still need to go through her things and I want to be gone before he gets back."

"Okay, I won't take much more of your time."

They moved to the living room and settled in. Brian sat at the end of the sofa and Diane took the recliner to Brian's left across from the jumbotron. The shades were drawn, the room dark, yet it was still apparent the room needed dusting badly. There were aging overlapping rings on the coffee table and side tables. The TV screen had numerous smudges and handprints that were clearly visible on the black surface. The room was cluttered. The cheap furniture was old, worn.

"I still want to know what actually happened," Brian said. "I'm still a little confused."

Diane clicked on a table lamp to dispel some of the gloom, but it didn't seem to help much.

"Can you walk me through what actually happened?"

"Well, I don't know much either. Trying to get Mickey to talk is like pulling teeth. He told me the basics, and I would be surprised if it was any more than you already know. I talked to the kids and they've given me a few more details, but not much."

"I've been very concerned about the kids, especially Kyle. I can't imagine what it would be like to find your own mother like that."

"I know. It breaks my heart to think about it," she said. "He's a lot like his father. He's not saying much. He's pretty shut down. Hannah has told me more than he has."

"Would it be okay if I stopped by your place and visited with them?"

"Yes, of course, I think that would be great. I don't know about Kyle, but Hannah would think that was pretty exciting to have a pastor come see her. She's at that age."

"I'm glad to hear you are open to that. I would like to see them as soon as possible, maybe when they get out of school today?"

"No, that won't work," she said. "Mickey is picking them up and they are staying with him tonight. They are not thrilled about coming back to this house. But I will have them again tomorrow, so you can see them then."

"I will plan on it, thank you," he said. "Would you mind telling me what you know about what happened?"

"Well, I know they had a big fight the night before. There was a lot of screaming and Mickey ended up stomping out the door with Candy yelling after him."

"Do you know what they were fighting about?"

"No, but Hannah said when he walked out she screamed out the door at him, 'If you do I will kill you. I mean it, Mick. I'm serious.' Mickey was gone until late that night. Nobody is sure when he got home but he was there in the morning helping to get the kids ready for school. Candy was still sleeping, or so the kids thought. Because of her chemo treatment, Mickey had to pick up a lot of the housework, like getting the kids to school, driving them around, and fixing meals. It's been a hard time for them all," she said. "I tried to help when I could, but Mickey doesn't like me involved, so I don't push."

"Then I guess Mickey went to work and sometime during the day Candy decided to hang herself. She took some rope from the garage, tied one end to a wall hook, and other end she made a loop and put it around her neck. She sat down in the closet and let the rope tighten so that she passed out, and when she did the weight of her body did the rest." Diane was tearing up through the whole explanation, pulling one Kleenex after another out of the box. Wads of crumpled tissues began to pile up on the coffee table between them.

"Then at about 3:45 Kyle comes home," she continued, "and calls out for his mom. He knows she's home because her car is in the garage. He figures she's in bed not feeling well, so he comes to check on her. He opens the door to her bedroom and there she is . . . his own mother, my little girl . . ."

She lost control again and Brian waited patiently for her to let it out.

When she recovered she said, "So Kyle turned and left the room. He took out his phone and dialed 911. They asked him if she had a pulse, so he had to go back in there and feel her wrist while the paramedics were on the way, can you imagine? He did and said he couldn't find a pulse. He told them she 'looked pretty dead.'

"The paramedics came and then the police. They tried reaching Mickey but he was not answering his phone. He almost never does when he's working. They had Kyle contact me and I went right over. Then Hannah came home to this big circus going on. It was all so unreal, like a bad dream. The coroner came and they put her on a gurney and took her away. The police asked everyone questions and then they left." She sniffed and waved her hand, clutching several tissues. "Then the house was quiet again and we three just sat there in shock, crying and staring and crying again. It just didn't seem real. It didn't seem possible. We just sat there in the dark until Mickey finally came home." Diane paused and gave a quick glance at the pastor.

"When we told him he just went pale. He didn't cry; he just went pale and went to his room. He stayed there for so long. I didn't know what to do. I finally went up and knocked on his door. I told him he needed to come down and be with his children. He just said he couldn't. I told him I would stay as long as I could. He didn't say anything and he didn't come out of his room at all. I fed the children, but they weren't hungry, and when it was time I put them to bed. I then called everyone I could think of to let them know. I finally went up and knocked on Mickey's door. I told him I was leaving. There was no response, so I was more insistent. I told him that I needed to know if he was okay before I could leave. I needed him to answer me. Finally, he just said, 'I'm fine. Go.' I stood there a minute, afraid to leave. I thought about taking the kids. I didn't feel good about leaving them in this situation, but I didn't know what else to do. I told Mickey if he needed me to take the kids to just let me know, that I would take them as much as he needed me to, but he didn't answer. I asked if he heard me and he said he had. Then he thanked me. He didn't say anything else, so I finally left.

"The next day he said he had to go to the funeral home later that day and asked me to take the kids. I was there when they came home from school and they seemed glad to be able to leave with me. I've had them pretty much the whole time since and have heard very little from Mick. I'm worried about him and I don't much like leaving the kids with him. He doesn't seem very stable right now."

"No, he doesn't," Brian agreed. "Do you think he's a danger to himself or the kids?"

She thought for a moment. "I can't really say," she said. "Who knows? Maybe so. I do know he loves his kids, but he might be a danger to himself."

"She didn't leave a note of any kind. You have no idea what she was thinking?"

"Nope. Nothing. The police asked me that several times. I talked to her at least once a week and I've known her all my life, so this is a complete shock. I would have thought I would have seen it coming. But then…well not a complete shock when I think about it, but I had no idea she was this bad."

"What do you mean, 'not a complete shock'?"

"Well, she was always complaining about things, her health mainly. As I said, a lot of it she did for attention and pity. I could see her pretending to commit suicide for attention, but I can't see her actually doing it."

"So she's never tried it before?"

"Oh, she used to threaten it, but no. No actual attempts that I'm aware of . . ."

"What about having her son find her? That seems unusual. I would think, even in all her pain, she would be careful not to let the kids see her that way, wouldn't you think?"

"She loved her kids. I don't know what she was thinking. I've thought about that too, how stupid and thoughtless it was. She must have been a mess not to think about that. It makes me angry every time I think about it. Kyle is such a sensitive boy, I just don't know how he's going to deal with that for the rest of his life."

"There was one other thing I was wondering," Brian said, "if you don't mind my asking."

"No, I don't mind."

"It's the way she killed herself. Hanging is so unusual for a woman. I've looked it up and hanging is usually how men kill themselves. Women typically use less violent means. I just wonder why she would hang herself . . ."

With that, Diane began tearing up again. She reached for a Kleenex and the tears began to roll.

"I'm sorry, I've gone too far."

She shook her head. When she was able to compose herself she said, "No, it's fine. I just can't help wondering about what she must have been thinking and how much she must have been hurting to do that to herself. I thought, why didn't she pick an easier way? That seems like such an awful way to die . . ." She seemed to choke on her last words.

They both sat in silence for a moment, and then Brian said, "Well, I should let you get back to it. Do you want company? I could help you if you like. This seems like a hard thing to do alone."

"No, I appreciate it, but I think I would prefer to be alone, thank you."

"I know you don't like the church and don't believe in God, but would you mind if I said a little prayer before I go?"

She looked up at him, eyes still brimming with tears, and said, "I was actually hoping you would offer. I was afraid to even ask you after the things I've said."

"Please don't worry about that. Is there anything in particular you want me to pray for?"

She seemed thrown by this question and had to think for a moment. Then she said, "The kids. I would like you to pray for the kids."

He took her hands in his and began, "Dear Lord, you know what's happened here. Candy has taken her own life and left her mother, husband, and children behind. We don't know what kind of pain she was in, but we entrust her now to your care. Give us some comfort to know she is with you now and that her pain is now gone and that she is free from all earthly cares. We don't understand the full mystery of that but we believe she is still alive and with you and we shall see her again. In the meantime, Lord, we need your help down here. There is a lot of pain that is too big for us to handle. Candy's mom here, Diane, needs some strength and healing. Lord, you know the pain of losing a child and we know you feel Diane's pain in this. Help her through it please. We ask that you watch over her grandchildren, Kyle and Hannah, that through the pain and shock of this loss they will come to love and appreciate each other more. Lord, we know bad things happen in this world and sometimes those things are terrible. We also know that you can take bad things and turn them into good ones. Use this terrible event to make good things happen in their lives. Watch over them, give them healing and peace. We pray also for Mickey, who seems so very lost right now. Please keep him safe and help him to find himself in the midst of all this sorrow. We know you can do these things and we know that you will because we ask in Jesus's name. Amen."

Brian looked up and saw Diane's head still bowed. Her shoulders were heaving and she was sobbing. He was deeply moved. He stood by her chair and put a hand on her shoulder and encouraged her to let it flow. When she was done, she wiped her eyes and smiled up at Brian. She did seem better now, and said, "Thank you, Pastor. I'm glad you came."

"I am too," Brian said. "I actually came to see if I could talk Mick out of having a private service, but I don't think I'm going to be able to do that. We've begun to make plans for a candlelight vigil service for Sunday night at 7:00 p.m. I hope you will come and bring the kids. If you could get Mick there it would help him greatly. It will be a healing service and you are likely to hear a lot of wonderful things about your daughter. I guarantee you will be glad you came. The kids need to hear those things too."

"What is a candlelight . . . what did you call it?"

"A vigil. It's just a time of remembering and celebrating Candy's life. She was a member of the church and so we will spend a little time remembering the gift she was to us and to say prayers and sing and remind ourselves that death is not the end of life."

"I will think about it."

Brian offered a hug that she gratefully accepted as they said goodbye.

CHAPTER 23

WHEN BRIAN GOT back to his office it was nearly time for his noon meeting with the FRLC, the Fellowship of Recovering Lutheran Clergy. The meeting was essentially an AA 12-step meeting that happened over the phone. It was private and by invitation for clergy only. Brian had been involved with the FRLC since its inception in 1991. He helped start the phone-in meeting that had been going on for the last ten years. The phone-in meeting was a great way for pastors to meet to talk about recovery in the privacy of their own office or home and not worry about damaging rumors that could hurt them in the community if they shared too openly. Small-town life could be hard for a pastor and his or her family. This meeting was a safe haven.

There were four pastors there besides himself, one from Florida, one from Wyoming, one from Washington, and one from California. The topic was "maintaining sanity in an insane world," and Brian marveled at how well the topic fit with what he was dealing with. The meetings made him realize he wasn't the only one dealing with more than he could handle and that all he needed to do was trust God, do what he could, and let the rest go. He felt refreshed and renewed by the meeting, as always.

After lunch, Brian was able to clear things from his desk before his appointment with Jeffrey Stephens. He also wrote his prayers for Sunday and wrote some more notes for his Sunday message. It was shaping up to be a funeral sermon, which was fitting since it didn't look like there would be a public funeral for Candy after all. He wouldn't preach at the vigil but only read Scripture, pray, and make a few brief comments.

When Jeffrey Stephens showed up Brian could tell he was as nervous as you can imagine any fifteen-year-old boy would be in a pastor's office to challenge his faith. Brian tried to put him at ease by asking him about school, his teachers, his favorite subjects, any sports he was involved with, and did he have a girlfriend. He had visibly relaxed by the time Brian got around to the subject of the meeting.

"So, Jeffrey," he said, "I understand you are having some issues with confirmation. You want to talk about that?"

"Sure, yeah, I guess so."

"First I want to tell you that I fully support you on this. If you aren't ready or don't think you want to confirm your faith, then I think you are right to back out. In fact, I admire you for it. Okay?"

Jeffrey nodded his head. "Okay," he said, seemingly thrown off by the pastor's openness to his rebellion.

"What I do want to make sure, however, is that you are certain about what it is you are not believing. Oftentimes students your age hear things they don't believe but maybe heard them wrong. I just want to make sure you haven't heard the wrong thing. It happens all the time. Confirmation is a big deal, and before you miss a chance to celebrate with your friends and family I just want to make sure we are on the same page and not confused about your understanding. Fair enough?"

He nodded again.

"Okay," Brian said, "where should we start? Did you manage to write down some things that you have a problem with?"

Jeffrey was clearly nervous again, likely afraid of confronting the pastor with his criticisms of religion.

"Well," he began, "I didn't write them down, but I know what they are."

"Okay, that's fine," Brian said. "Why don't we start with the first one?"

"Well, I guess the first thing I would say is that I'm not sure about religion. For me it just doesn't seem very logical or real. I think I would say I believe more in science."

"Okay," Brian said, "that's a great topic. Go on."

"Well," he said, "I just think that we probably evolved from animals. That just makes more sense to me."

"I don't have a problem with that," Brian said. "I would agree with you."

"But in the Bible it says God created people from dust and made the world in seven days."

"Yes, I know and there are some people, some Christians, who think that's literally true, but I'm not one of those Christians. I think science and the Bible are very compatible. What you have to understand first is that the Bible is not a science book. It is more of a poetry book. It talks about God and creation through metaphors. It says God made us out of dust, and that's actually very true when you consider scientifically speaking all living things are literally physically made out of dust particles. Scientifically speaking, everything really is made out of dust and then returns to dust. The Bible says the same thing as science does but says it in a different way. What's amazing is these are things that were written and believed by people way before science came along and even so it's still accurate. The difference comes when we understand the Bible is not about science at all. It's a book that tries to make sense of God and our relationship to God." Brian realized he was being preachy and reminded himself to dial it down a little. "Sorry, I get a little carried away sometimes," he said. "Were you able to follow that?"

"So, you believe in evolution?" Jeffrey said with an expression of confusion on his face.

"Well, yes, I do. I don't think it answers everything yet, but I think it's on the right track. But just because we evolved does not exclude the idea that someone or something bigger is at work making all this happen."

"What do you mean? Why do you say someone or something had to make it happen? Couldn't it just happen naturally?"

"Well, they do say that's possible, but the odds of the life as we experience on earth happening by chance are so huge, remote, that most scientists and mathematicians are beginning to say it's extremely unlikely. A growing number of scientists believe there has to be some kind of intelligence at work in the universe. They are finding so many things are too exactly right for life to just happen. It points to something greater at work we don't know about yet, some kind of creative intelligence at work in creation. Here, let me show you some quotes I have from some of today's top physicists and mathematicians." Brian rummaged around his file box and then turned to his computer. "I think I know where to find it."

After a few moments of searching his files, he came up with what he was looking for. He scanned it and said, "I can't read all this to you, but I will print it out for you to take. I'll just read a few. These are all Nobel Prize-winning physicists, mathematicians, and rocket scientists, some very smart people. They don't speak about Christianity necessarily, although some do, but they are saying there is some really big mystery at work in the universe, which I believe is God, of course." He printed a copy and went down the hall to get it out of the printer.

Brian came back and placed a copy in front of Jeffrey and said, "Let me just highlight a couple. Here is one I like from Wernher von Braun, who is a Nobel Prize-winning rocket engineer. He says, 'I find it as difficult to understand a scientist who does not acknowledge the presence of a superior rationality behind the existence of the universe as it is to comprehend a theologian who would deny the advances of science.' Kind of fits exactly what we are talking about.

"And this is one, Tony Rothman, a physicist, another Nobel Prize winner: 'When confronted with the order and beauty of the universe and the strange coincidences of nature, it's very tempting to take the leap of faith from science into religion. I am sure many physicists want to. I only wish they would admit it.'

"And then, of course, you've heard of Albert Einstein? He said, 'Everyone who is seriously involved in the pursuit of science becomes convinced that a spirit is manifest in the laws of the universe—a spirit vastly superior to that of man and one in the face of which we with our modest powers must feel humble.'"

Brian looked at Jeffrey, who was reading the other quotes with interest, and realized he might be overwhelming the boy. "What do you think?"

Jeffrey shrugged his shoulders and simply said, "This is interesting."

"So, Jeffrey, my point is that I also believe in science. I think science does amazing things. Even so, it still can't answer all our questions, and in fact, the more they discover the more questions we get. This universe is not as simple as we want to think. It's vast and complicated. I just believe there is way more going on than we will ever know in this lifetime, and at some point we learn to trust there is something out there bigger than us. I believe that it's a something we can trust, that cares about us. I believe rather than disproving God, science is confirming the existence of a God. For example, the complexity of DNA. A single strand contains digital information equivalent to half a million pages of information and is mathematically identical to an actual language. Think about that! I think this argues strongly for an intelligent source behind everything. How could a thing like a million pages of information in the form of a language contained in a microscopic cell happen randomly and by chance? And that's just one example. There are a million more." Brian was getting worked up. This was an exciting topic for him.

"The thing for me is," Brian continued, "if the universe is a place where only physical matter exists, then how can an impersonal, nonconscious, meaningless, purposeless, universe accidentally create personal, conscious, moral beings who are obsessed with meaning and purpose? It isn't logical, and atheists know that. I can understand their hatred of religion; there are plenty of reasons for that, but in the end they must concede to some kind of intelligent design."

Brian again felt like he was preaching and overwhelming Jeffrey. He couldn't seem to help it. "Anyway, the point is you can believe in science and God too. They can go together."

Jeffrey was taking it in, but saying nothing. He was looking uncomfortable, like any fifteen-year-old would.

"Anything else about science and religion? What are you thinking?"

"I don't know."

"Do you realize you can believe in both?"

Jeffrey was thoughtful, and then said, "I guess. I wasn't sure."

"Okay, what other issues are you wrestling with?"

Jeffrey pulled himself upright in his chair and looked thoughtful for a moment. "Well," he began, "I guess I just don't think I believe all of it."

"All of it?" Brian asked. "All of what?"

"The Bible," Jeffrey said.

"Anything in particular?"

"I don't know. Just some of the stories don't seem real to me, like they were made up."

"Give me one example," Brian said, knowing he was putting Jeffrey on the spot, but he wanted to make sure he was addressing the right issue.

Jeffrey was struggling to come up with an answer and Brian felt bad for him. He didn't want this to be a negative experience for Jeffrey. He wanted him to leave feeling he had all his concerns addressed. Brian admired and respected Jeffrey for his willingness not only to talk to an adult about this, but to a pastor no less. He never would have done that at his age. That takes nerve. He had to give him credit.

Brian was about to makes some suggestions to help Jeffrey remember stories, but Jeffrey blurted out, "The story of that guy being eaten by a fish. I don't think that's possible, to live inside a fish."

Brian nodded in agreement. He thought for a moment and then said, "But what if I told you the same thing happened to me?"

Jeffrey looked at him suspiciously. "What do you mean? You were swallowed by a fish?"

"Well, not literally, but that story is my story of faith," he said. "I know what it's like to run from God. I know what it's like to be thrown into the sea. I know what it's like to be in the belly of a fish and then spit out in a pool of vomit. It's not literally what happened to me, but it is figuratively and metaphorically. In fact, that's exactly what happened to me. It tells my story quite well," Brian said. "I was an alcoholic and I was using drugs and alcohol to run from God and from the world. It just about killed me. Then God saved me and gave me a second chance and a new life. Now, instead of running, I try to do what God wants me to. When I read that story of Jonah and understand it as an allegory, it makes a great deal of sense. It's a parable that tells a story of what life is like for some. It's like poetry. A lot of the Bible is like that."

Jeffrey seemed to be thinking hard about that.

"As I said before," Brian went on, "the Bible is true, but not always in a literal way. It tells stories about life and God and they are true, even if some of them didn't really happen. The Bible isn't a history book and it's not a science book; it's a book of poetry and metaphors and figurative speech. It speaks of truth but it speaks of truth in code. That's why so many people get it wrong. People either take it literally or they misinterpret its meaning. You have to look past the literal word to get at the spirit of the word, and that's not always easy or simple."

Jeffrey seemed thoughtful again, apparently running this new information around his brain.

Then Brian jumped in again, unable to hold back or give Jeffrey time to absorb the new thoughts. "You also need to know it's okay to have doubts. In fact, you are expected to have doubts. I have doubts about many things Christians teach and believe. So it's okay to get up and confirm your faith even with a lot of doubts and unanswered questions. I still have many myself. You can essentially say, 'I'm not sure I believe all of this and I am still learning, but I am open to it.' That's perfectly fine."

He watched Jeffrey mull this over for a bit and then said, "What are you thinking, Jeffrey?"

He shrugged and said, "I don't know."

"Are there other things you wonder about?"

Jeffrey shook his head. "No, those were the main things."

"Did I answer them for you?"

"Yeah, I guess so."

Brian stared at Jeffrey and Jeffrey looked around the room, an awkward silence hanging there.

"So what are you thinking Jeffrey? Do you want to think on this some more before you decide for sure about being confirmed or not?"

"Yeah, I think that's what I want to do."

Brian looked at him and was impressed. Brian had a personal theory that those who wrestle greatly with their faith are the ones who end up serving God the most. Ironically, he believed Jeffrey, like Jonah, was being called by God and that's why he was wrestling so mightily and trying to run from his faith.

"Jeffrey, I want to commend you for coming in here. Struggling with your faith and asking questions is what the life of faith is all about. It means you are smart and willing to take a stand. Those are excellent qualities. I want you to know I will support and defend whatever decision you make. I know your parents are putting a lot of pressure on you to do this, but by all means please don't do it if you can't do it with a good conscience. I will defend you and I will talk to your parents and help them understand. I would never want anyone to do this if they weren't ready or serious. I want you to know you impress me, because most kids would just do this to get it over with whether they believed it or not. By challenging these things, you understand this is important and it matters. It means you have a lot of integrity. I salute you for that."

Jeffrey made a tight smile, but Brian could tell he appreciated hearing this. "Can I offer a word of prayer before you go?"

"Okay."

"Is there anything in particular you would like me to pray for?"

Jeffrey thought for a moment and said, "Just that I make a good decision, I guess."

Brian bowed his head and began to pray. "Dear God, we don't understand the full mystery of who you are. We really don't know much at all. All we really have is our faith. We have faith that you exist, we have faith that you care, we have faith that you are listening. Please give Jeffrey your guidance as he prepares to affirm his baptism and proclaim his faith in you, that you really exist and that he can trust you with his life. I pray and trust you will help him make this important decision. Give him the strength and courage to stand by his convictions always and to do what his heart tells him to do. My heart tells me that you are doing something important in Jeffrey's life and I pray he will see it too. Help him to believe and trust in you, we pray in Jesus's name, amen."

Jeffrey said, "Amen."

The two stared at each other for a moment and then Pastor Matterson said, "Thanks for coming in, Jeffrey. I hope you know that I am here for you any time you need to talk, okay?"

"Okay, Pastor Matterson, thank you." He got up to leave, looking relieved to be getting away.

CHAPTER 24

A S SOON AS Jeffrey was through the door, Maureen came swishing in with a pink piece of paper and handed it to Brian. "Mike Hemsley just called and he wants you to call him back as soon as possible."

Brian took the note and pecked in the number. Mike was there on the second ring, "Officer Hemsley."

"Hello, Mike, it's Pastor Matterson. You called?"

"Yes, Pastor, thanks for calling me back. It's about Mick Vinter."

"I figured. What's happening?"

"It looks like we are going to pick him up for questioning. The investigation is turning up some things and it's not looking so good for him right now. I just thought you should know. His family is going to need some support."

"Will he be arrested?"

"It's not certain yet. They have several questions they need him to answer and it all depends on what he has to say. He's certainly going to know he's under suspicion after this," Hemsley said. "Either way, he's going to need a pastor too, I'm thinking."

"You're a good man, Mike. I know you shouldn't be telling me this, but I sure do appreciate it."

"Just remember, this is very privileged information. Nobody can know, not even your wife."

"Got it. No problem. If they do decide to arrest him, will they wait until after the funeral? It seems like the thing to do."

"If they think he did this then no, they won't care about that. But right now they just want answers."

"Well, the question I have is how does someone hang someone against their will? That doesn't seem very feasible . . ."

Hemsley was silent for a moment and then said, "Not if that's not how she died."

"Oh," Brian said, "I hadn't thought of that. Is that what happened? Was she already dead when she was hung?"

"I'm not saying anything, just that you just never know," Hemsley said. "Look, I gotta go."

"Okay, Mike, thanks for the heads-up," Brian said as Hemsley hung up the phone.

Brian was grateful he didn't have Mike's job. He wondered what to do now and what to think. He still could not imagine Mickey Vinter hurting anyone, nor could he imagine Candy taking her own life. But then, he also couldn't imagine how anyone could fake being sick to the degree Candy did either. What people were capable of was constantly catching him by surprise, even though he himself knew his own past and some of the outrageous things he had done. He was sure those things would surprise many people if they only knew.

CHAPTER 25

O NCE AGAIN, THE day was getting away from him. He had lots of unfinished business and he had to determine how much absolutely had to be done before he could go home. It was another day he would go home feeling little got done and the list grew longer. He hated that feeling. His sermon writing would have to wait until the next day, which was normally his day off, but sometimes he had no choice. This was one of those times.

* * *

On Saturday, Brian called Mick to see how the funeral had gone and to offer support, but there was no answer on his phone. He wanted to know what happened with the police. *Was he arrested?*

He called Diane, Candy's mother, to see if she had heard anything. He also wanted to know if he could come see the children, but she didn't answer either. He left a message and a number where he could be reached. He also reminded them of

the vigil planned for the next day and strongly encouraged them
to come.

*　　*　　*

Sunday morning services were fuller than normal, as they
usually are after something terrible like the death of a young
person or a suicide or other big tragic thing. Brian was nervous
about his sermon. He felt it was too much of a funeral sermon and
wondered if that was what the day called for. He knew better than
to be anxious because what he had was what he had. How many
times had he written a sermon and felt the same way? He would
say to God at times like this, a bit defiantly, "If this isn't good
enough then you need to get someone else because this is all I
got." Then he would give the sermon and he would get supportive
comments. In fact, some of the sermons he felt worst about were
the times he would get the most encouraging comments.

Nearly every week his wife asked, "Do you have your sermon
done?" and he would reply, "Yes, but it's crap." He almost never
felt it was any good. She would say, "You always say that and it's
always better than you think," and she was always right. Almost
always.

Brian didn't think of himself as a preacher. He thought his
style was more conversational, as a teacher really, or as someone
sharing from his heart as they do in AA. It was in 12-step groups
where he learned to talk openly and sincerely in front of other
people, and that was the style he adopted for his preaching. He
felt it was the most genuine way to communicate. He had a strong
distaste for pastors who took on a persona when they got into the
pulpit. To him it rang as phony, as an act. It turned him off. He
liked when people were themselves.

*　　*　　*

Brian got up in the pulpit with a knot of butterflies in his
stomach as usual. He read the text for the day, the story about

the Sadducees challenging Jesus about life after death. He closed the Bible and looked around the room. All faces were turned up to him, like baby birds in a nest waiting for food. They wanted to know what he would say. Could he answer their questions?

He looked across the room at all the familiar faces and then felt that familiar sense of peace envelope him as it always did once he began. He was a wreck until that moment each time he preached, but when the moment for speaking arrived, so did the peace. He hated that he had to wait for it and he was terrified of what might happen if it didn't come. *What if the well runs dry?* As of yet, twenty-one years and counting, it had not failed yet. The peace enveloped him; he took a deep breath, looked out at all the eager faces, and began:

"As I prepared my sermon for this week all I could think about was the death of Candy Vinter. As many of you know, Candy Vinter was a longtime member of this congregation, a wife and mother of two. She was fighting cancer,"–Brian had decided since he didn't know the truth of this he would stick to common beliefs–"Candy took her own life last week, shocking us all.

"When something like this happens it's hard to know where to begin. There are so many feelings involved. All of us are stunned. It's as though a bomb went off in the community. Our hearts of course go out to those closest to that bomb–Mickey, her husband; Kyle and Hannah, her two children; Diane, her mother. Their hearts are torn wide open. They have been shattered. We hold them close to our hearts in prayer.

"But it's not just the family. All of us are hit with mixed emotions after something like this. We are stunned and in pain. We may be angry that this had to happen. We may be asking ourselves: 'What could I have done?' We may feel angry at Candy for not letting us help her. We may be sad to know she was in that much pain and we didn't know. We may feel helpless because she had that much pain and we couldn't fix it.

"I wonder if she knew how much she was loved? Did she know she has a mother that would do anything for her? Did she know she had a husband and children who adore her? Did she know she had friends and a church community that treasured her?"

"There is so much in life that is unfair and unacceptable. These tragedies are all around us. Life is unfair, it is painful, it is precarious, and it is dangerous. We take all the precautions we can, we buy insurance, we do what we can to be safe, but still death is hanging over us every day and we are powerless to stop it. We do walk through the valley of the shadow of death. Death is that dark cloud sitting just over every horizon. We don't want to see it, but we know it's there. We never know what might be around the next corner for any of us.

"This last week a one-year-old baby we have been praying for, little Tyler Swanson, died from a brain tumor. On Thursday, a twenty-two-year old baseball player in California pitched his first-ever major-league game and was then killed by a drunk driver on his way home. Every parent knows what I am talking about; every parent has those moments of dread when the phone rings. It could happen. It does happen. Death is all too real and awful, and we all know it.

"It's no accident that the most prominent and powerful image we have of God and God's love is this: 'For God so loved the world that he gave his one and only Son, that whoever believes in him shall not die, but have eternal life.'

"If God wanted to communicate how greatly he loves us, he could not have given a more powerful example of how much, or an image more potent than giving his own child. There is no love stronger on earth than the love of a parent for a child.

"I don't know about you, but I would not give my child's life for anything, not even to save the world. I would give my own life, but not my child. I could not. But God would, and God did. That's exactly what God did. That's how much God loves us."

"In just a few short weeks we will celebrate Easter, the high holiday for all Christians and the center of our faith. God sent Jesus Christ, God's own Son, to us as a gift of love. Even so, the world turned on him and hung him on a cross to die. The whole world was complicit in his death, even his closest followers.

"God's innocent and precious Son was humiliated, beaten, and hung on a cross in the blazing sun to die a terrible and painful death. We buried him in a tomb. That's what we did. That's the bad news.

"The good news is after three days he rose again. He returned to his followers with forgiveness, love, and promise, the greatest promise of all time–eternal life for all.

"If this story is true, then what it means is the best thing we could ever hear: We are all saved from death. God sent his Son to save our lives so that when we die and are buried in the ground we too, like Jesus, will be raised up. I don't begin to understand the full wonder of what that really means, but I believe it's true.

"The Sadducees in our Gospel lesson today thought resurrection and heaven and life after death was a joke. That's how they are treating it in the question they put to Jesus. They present a scenario that suggests they think the whole idea of an afterlife is ludicrous. They ask Jesus about a woman who marries all the brothers in a family and then say, 'In heaven, whose wife will she be?' You can almost see their smug faces as they think they have him in a trap, as they think they have demonstrated the absurdity of the afterlife. They believe they have just made it the joke that they thought it was.

"Jesus, however, surprises them. He turns the tables. They want to make him look foolish, but he ends up making them look like they don't really know much. He says, 'You don't understand God. In heaven you won't be worried about worldly things like marriage. Heaven is so far different from here, our earthly categories won't apply,' Jesus says. 'You become like the angels. You become spiritual beings!'

"Imagine that. Was Jesus making that up or is he telling the truth?

"Jesus was unequivocal about the question of life after death. In fact, his sole purpose for coming to earth was to open the gates of heaven to everyone. That terrible thing we did to Jesus, God turned it into our salvation. Isn't that the way of God? God turns our troubles and even our terrible deeds into blessings.

"We don't understand why terrible things happen on this earth, but they do. I don't need to convince any of you of that. However, I do know that all things work for good in God's economy, so that even terrible things become gifts in ways we cannot always understand. I don't know what the gift is from Candy's death, but I am sure of one thing—she is no longer in pain and she is with God, and we shall see her again. Many other things will come from her death. I don't know what they will be but I am very certain God will turn this terrible thing into something good, because that's what God always does.

"Candy was loved by her family. She was loved by her friends. She was loved by this community. Mostly, Candy is loved by God. God claimed her in her baptism right here at this font. She was loved and claimed by God, and God has always been with her and she will always be with God.

"That's because nothing on heaven or earth can separate us from that love, not even death. For this we say, thanks be to God. Amen."

CHAPTER 26

BRIAN FELT POWER in his words and in the room, power he did not feel when writing them. There was a silence when he sat down knowing his message had hit home. He could feel the power of the Spirit at work. He always marveled when it happened. He would replay it in his mind for days afterward, savoring the feeling. He was awash with a deep sense of relief and gratitude that God had provided for him once again.

Thank you, Lord, he said in his heart. *I don't deserve it, but thank you.*

Brian got high praise for his message. As people filed out, they shook his hand and told him, "Great sermon, Pastor." They said the same thing every week, so the only way he could measure their sincerity was whether they looked him in the eye when they said it. If they didn't mean it, they would shake his hand, look away, and say it. He made a lot of eye contact that morning.

After the service, he tried calling Mick again with the same result. He then tried calling Diane's house, but still no answer there either.

He had lunch with his family as he did every week if he didn't have a meeting or an emergency. They ate at one of their favorite fast-food restaurants, Chipotle. Burritos as big as your head. Brian was feeling magnanimous after feeling God's Spirit all morning, so he let the kids order pop with their meal. They usually ordered water because buying pop for a family of four every time you eat out starts to add up.

The Sunday meal was always special, and it was one of the reasons the kids went willingly to attend church each week. They knew if they resisted and wanted to stay home they could, but they would miss the meal. It wasn't just the meal they missed, it was time together with family. They didn't know that's what made the Sunday time together special, but Brian and his wife, Donna, knew because she was the one who taught him. They had many meals together during the week, mostly dinner, but for some reason the Sunday meal had a special feel to it.

After lunch with his family, Brian made visits to the hospital and nursing homes. He took communion to those who could not make it to worship. They were always grateful to see him and he loved visiting, but he was so drained after worship he couldn't last long. He would make three or four visits before he was completely wiped out. He would normally head home and take a late afternoon nap at that point, but he had the vigil that night and wanted Mick and his family to be there. He drove by Mick's to see if he could catch him there. The house looked vacant, no Mick, no kids. He knocked, looked in windows, but saw nothing and heard nothing.

He tried Diane again, but no luck there either.

He wanted to call Mike Hemsley to see what happened with the interview with Mick, but didn't want to be a pest. Mike would call when he could.

He gave up, went home, and took his nap.

That evening the church was nearly full for the candlelight vigil. Brian had never planned or presided at a service like this before and wasn't sure what kind of response to expect. He was happy so many came. He knew it would be well attended, but didn't expect this many people. As he looked out at the growing crowd seated in every possible place, even in the choir loft and overflow chairs outside the entrance, he saw members of his faithful flock, the ones who come to every service, but there were mostly faces he didn't know. They were people from the community and people Candy worked with and people who knew the family, who needed to do something in response to the terrible situation. These were times a pastor could reach those who may never go to church. Seeing so many visitors and guests, he thought about repeating his sermon from the morning so people would know there were Christians who believed Candy was with God without a doubt. He knew his regulars wouldn't mind hearing the sermon again and he didn't want to miss an opportunity for these people to hear a pastor say that Candy was loved by God and is now with God. People tend to think the church just condemns everything, and Brian wanted to counter that with a message of unconditional love, forgiveness, and acceptance for all, without any if's, ands, or buts.

When the organ prelude finished, Brian welcomed everyone and reminded them they were there to honor Candy's life, to give thanks to God for who she was, for the gift she was to her family and friends, but also to hear words of hope and promise. They were there to remember Candy's life was not over, and for her, there was more.

They sang "How Great Thou Art," then Brian prayed. He invited everyone into a time of remembering and appreciating Candy Vinter. He asked if anyone wanted to come forward. After a long, awkward silence, he mentioned he also had a cordless for those who didn't want to come forward. Again, the awkward silence; then a hand went up.

As Brian walked toward the raised hand, he saw Diane and Hannah sitting near the back of the church. He asked the person to stand. A woman around Candy's age, heavyset, distraught face, wearing a black dress, stood and took the microphone from Brian.

She was a coworker of Candy and talked about what a trooper she was, how she always had a smile no matter what she was going through. She had never known anyone who had more difficulties, but she never let it get her down, and she was always thinking of others.

Other hands began to go up and Brian made the rounds of the sanctuary with the microphone. He was hoping to get close to Diane and Hannah so that he could make sure they would be around after the service so that he could talk to them.

Many spoke about how great Candy was, and it was a moving tribute to her. Brian was very glad Diane and Hannah were there to hear all these things and wished Mick and Kyle were there too. He had been looking for them after he saw Diane and Hannah, but could not locate them if they were there.

When the comments wound down, Brian encouraged everyone to continue talking about Candy and share stories. He told them how important it is to keep the memories of those we love alive. He read Psalm 23 and then from John's Gospel, words that assure us of a place in heaven. Brian gave an abbreviated version of his morning's sermon reminding everyone that life is filled with terrible things, tragedies that we don't fully comprehend, and that's just the way life is. But when this life is over, no matter how long it lasts and no matter what happens along the way, when we die we have a promise that Jesus will be there to greet us and take us to a place especially prepared for us. Jesus would not have said this if it were not true. "Let's hold on to that great promise," he told them.

The ushers then came down the aisle and lit candles. The overhead lights, already dimmed, went out completely. The room sat in silent candlelight for several moments. It was a deep and heavy silence, interrupted only by an occasional cough. Sacredness was thick in the air, it was palpable. Brian led the room in prayer and concluded with the invitation to mention aloud the name of a loved one who has gone to be with the Lord. It started slowly at first, a few names here and there, more whispered than spoken, then louder and more often. Soon the room filled with a cacophony of names flowing through the room: Angela, Eva, Harold, Donald,

Mary, Inga, Jonathan, Candy, Barry, Andrew, Bessie . . . It went on for several minutes and then slowly died down.

When it was quiet again, Brian nodded to the organist, who slowly began playing a familiar hymn. Right on cue the whole room joined in: *"Amazing Grace, how sweet the sound, that saved a wretch like me . . . I once was lost, but now am found was blind but now I see . . ."*

They sang four verses in a darkened room, faces illuminated golden by candles, tears in their eyes, and you could feel the presence of all those saints named aloud. They were there. There was no mistake, they were there, Brian would swear to it.

As the song came to a close there was silence. Brian was reluctant to break the mood, but also knew the candles were burning down and if wax was everywhere he would never hear the end of it from the pew crew.

Brian stood in front of the congregation and said a closing prayer, then a prayer of commendation for Candy. "Into your hands, O Lord, we commend Candy Vinter. A lamb of your own flock, a sheep of your own fold, a sinner of your own redeeming. Receive her into the arms of your mercy and the presence of all the saints in light. Amen."

Candles were extinguished and Brian grimaced, seeing some people shake their candles to extinguish them, knowing they were flinging hot wax on everything. He should have told them not to do that, but too late now. Brian invited everyone to stay for conversation, coffee, and bars. They closed the service singing "Beautiful Savior," then filed slowly out. Brian cut through the back of the sanctuary so he could get to Diane and Hannah before they got away, but the crowd coming out was too large. People stopped him to shake his hand, thank him, and he found himself trapped. He saw Robin Rawley, the education director. He caught her eye and waved her over.

"I need your help. Can you please see if you can find Candy's mother? Her name is Diane and she is with Hannah. I need to talk to them." She readily agreed and went off looking for them.

After several greeted Brian, he saw Robin escorting Diane and Hannah to where he was standing. Diane gave Brian a hug and thanked him for the service and the message. She said it meant a lot to her. She also thanked him for the earlier conversation they had had.

"You've given me a lot to think about. I've never heard a pastor who talks like you," Diane said

Brian was again grateful to hear these words. Getting someone to reconsider their faith after they had rejected it always felt like a major victory to him.

"How was the service at the funeral home?"

"Not very good," Diane said. "It was just so sad. There was nobody there to lead us, so we were just lost. Nobody knew what to say. The funeral director read some things, but they were just words. They didn't mean anything. I'm just so glad I came tonight. I feel a lot more hopeful after that service. I just wish Mick and Kyle could have been here."

"Me too," Brian said. "How are they?"

"It's hard to tell. I don't see Mick and he didn't say two words at the funeral. Kyle is very withdrawn and isn't talking either, just like his dad. I am worried about both of them."

Brian squatted to get at eye level with Hannah. She had pretty blue eyes like her mother, which were red and tired from crying. "How are you doing, Hannah? Pretty awful, isn't it?"

Hannah looked back at Brian, then dropped her eyes to the floor and just nodded.

"Would it be okay if I came to visit you in the next day or two?"

She didn't look up but nodded her head to indicate it would be okay.

CHAPTER 27

AFTER A MUCH-NEEDED day of rest on Monday, Brian was on his way to the church early Tuesday morning after dropping his son off at school when he his phone went off.

Yo, listen up, here's the story
About a little guy that lives in a blue world
And all day and all night and everything he sees is just blue
Like him, inside and outside
Blue his house with a blue little window
And a blue Corvette
And everything is blue for him
And himself and everybody around . . .

"Good morning, Pastor, have you got a moment to talk?" It was Officer Hemsley.

"Yes, Mike, I'm on the road."

"You know you shouldn't talk on a cell phone when you are driving, don't you?"

"I have hands free, not holding a phone. That's okay, isn't it?" Brian responded.

"I'll let you off with a warning this time."

"Thank you, Officer Hemsley, I really appreciate it. I've been anxious to hear from you. What's happening?"

"Well, first of all we had the hardest time finding Mick. He's hardly ever home and he's not answering his phone, but we finally tracked him down at one of his job sites. He's not a big talker. It was hard getting anything out of him. He answered our questions but he changes little things in his story, and that's not what we like to hear. He's not telling us everything. We don't know what he's hiding or why he's hiding it, but something's not right. We have a few things that point to him, but there are other things that don't add up. Sorry, that's so cryptic, but it's all I can tell you . . . I shouldn't be telling you anything, but I trust you and I care about this family, especially those kids. And there's another thing . . ."

"What's that, Mike?"

"Well, again, strictly confidential. Our office was just undergoing a major audit. As you know, Candy worked in accounting. In the course of our investigation, we became aware of some financial discrepancies that might involve Candy. Not sure how that's relevant, but it would point to motive for suicide if she thought she was about to be caught. Again, please keep this under your hat."

It occurred to Brian this might have been what Candy and Mick fought about. Maybe Mick was threatening to turn her in? "Wow," Brian said. "How sure is that, Mike? And how much are you talking about?"

"Pretty sure, and it's a lot, but that's all I can say. I'm not sure how this is going to come out, but when and if it does that poor family is going to need even more help. That's why I'm telling you."

"So, no arrest yet?"

"No. As I said, we are still investigating. It's a lot messier than we thought. We'll get if figured out though."

"Well, I appreciate you keeping me apprised. You have my complete confidence and I will be there for the family. I am going to see the kids today if I can and see how they are doing. Please keep them in your prayers."

"Oh, I am. Believe me, I am."

"I've got to believe you wouldn't lie to your pastor. There's a big penalty for that. But I will let you off with a warning this time."

"But I wasn't lying. How can you let me off when I wasn't doing anything wrong?"

"Tell it to the judge, tell it to the judge," Brian said.

"Goodbye, Pastor," Hemsley said and clicked off the phone.

As Brian pulled into the church parking lot, Aksel Erickson was there waiting for him. He thought about the fake phone call trick, but decided to get it over with.

"Good morning, Aksel," he said as he got out of his car and pulled his briefcase from the backseat.

"Good morning, Pastor. Well, I got those bids you wanted. It was just like I said it would be. I got bids from two other places, just to be safe. They all said about the same thing, more or less. I have them here in writing," he said, offering Brian a folder.

"That was fast."

"Well, it's early spring still and many of these guys are hungry to line up work."

"The numbers are what you thought?"

"Yes, pretty much," he said. "One place was a little lower, but I didn't like them and I think they were lowballing to get the work. I would bet they would find other things to charge us for. I just didn't trust them."

"What was your guys' final numbers?"

"A guaranteed bid of $34,355 for the full rubber membrane replacement. They could start right away. To patch, which they don't recommend because they see that lasting just a few short years, and I agree, $11,500. The full replacement comes with a twenty-year guarantee," Erickson said.

"Which option do you think we should go with?" Brian asked, knowing full well what Aksel thought.

"I think we have to replace the whole thing, Pastor," Erickson said, not catching Brian's jest.

"Okay, Aksel. I appreciate you going the extra mile on those bids. Would you be willing to present them at council? With you there the chances of it passing and them not taking the cheap route would go way up. It would also really help with any delays. They may ask me something I don't know and we will have to table it another month. Could you make it?"

Aksel looked distressed. "You know how much I love those meetings, Pastor. I really would rather not."

"How about we just have you come to the beginning? That way you wouldn't have to stay for the whole thing. I will put you at the top of the agenda so we deal with this first and then let you go. You wouldn't have to sit through the whole meeting. It would be quick and easy for you."

"I just don't know . . . I really don't like talking in front of a group of people, you know that. I told you I would do anything you ask, just don't make me come to any meetings."

"How about this? I do all the talking, I explain everything, I answer all the questions, and if there is anything I can't answer then you will be there. You don't have to say anything unless there is a question I can't answer," Brian proposed.

Aksel looked in agony, but finally relented. "I suppose I could do that."

"Thank you, Aksel. If we really want to get this done this is the way to do it. It won't be bad, I promise."

"Okay, okay, but you will owe me for this," Erickson said, not smiling.

"Of course, Aksel. Of course. Do you have any sins you need forgiven? Or maybe you have some rotten relatives who need to get into heaven? I can fix that for you."

"Oh, I have lots of rotten relatives," he said, "I'm just not sure I would waste a favor on them."

"You're terrible," Brian said. "I'll just pretend you didn't just say that. Oh wait, I forgive you. There, now we're even."

"I don't think so," Erickson said, "You're not getting off that easy. If I'm going to a meeting then you owe me big."

"Okay," Brian said, "but it was worth a try."

"You have a great day, Pastor," Aksel said, turning away.

"You too, Aksel, God bless you."

When Brian walked into the office Maureen handed him his messages, and before he could think about what he was saying he asked, "How are you, Maureen?" and then silently kicked himself for opening that door. When will he learn? He braced himself.

"Oh, I'm fine. I still don't have the newsletter done because nobody's given me their articles as usual. I have to chase everyone down every time, including you! Every month it's the same thing. The volunteer who helps fold and stuff is not able to come in today, so it looks like I will be doing that all by myself. My computer keeps doing funny things. I just don't trust that thing anymore. Can we talk about getting a new one? Oh, and the phone won't stop ringing. It would be nice just to have someone to help answer the phone."

Brian grimaced inside and said, "Let me know when you are ready to fold and stuff. I will come out and help you." He knew she would never do that because that would be giving up her complaining rights. He moved swiftly past as he knew standing there could tie him up endlessly.

He settled in his office and noticed one of his messages was from Diane. He called right away. Diane answered, "Hello?"

"Hi, Diane, this is Pastor Matterson. I see you called."

"Yes, hello, Pastor. Thank you for returning my call so quickly. I really hate to bother you; it's just that I thought you might be able to help, but I don't know."

"Yes, of course. I will do what I can. What can I do?"

"Well, I don't know if this is really something you would know anything about; I just thought maybe if I could talk to you about it."

"Just tell me what it is. If I can help I will."

"Well, the police called today and they want to talk to the kids," she said. "I just wondered . . . I don't know, is that normal?"

"I don't know what's normal in police work, but I would assume they are doing what they normally do—just routine, I would think. Did they say what it was about?"

"No, they didn't say. Well, yes, they did say just what you said. They said it was just routine for their final report. They just needed to ask a few questions."

"Well, then I wouldn't worry too much about it," Brian said. "Do you know when they are coming over? I was hoping to visit with the kids today to see how they are doing."

"They want me to bring them to the station. That's why I'm so worried. That doesn't seem normal to me. I just worry there's something going on they're not telling me about. These kids have been through enough. I just can't imagine this turning into something else. I just don't want to think about that."

"Well, why don't you just wait and see. It's probably nothing. I assume you are going with them?"

"Yes, of course. Can you imagine them doing this alone? Hannah's only nine and Kyle's fourteen. He's big and puts up a tough front but he's still just a little boy."

"Will Mick be coming?"

"I wouldn't count on it," she said, "he hasn't been around much. I will call him, but he never answers. I really worry about him."

"Me too," Brian said. "If you do talk to him, please let him know I need to talk to him. I know he doesn't want to talk to me, but I am determined to be there for him whether he wants me to or not. I don't think he has anyone, and he needs someone."

"I think you are right. I will let him know he needs to see you. I can influence him sometimes and maybe if I come down on him he will listen."

"Would you? That would be great," he said, "It's for his own good."

"I will."

"If you can't reach him or he doesn't want to be there, I would be glad to accompany you and the kids to the police station."

"Oh, you don't have to do that. You're a busy man," she said.

Brian knew she was anxious and needed support herself. "No, I insist. In fact, even if Mick is going I would still like to be with you. This is a terrible situation for the whole family, you included, and I think you would all benefit by having someone there who can help you think things through. Times like this everybody feels so lost. I can help with that."

"That would be wonderful," she said. "Thank you."

Brian could tell she really meant it. "Let me know what time and I will be there."

"I told the kids they didn't have to go back to school yet, but Kyle wanted to go. Hannah stayed home today. So we will go down there as soon as Kyle gets home from school, around 3:45."

"Okay. I will come over about 3:15 so I can visit with Hannah a little before we go."

"That sounds perfect. Thank you so much, Pastor."

"Just remember, there a lot of people who care about you and are praying for you. I'm praying for you and Mick and the kids all the time."

"I appreciate that."

"Okay, I will talk to you later. God bless you."

"God bless you too. Goodbye," she said and clicked off.

CHAPTER 28

BRIAN TURNED ON his computer, hung up his coat, and was getting ready to address his daily list when Barney came through his door.

"Barney, you didn't knock."

"The door was open."

"Okay, fine. What's up?" Brian asked. He didn't have the energy for another round with Barney.

"The coffee machine is working great. We got the bill, $645.00. Not as bad as we thought."

"You said between six and seven hundred. That's exactly what we thought."

"Well, it wasn't seven hundred and we didn't have to buy a new one."

"Well, yes, that's looking at the bright side, I guess. Can we make sure people don't pour water in it again?"

"Oh, I hadn't thought of that. That's a good idea. I will figure out a way so that the top don't come up no more."

"I think that would be good. And also maybe a note saying 'If you don't know how to operate this machine ask somebody.'"

"That's a good idea too. Could Maureen make me that note? I could tape it on there."

"Great. That would be great, Barney. I will let you ask Maureen to make you a sign. Thanks."

"Thanks, Pastor," Barney said, walking toward the front office.

Brian spent the rest of the morning in meetings. He met with the worship planning team to review the previous Sunday's service and to plan for the upcoming one. They reviewed the lessons for upcoming Sunday, selected hymns, and checked to see what special things might be coming up, such as baptisms, special focus Sundays, or other celebrations. They reviewed announcements and as usual tried to keep them to a minimum, which was always a challenge. Everyone wanted something mentioned on Sunday morning, and if they weren't careful announcements could run ten minutes or more. It was a never-ending fight to keep them at a minimum. Even when pared down to as few as possible, there were at least three of four last-minute urgent requests on Sunday morning. Brian hated saying no to these but learned he had to be firm. It was one of those things that continued to make people angry with him. Members felt entitled to have their information announced, and when told "no" they took it personally. He was not saying "no" to their announcement, he was saying "no" to their poor planning. But nobody likes that either.

Brian then met with the pastoral care team to review prayers from the previous Sunday and any new prayer requests that came in during worship or over the phone or through email. Appropriate prayer requests went out through the email prayer chain to more than 300 people who prayed over them. They reviewed the pastoral care board, a whiteboard kept in the hallway that showed who was in the hospital or in nursing care. They decided who needed a visit and who should still be on the board and whether to add anyone new.

He met with the ministers of communion, volunteers who take communion to the elderly and homebound who can't make it to worship anymore. They shared stories, asked questions, and made sure they all had assignments.

He met with Beki, the financial administrator, to talk about the budget and warned her about the upcoming roof repair bill and the coffeemaker. She was not thrilled with this information, but who would be?

"We don't have the money for that," she said, "we aren't even keeping up with the regular expenses."

Brian looked at her and smiled. Beki had been doing this for a long time and she knew how it worked. Typically, most churches ran behind on the budget until the end of the year, then hopefully made up the difference in the last three months. It happens every year in every church with few exceptions. Church council consisted of regularly changing leaders who were mostly from the business world and not as familiar with typical church cash flow. Consequently, Pastor Brian spent every single church council meeting of his life watching anxious speculation, hand wringing, and problem solving around money problems. It never ended.

In his earlier days as a pastor, he tried hard to calm the anxiety and refocus around ministry challenges, but money always stole the show. He finally learned that people needed to feel anxious about money. It's what they know and it's what they do best. Now he expected it and just let it run its due course.

When it happened, and it happened every single meeting, he would just sit back and listen. The conversation was so predictable. People would look through the expenses and wonder why they were behind. There would be several suggestions on how to cut expenses even though there was nothing in the budget that was over. There would be talk of fundraisers and ideas about how to get people to pay for particular things. It would run on like that for a while and then finally everyone would conclude, "I guess we just have to have faith."

Brian had so many times tried to tell them that to begin with to save them all the time and energy, but he learned they just needed to find their way there on their own. There were no shortcuts to faith.

"Since when have offerings kept up with expenses?" Brian said to Beki with a knowing grin.

Beki smiled. "I know, but I don't know how we pay for something like this. This is a major expense."

"Well," Brian said, "we do what we have to. There's really only a couple options. We do a fundraiser, we take out another loan, or we do a cash-out refinance on the building. What else is there? We could do a line of credit, but I don't think that will fly."

"No, I don't either," Beki said. "I could run the numbers on what a refinance would look like so we have that for the meeting. Nevertheless, I think we should start with a fundraiser. I just hate taking out credit every time we need money."

"I know, but you know how everybody reacts to fundraisers, 'the church is always asking for money,' they will scream. And you know the thing that drives me crazy about that?"

Beki shook her head.

"The people who scream the loudest about 'the church is always asking for money' are always those who aren't giving much anyway. The people who are the most generous never complain about giving more and they're the ones who do end up giving more, not the complainers. Why is it we always seem to let a minority of voices have so much influence?"

Beki nodded in agreement. "It's true."

"Yes, having those refinance numbers for the meeting would be great. I will let the president know this is coming up so he isn't surprised," Brian said.

They reviewed the budget and the giving report and saw that everything was normal, or at least part of a new normal. For the last thirty years, mainline churches had been losing members, losing worship attendance, and of course, losing money. It was an epidemic felt in every mainline denomination. Congregations were fighting a war of attrition as once again the culture drifted away from the church. This wasn't a new phenomenon, at least not according to the Bible.

CHAPTER 29

BRIAN MADE HIS way to Diane's house praying the whole way God would help and guide him with the kids. Dealing with death was hard, but working with kids was especially challenging. Knowing how important it was for them to open up and talk, Brian knew he had to do his best to make that happen, no matter how tricky it was.

He arrived at Diane's twenty minutes early. He had checked with her about this as he hoped to use the extra time to approach Hannah. Parking at the curb in front of the cozy rambler located in an older neighborhood, Brian took a look around. The houses here were the first built in the suburb, probably early fifties, shortly after the war. The lot sizes were smaller and homes were basic and practical, looking to be around 1,200 square feet, give or take.

Brian recalled his own childhood home, which was much like those on this street. Six kids and two parents packed into a three-bedroom home, sharing one bathroom. At the time, that didn't seem unusual. Now? It seemed impossible. Brian allowed himself a moment to stop and marvel at how "usual" had changed over the years. He mused briefly on his current life and how it compared with the world of his childhood. He thought of his father declaring that old line: "When I was a kid, life was hard!" And then he would describe having to milk all the cows before walking five miles to school in the snow with no shoes.

Brian smiled and wondered what he would say to his grandchildren. Probably something like: "When I was a kid, life was hard! We had to get up to change channels—and there were only four!"

Diane answered the door after his knock and showed him into the living room with an offer of coffee.

As he scanned the inside of the home, he said, "I think I've had enough coffee for today. I would love a glass of water."

He noted that the house was nicely updated, with new carpet and cabinets, and contemporary colors throughout. She had done a good job making it feel modern and cozy.

Diane returned from the kitchen with two glasses of water, and sat down on a gray contemporary sofa across from Brian, who sat in a floral print wing chair. He could see she was much better than at their last meeting. She was still wearing the weight of her grief, but it did not seem as oppressive. She was much calmer, and maybe even had a little glimmer of hope in her eyes.

"I have to tell you," she said, "Hannah is really nervous about meeting with you. I told her you were coming to visit and that you wanted to check on her, and she has been obsessed about it all day."

"Oh," Brian said, "I hate to hear that. The last thing I want to do is add to her problems. She doesn't have to talk with me."

"Well, she's nine and you are a pastor. That's intimidating for any little girl, no matter what she's going through. She is nervous, but I also think it makes her feel special. I think she would be very disappointed if it didn't happen."

"I have kids," Brian said, "I think I understand that."

"Do you want me to get her?"

"Well, why don't you and I just visit for a minute? I wanted to check on you too, see how you are doing."

"Oh. Well . . . I guess I'm doing better. I have my moments. They just wash over me and I never know when it's coming. The stupidest things will set me off. I'm not sleeping well. I lie in bed and things run through my mind over and over. I dread going to bed."

"I can understand that."

"But I have to tell you," she said, "that service the other night really helped me a lot. The funeral at the funeral home was just depressing. They had recorded music and someone read Scripture and said some nice things, but it just left me feeling hollow. I'm so glad I came to the vigil at the church. Just listening to all those people go on about Candy meant so much to me. I know it meant a lot to Hannah too. And your message made me cry."

"That's why I was trying so hard to get Mick there and would like to have seen Kyle there too. They needed to hear all of that. We did record it. It's not the same as being there, but it might help them to listen to it," Brian said. "It's an important part of the healing process and being able to let go, listening to people talk about how much people appreciate your loved one and feeling a connection with something bigger. I don't think we ever know how loved and appreciated we are until we die. It's one of the sad realities of life."

"It helped me. It made me cry over and over, but not in a bad way. And your words, the things you read and what you said made me feel hopeful. I was so sure there would be some kind of condemnation of what she did. I only came for Hannah's sake. I was expecting some kind of condemnation, so was dreading it. But not only did it not come, it was just the opposite," she said. "Anyway, I'm really glad I was there and I want to thank you for that."

"I was just so happy when I saw you and Hannah there and I'm glad you liked what you heard. It's all true." He gave her a sincere smile, and then said, "So tell me about Candy. I'm realizing I didn't know her like I thought I did."

Diane set her glass down and stared out the front window.

"I sometimes wonder that same thing," she said, as if she was talking to herself. "I have a lot of guilt about my children. I wasn't the best mother."

"Nobody's perfect. If you can, tell me what you mean."

Her downcast eyes and the beginning of tears showed the torment in her heart. "Oh, I don't know," she said. "It was such a mess back then. Candy's father was a drinker. Her older brother and sister were always fighting and their father was always riding them and I was just always trying to keep the peace. I think Candy got forgotten a lot in the middle of the drama," she said, heaving a sigh. "It was like she didn't exist. I could see that, but I had my hands full and couldn't do anything about it. I was just trying to survive."

"That sounds awful," Brian said, then added, "but not that unusual."

She looked at him with her misty eyes, giving him a questioning look. "What do you mean?"

"I've been a pastor for a long time now and I've found very few families that haven't been very messy, including my own. What you describe sounds very familiar."

After a moment, Diane asked, "Do you mean that?"

"Oh yes," he said. "My family was a train wreck. Sometimes I wonder how I ever survived it. I have a few siblings who didn't."

She looked out the window again, slightly shaking her head. "You mean all those people in your church aren't as perfect as they seem?"

"Well," he said, "there are some really solid families I admire. There are some great parents and kids, but they are the exception. There are a few like that, but even the best ones have their issues and problems. Mostly, the families I've seen all have very real problems, even some worse than yours and mine."

"Really," she said. "That's amazing. I always resented those other families in church. They all seemed to have it together and I knew what my family was like, so I resented them for it. I also hated God because it wasn't fair." She shot Brian a sideways look. "I can't believe I'm telling you this."

"It's okay. I'm a pastor. Anything you tell me stays with me. I also totally understand what you are feeling, because I have felt the same things."

"I find that hard to believe."

"I'm a recovering alcoholic. I come from a very messed up family. The only reason I have a life today is because of God and a lot of very broken and beautiful people who helped me get my life back," he said. "You can believe it."

"But you're a pastor. You're a pastor of a large church. How can that be? In my parents' church, you wouldn't be allowed."

"Yes, I know. But I would never want to be in that church," he said. "I'm in a church that understands we humans are broken and need healing. People like me are accepted, welcomed, and forgiven. And isn't that what the church is supposed to be?"

"Well, you would think."

"So tell me about Candy," Brian said, gently guiding the conversation back to Candy. "What was she like?"

Diane looked at her watch and saw the time. "You won't get to talk to Hannah if you keep talking to me."

"I've got lots of time. I can talk to her after we go talk to the police. It might be better then anyway. She will be more open to talking after we ride together and meet with the police."

"Candy?" Diane began, "Let's see . . . What do you want to know?"

"Start with when she was born."

"Oh Jesus!" She shot a hand over her mouth, looking horrified at Brian, then said, "Sorry!"

Brian laughed at her reaction. "It's okay, Diane. It's not a big deal."

"Wow. You *are* different. That would have gotten me a beating in my home, saying something like that in front of the pastor."

"That's pretty wrong, isn't it?" he said. "I'm so sorry that's how you were taught about love and forgiveness. It's just sad and crazy, isn't it?"

She relaxed visibly. "Well, Candy was born in Minneapolis. Durk, my husband, was working for 3M as a custodian. He drank heavily. I was working at the school cafeteria and trying to raise two kids and a newborn. I wanted to cut back on my hours but Durk was just not willing. He was always worried about the money. He said we couldn't afford it, but we could have. Candy was a fussy baby, and I hate to admit this, I wasn't very patient with her. When she would fuss I would just leave her and let her cry." Diane began crying. "I am so awful," she said. "What kind of mother does that?"

"The only kind of mother that does that is a mother who is doing the best she can and has way more than she can handle. You were just trying to survive a terrible situation and doing the best you can. You can't beat yourself up for that. Besides, how old were you then?"

"I was in my early twenties. I was still just a child myself. Still, I can still hear her crying and crying, and it would just make me want to scream. I just wanted to shake her. I think I hated her." She gasped. "I can't believe I just said that!" And burst into heavy sobs.

When she had spent herself, Brian said, "Think about what you were dealing with. An alcoholic abusive husband, a full-time job, two little children, and a fussy newborn. You were pushed to your limit. It's what anyone would feel in that situation. And yet in spite of all that you found a way to survive and get the job done. That's what you did. That's all you could do."

Diane cried some more, then wiped her eyes and blew her nose.

"There were times I thought about taking my own life," she said after she regained her composure.

"Which just means it was pretty bad."

"But now I think about Candy. It was that bad for her and I wasn't there for her . . . again," she said. "It's just that same thing." Brian waited a moment, then softly urged her by asking, "What exactly was so bad for Candy that she would choose to die?"

"I'm not exactly sure. She really didn't let me into her life much, and I think that had to do with Mickey. He and I don't get along and so we've never been all that close. I've just been a babysitter for them for whenever she got sick, but not much more than that, but it's the least I could do," she said. "I think she was stressing about work. I think there were some things happening there. She was stressing about her cancer. She was getting chemotherapy and radiation and that was making her sick a lot. She was missing work and in bed a lot. Mickey was doing everything for the kids because she didn't have the energy for them. I think she and Mickey were not getting along. The kids would tell me they were fighting almost every day. The night she took her life she and Mickey had a huge fight and he left the house. He had never done that before. Hannah told me that Kyle got really mad at her."

"Kyle got mad at her? Why?"

"Well, when they fought it was mostly Candy who did the fighting. Mick would just take it. But this time was different and I think Kyle got mad at her for driving Mickey away. After Mickey left, Kyle and his mom got into a big yelling match too. Hannah said it was scary. She never heard Kyle yell at his mom that way."

Just then, the back door suddenly opened and Kyle walked in with a rush of cold air. He was bundled in his heavy winter coat and carrying his fully loaded school backpack.

CHAPTER 30

"HI, KYLE," BRIAN said. Kyle looked at Brian, then looked away, and said hi with little enthusiasm. He dropped his backpack and coat by the door, kicked out of his boots, and made his way to his room without looking back at the adults.

Diane called out to him, "Kyle, we have to go down to the police department. If you want anything to eat before we go you need to get it now."

"Why do we have to talk to the police again? We already talked to them," he yelled back defiantly without turning around.

"We already talked about this," she said. "It's routine. They have to write a report and they have to know all the details."

"I already told them everything!" His voice now petulant.

"Well, you have to tell them again. We don't have a choice. Please just get ready to go."

His door slammed. Diane looked at Brian as if to say, "See what I'm dealing with?"

"Hannah," Diane yelled, "it's almost time to go. Come out and say hi to Pastor Matterson."

Hannah came out of her room as though she had been standing by waiting for her cue.

"Hi, Hannah," Brian said as she came into the room. "I was so glad you came to the service on Sunday. Did you like it?"

Hannah shyly nodded but did not smile. It was clear she was very nervous.

"Wasn't it nice to hear all those things people were saying about your mom?" Brian asked her.

Hannah nodded again.

"Why don't you come in here and keep Pastor company a moment while I get ready to go?" Diane got up and Hannah cautiously took her place on the sofa.

"So, what was your favorite thing you heard about your mom the other night?"

Hannah thought for a moment and looked troubled, like somehow this was a test. He knew she was just shy and afraid, so he prompted her. "There was that one lady who said your mom helped her through a hard time in her life and said it was the nicest thing anyone ever did for her. Do you remember her?" Brian asked. "She was sitting close to where you were."

She nodded again, a smile playing at the edges of her mouth.

"So, Hannah, what grade are you in now?"

"I'm almost done with the fourth grade."

"Do you like school?"

She nodded.

"Do you like your teacher?"

She nodded.

"What's your teacher's name?"

"Ms. Albers."

"Is she nice?"

"She's real nice,"

"Do you have a favorite subject?"

"Um . . . I like spelling."

"Spelling? Really? I didn't like spelling when I was your age. I wasn't very good at it. Are you a good speller?"

"Yes," she said, brightening, "I've won the spelling bee twice."

"Wow, that's amazing," Brian said. "I was always scared of the spelling bee."

"It's not scary."

"Well, it's probably not scary if you are a good speller. How did you get to be such a good speller?"

She shrugged. "I don't know, I just am."

Diane came back into the room and yelled for Kyle. There was no response and she looked at the pastor with clear frustration. "I don't know what to do with him."

"Let me see if I can get him," Brian offered.

As he passed her, Diane whispered, "Doesn't this seem strange to you, the police wanting to talk the kids at the station? I don't understand why they just don't come here."

"I don't know either. I presume it's just routine."

Brian went to Kyle's door, the only one closed, knocked softly, and said, "Hey, Kyle, it's Pastor Matterson. Listen, I know this is hard, but it's best just to get this over with. It won't take long and I'm going with you so you will have a friend there, okay?"

There was no answer and Brian waited several moments. "Kyle, can you hear me?"

"Okay! I'm coming . . ." His irritation showed in his voice.

CHAPTER 31

BRIAN DROVE THE three of them to the police department and on arriving they were told to sit and wait until one of the detectives could come out and get them. They sat in silence in the waiting area. Kyle had his phone out, playing a game. Hannah sat looking around the room with somber curiosity. Police departments are serious places with lots of cold hard surfaces.

Brian looked at Diane and raised his eyebrows, but he couldn't think of anything to say that seemed appropriate, so the silence hung in the air.

Minutes dragged by.

Kyle finally said, "How long is this going to take?"

He had no sooner spoken when a door opened and a stocky middle-aged man with a large mustache, balding head, and ruddy, pocked complexion came in. He turned to Brian and the Vinters, the only people in the room, and announced that he was Detective David Walters.

"Are you the Vinters?" he asked.

Diane stood and said, "These are the Vinter children, Kyle and Hannah. I am their grandmother, Diane Gunderson," she said.

Walters turned to Brian and said, "And you are?"

Brian extended his hand and introduced himself, "I'm Pastor Brian Matterson. I am the Vinters' pastor."

"Nice to meet you, Pastor. We'll need you to wait here. We are just going to take them back and get a statement from each of them. We won't be long."

"If you three would come with me please," he said, nodding to the Vinter family.

Brian wanted to protest, but was caught off guard by Detective Walter's forcefulness, and his reaction was to obey. He later wondered if this was a technique they taught them, thinking he should maybe learn some of that.

The detective herded them through the door, and just like that Brian was there alone, waiting and wondering what was going on. He wondered if he could ask for Officer Mike, but thought that was probably not a good idea as that might put Mike in an awkward position. He tried to relax, but he hated the idea that the kids were in there talking to the police and he couldn't be with them. After all they had been through this must be terrifying. He felt like he should be in there just to offer some comfort. It was clear the detective didn't want him in there, however. What should he do?

He became agitated. He tried to be patient, but then finally went up to the uniformed woman seated behind the bulletproof Plexiglas and spoke through the metal speaker. "Hi," he started, when he got her attention, but wasn't sure what to say next. "I am Pastor Brian Matterson from All Saints Lutheran Church and I am the pastor for the Vinter family. Those kids in there have just lost their mother and their father is not here. I came to help them through this and really feel I should be in there with them. Could you check and see if that would be possible?"

The stern-looking uniformed officer looked at Brian's askance. as though she didn't have time for this. "It won't take long. They'll be out shortly. You can just wait for them," she said in that matter-of-fact, forceful way that the detective had used, a way that seemed to call for his immediate obedience. It made him think of *Star Wars* and Obi-Wan Kenobi and the Jedi mind trick "These aren't the droids you are looking for."

Brian stepped away from the window, not wanting to be too pushy. He knew it was the intimidation of the police that made him back off too easily. He knew if he refused to take no for an answer and made a fuss he could get his way to some extent, but instead went back to his seat, hating himself for being dismissed so easily.

He sat back down and after a few agitated moments went out to into the city hall lobby, pulled out his phone, and called Mike Hemsley. The phone rang three times and went to voicemail. Brian hung up, not knowing what he would say anyway. He just didn't like feeling powerless and needed to do something. He took a deep breath, said the Serenity Prayer–the long version–and went back inside and sat down. He just needed to hand it to God.

Time dragged on and he grew anxious again. He went up to the officer in the window and said, "It's taking a long time. Do you know how much longer it will be?"

The officer again looked annoyed but didn't look up. "It shouldn't be much longer."

Brian was about to turn away but then stopped. "That's what you said last time. It's been almost an hour since then. Can you please check and see what's going on?" he insisted.

"Sir," she said, "they are taking statements. When they are finished they will be out. That's all I can tell you."

Brian turned away exasperated, but reminded himself to let it go. He checked his calendar on his phone to see what he had coming up. He saw he was to meet the council president in forty-five minutes to talk about the roof situation. After that, he needed to pick up his son from band practice and take him to swimming practice. He could still keep those appointments, but this was dragging on too long for him. He was pushing it.

After another twenty minutes, he decided to call the council president to let him know he was running late. He really was stuck there since he had agreed to drive. Instead of meeting with the president in person, he offered to discuss the roof situation over the phone instead.

He went back out the city hall lobby and found a quiet corner.

CHAPTER 32

BOB ANDERSON WAS the president of the council and had been a member of the church his whole life. He was an insurance salesperson for a big-name insurance company and an easygoing guy. He was young, in his early thirties, bright faced and energetic. He was married and had his second child on the way. Brian thought he was the ideal insurance man as he had all the right qualities.

Bob had been a reluctant church president, as so many are, but in his case, he became president by default. He missed a meeting, got nominated and elected, and found out about it later. When he heard about it, he refused initially but eventually caved and said yes. He declared he knew nothing about being a church council president, but Brian convinced him that nobody ever does. It's a job learned only by doing.

Essentially, the president is a confidant to the pastor. He helps plan the council agenda and presides over the monthly meeting. The pastor keeps the president apprised of what's happening in the church and the president then leads the council to solve any problems facing the church. As might be expected, most problems were financial in nature.

This month, it was the coffeemaker and the roof. The coffeemaker was easy. Any extra expense up to a few thousand dollars was fairly easily managed. However, a major expense like the roof creates real anxiety in the council.

Brian had learned his role was to not worry so much about the money, because he knew God would always provide somehow, but rather to manage the anxiety associated with it. He began by making sure the leader wasn't made anxious by news of financial setbacks. If the leader was anxious, then the group could spin out of control. Fear and anxiety are the enemies of the soul and the church, and really the whole world when you think about it. Letting the council president know there is a big problem in advance of the meeting, thinking through some of the solutions and helping him or her know it's going to be okay are the most important steps when introducing a new challenge.

Bob's secretary put Brian through. "Hello, this is Bob Anderson, your friendly neighbor."

"Howdy, neighbor," Brian said.

"Hello, Pastor, how are you? We have a meeting coming up shortly."

"That's why I'm calling. I'm getting tied up here and won't be able to get away in time to meet you. I have time now to talk, if that would work. Otherwise, we can reschedule."

"That's fine. I can talk now."

"I need to let you know that we have a very serious problem at the church," Brian said. He knew it always helped to make it sound worse at first so that when he said what it was it didn't seem so bad.

"Oh no," Bob said, "sound's bad." He had his full attention.

"Well, it's not good."

"What's going on?"

"I think you know we had water leaking into the nursery?"

"Yes, I heard that."

"Well, we've had it looked at and we have two choices. We can put some patches on our roof as a temporary fix that may last a year or two, or we can replace the whole thing."

"Replace the whole roof?" Mike asked, alarmed.

"No, no, not the roof. We just need to replace the rubber membrane on the roof. The roof is fine, it's the rubber coating that's leaking. We knew this day was coming and it looks like it's here."

"Do we have insurance for that sort of thing?"

"No, nothing that covers replacement. If we could get a tree to fall on the church that might do it."

Bob chuckled. "I don't want to know about that," he said. "So what are we looking at?"

"Well, Aksel got a couple of quotes for us. It looks like about twelve-grand to patch and about thirty-five grand to replace."

Bob whistled. "Wow. That's a lot. How can we possibly do that?"

"Well," Brian said, "I don't think we have a choice. I don't know how we do it, I just know that if something like this happens to my house I don't like it but I'd find a way to get it done. We just need to do it."

"Yes, but how?" Bob said. "I just don't see how. We don't have that kind of money."

"We do have some options," Brian said. "We can do a fundraiser. People won't like it. Heck, I don't like it. But I would give if asked. The only other option is to look at refinancing our current building loan and do cash out refinance to pay for it. One more idea might be to see if we can get a short-term line of credit and pay if off over a couple years."

"Wow," Bob said. "The council isn't going to like this."

"Nobody likes things like this Bob. It's just life. You do what you have to do and trust God to provide, right? We'll be fine," Brian said. He found himself wondering how much he really trusted those words sometimes. He knew God had provided for him constantly through the years both personally and for his churches, but he also knew from experience sometimes things could get so bad you wouldn't be fine—at least, not in this life. He knew this honest knowledge of reality was the basis of all fear and anxiety for humans, the only creatures on earth who have the ability to obsess about the possible bad things that can happen. Brian knew his dog didn't lose any sleep worrying about retirement. For that matter, he didn't even know he was naked!

"What do you think the council will say?" Bob asked.

Brian knew Bob was still uncomfortable in his role as council leader. He had not felt ready to be such a leader, and Brian could certainly understand his reluctance to lead. As he was fond of saying, "God calls the brightest and best to serve, but since they won't do it he has to settle for people like you and me." The Bible is filled with reluctant leaders who do amazing things.

"They won't like it any more than we do, and the congregation won't like it either," Brian said, "But, again, it is what it is. We have a wealthy Father who can afford to pay for this. We just need to trust him."

"That's right, Pastor. That's right. Okay, we can handle this. So how do we proceed?"

"I have Aksel coming to the meeting on Thursday. We need to move him to the top of the agenda so that he can get out of there. He hates meetings and I promised we would get him through this as quickly as possible. I will present the situation, Aksel will be there to answer questions, and then we will need a motion to authorize the action that stipulates how it is to be paid for."

"Do we do the repair or do the whole replacement?"

"Well, that's up to the council. Aksel will recommend the full replacement and I have to agree with him. I can't see paying that much for a two- or three-year fix that we will need to repeat before long. If we do that we will still need the full replacement in three years, and who knows what the price will be then," Brian said. "The full replacement comes with a twenty-year warranty."

"That makes sense. I would agree with that I think," Bob said. "So, how do you think we pay for it?"

"Beki is looking into what a refinance would look like. I would recommend we do a fundraiser and cover any remainder with a refinance, depending on what those numbers look like, or a short-term loan," Brian said. "The council will need to decide on what kind of fundraiser we do. I will try and have a few suggestions."

"That sounds good," Bob said. "I feel better. It sounds like we really can do this after all."

"Oh, I think so. It's just that initial shock. But like I said, it's really not a choice. We just have to bite the bullet and do it."

"Yep, I agree," Bob said. "So anything else?"

"Nope, that's all I got. You could say a prayer for the Vinter family."

"Yes, of course. That's just so terrible. I will pray for them. I have been."

"Okay, Bob. Thank you. I will email you later with some agenda items."

"That sounds great Pastor. I will talk to you later."

"God bless you, good neighbor."

Bob laughed, "You too, Pastor," and he hung up the phone.

CHAPTER 33

BRIAN CHECKED HIS watch and saw it was 4:15. Time was running out.

Back at police reception, he once again approached the woman at the window. "I really hate to be a pest, but this is taking a lot longer than I thought it would. Can you check and see how much longer? I have other appointments I need to consider and I am their ride."

The officer held up a finger and finished whatever she was typing on her keyboard. "I can check and see," she said, "but it will be a moment."

Brian took a seat, fuming. He was sure they were being difficult on purpose, but he knew it would do no good to try to push them.

The officer picked up the phone, spoke to someone, then hung the phone up and said, "Excuse me, sir."

Brian approached window.

"One of the detectives will be out to talk to you in a moment."

"Thank you," Brian said, wondering what was going on. He assumed they were trying to find evidence that Mickey may have been involved with Candy's death and were pressing the kids for information. He was worried they had them separated and were intimidating them with no parents or other adults to help them. *Could they do that? Probably not.* Brian didn't know what to think, but if Mick didn't do anything wrong this was a lot of trauma on top of trauma. He said a prayer for the Vinter children and Diane.

Another twenty minutes went by and Brian was trying his best to remain patient. He realized if this took much longer, he was going to have to figure out how to get his son picked up and delivered to soccer and get to the swim meet. He wasn't sure he had any options, however, as he knew Donna had plans and he didn't dare ruin those for her as he had done so many times before.

He was just about to get up and be a pest again when the waiting area door opened and the burly Detective Walters came through. He cocked finger at Brian and said, "Could you come with me please?"

Brian was taken aback by his brusque manner and said, "Can you tell me what's going on?"

"That's what we're trying to figure out," he said. "Maybe you can help us."

Brian followed the detective through the door and down a long hallway with many closed doors. The detective opened a door and ushered Brian through to a small square room with a metal table bolted to the floor, two chairs on one side and one on the other, also bolted to the floor. No windows, but a mirror that Brian assumed was one-way glass. It was an intimidating space.

Brian sat at in one of the chairs and Walters sat across from him.

"Pastor, we realize this is a difficult situation, but there are some things that are not making sense to us and we are just trying to understand the situation. Maybe you can help us."

"Of course, I will do what I can, but I'm not sure I have much that will be useful. I have to tell you I'm running very low on time. I have some other pressing engagements to attend to."

"This is pretty important and it shouldn't take too long. What I am about to tell you is confidential to the investigation and I ask that you not share it with anyone, especially anyone connected to the family."

"Okay," Brian said, "I think I can agree with that, but I'm not sure I feel completely comfortable with that arrangement."

"I know this is a little unusual, but we are just trying to get at the truth. We are concerned that people in the family are covering for each other and we don't want to see the wrong person charged with a crime, if there has been a crime. We think you might be able to help us get at the truth."

Brian could smell the detective's cheap aftershave in the confined space as he leaned across the table. He used too much. "Okay. Like I said, I will do what I can but I also don't want to be used to hurt anyone, so if I feel uncomfortable with anything, I may want to stop."

"That's fine. We won't ask you do anything to hurt or jeopardize anyone. We are just trying to get at the facts."

"All right then, go ahead, but I really do need to hurry."

"First off, please tell me what you know about this situation already."

Brian was thrown by this because he already knew more than he should have. Mike Hemsley had told him things in confidence, like the possible theft of money from the police department. Then there was the information from Sue Solberg about all the faked illnesses. He was struggling to sort out what all he knew and what all he could share.

Walters, a veteran detective, picked up on Brian's vacillation right away. "Why are you hesitating?"

Brian was impressed by the detective's acute powers of observation; he didn't think he was that obvious. "Yes, well, I've been told some things in confidence that I don't know I'm at liberty to share with you, so I am thinking about what I can share."

"Just tell me what you know."

Again, Brian felt pressured and intimidated, but decided he wasn't going to be manipulated.

"Detective, I've been patient, sitting out there waiting and wondering what's going on. You've been in here talking to members of my flock, minors, and I don't think I want to tell you anything until you tell me what's going on. This just doesn't feel right to me."

The detective glared at him, his black eyes seemed to penetrate right through him. Again, Brian wondered if that look was something that was taught or learned. It was powerful. It scared Brian a little. He steeled himself.

Walters' withering glare lasted longer than Brian liked, but apparently it was long enough for the detective to clearly indicate he was the one in control. "Okay, Pastor. I will tell you what's going on. We have a victim that at first appears to be a suicide. After forensics and autopsy, we find there was significant bruising on the neck which preceded the apparent suicide. This leads us to think there was an assault with strangulation preceding the apparent suicide. This leads us to believe maybe the suicide was staged to cover up the strangulation. The primary suspect is the husband, who we know had a highly charged argument before leaving the house. We also know that his wife is having trouble at work and a strained marriage. We know that she has a life insurance policy and a separate savings account the husband may or may not know about, with a large sum of money in it. He has means and motive. We brought him in for questioning and he was evasive. He reluctantly allowed us to take a DNA sample. We were about to charge him with murder when we discovered the job issues and financial issues which reinforce motive. However, the DNA results from material found under the victim's fingernails do not match the husband. They are close, but do not match. He also does not present with any defensive wounds consistent with the amount of material we found under the victim's nails. He should have scratches on his body. This has us a little confused. Are you following me so far?"

Brian nodded, suddenly realizing for the first time that this really does look like a murder. He had not allowed himself to really go there before, but now could see why they thought so. He suddenly thought so too.

"So," Walters continues, "we need more information. We think the kids might be able to tell us more. We think maybe they heard something that night or some other detail that might help us make sense of this. In the course of the conversation, we noticed the son being evasive and nervous. We also noted that the son has a few scratch marks on hands and wrists. We asked him to remove his shirt and we found several more scratches on his arms and shoulders consistent with the wounds we were looking for on the father."

"Kyle?" Brian blurted out. "Are you serious?"

"I'm as serious as a heart attack," Walters said matter-of-factly. "We want to get a DNA sample from the boy to see if he matches, but the law won't allow us to take his DNA without parental approval."

Brian's head was spinning. What did this mean? Kyle killed his mother and tried to cover it up? He felt overwhelmed by the implications, for Kyle, the family, the church, the community.

"My God," Brian said. "What will this mean for him?"

"It's impossible to say at this point. We don't know anything other than circumstantial evidence. The DNA would help us know the truth. That's where we need your help."

"My help? What can *I* do?"

"We are holding Mick pending charges, but now we think Kyle is the more likely suspect. We need Mick's permission to get Kyle's DNA, but for understandable reasons Mick is reluctant to give that permission. We think you might be able to convince him it's the right thing to do."

"I don't know," Brian said. "I think I might feel the same way if I were him. What would I tell him? Why is this the right thing to do?"

"If he is charged with this and found guilty he's going away for thirty years at least. His kids will have no mother and no father and no home. Mick will be at least sixty before he gets out. That's a big price to pay for something he didn't do," Walters said. "If Kyle is found guilty he will go to juvie and get the help he needs.

His father can see him regularly, plus continue to be there for his daughter and provide a home for her. Kyle could be released before he is twenty and still have his life ahead of him. If he did this thing, even if he had good reason, it's still the right thing to do. Can you imagine what kind of life Kyle will have knowing he is guilty of killing his mother and his father is paying the price for him? His life won't be worth a plug nickel and he will never find any peace. This is the right thing, Pastor, and I think you would agree."

These guys are good, Brian thought. He could find no fault with what Walters was saying. It really did make sense. And yet, Brian felt overwhelmed and lost. His emotions left him in no condition to be making these big decisions. Brian realized a lawyer was needed right now. He was in over his head and he needed good advice. It's not that he didn't trust the police, but he certainly didn't trust himself in this situation, not with how out of his element he was and the stakes were too high.

"So, you've presented this to Mick already?"

"Yes, sir, we have. He won't budge. He wants to take the fall and save his son."

Brian thought about the time and his other personal commitments and felt his anxiety growing too big. He needed to be here, but he also needed to be there for his own kids. He looked at his watch, 4:30.

"Well?" Walters pressed. "Will you help us?"

That question kept ringing in Brian's ears. *Will you help us? Will you help us?*

He didn't know if the detective meant it that way, but it sounded to him like he was being asked to help the police rather than the Vinters. He thought what the detective said made sense and yet he just didn't know. Perhaps he had seen too many television detective-shows and was jaded by police wanting to make their case regardless of the truth. Although he didn't think that's what was going on here, he just couldn't be sure.

"I will talk to Mick and see what he is thinking, although he isn't that easy for me to talk to either," Brian said. "Candy was the one who came to church, not Mick. I've tried talking to him many times, but he doesn't give me much. So I wouldn't get my hopes too high."

"That would be appreciated. We've tried everything we can think of, so it's worth a try," Walters said and quickly got up. "Wait here. I will set things up."

Brian checked his watch again and saw it was 4:35. He could get to the school in fifteen minutes at this time of day if he hurried. He had to leave at 5:00 at the latest. But then he had to take Diane and the kids home too; he was their ride. He really didn't have any time left. He hoped it would be quicker than things had been so far. Before long, the door opened and Walters came in.

"Right this way, Pastor Matterson."

Walters led Brian down the hall to an identical room. Mick sat in the single chair. Brian sat across from him. Mick's wrinkled clothes appeared to have been slept in for days. Brian was sure it was the same shirt he had been wearing the first day he went to see him. His eyes were red and puffy. From crying? Or not sleeping? He looked a mess. An empty Styrofoam coffee cup sat in front of him. He looked like a prizefighter slumped on his stool after losing fifteen rounds. Brian's heart went out to him.

This guy just lost his wife and now he may now be losing his son. What a total disaster. "Hi, Mick," Brian said as he sat down.

Mick looked up at Brian briefly and nodded his greeting, returning his eyes to the spent coffee cup.

"You look pretty rough," Brian said. "What a mess, huh?"

Mick kept staring. He might have nodded in agreement, but Brian couldn't tell. Brian wasn't sure how to proceed. Were they recording this? He imagined two detectives behind the glass, a video camera, the department chief, and a whole room of people waiting for Brian to get what they wanted out of Mick. It didn't feel right to him. He also remembered what Walters said and he was certain it made the most sense. Yet he couldn't shake the feeling of being a pawn.

Speaking quietly, he said, "So, Mick, I brought your kids and Candy's mom down here so they could give a statement. I thought I would be here for a half hour or so. That was about three hours ago and now I am in a room talking to you. I didn't even know you were here. Detective Walters explained to me the situation, and I'm sure it has been explained to you."

It seemed as though Mick was listening, but Brian couldn't be sure. Mick appeared to be in a state of shock, so who knew what he was hearing.

"They tell me they first thought you might have had something to do with Candy's death and they were going to arrest you, but your DNA doesn't match the evidence they found. Now they think Kyle might be the one who did it, and they want to check his DNA, but they need your permission before they can take a sample for testing. Is that right?"

Brian wanted to see if Mick was even listening. This time he saw him nod his head.

"And they explained to you that if they arrest you, you might get thirty years in prison. If they arrest Kyle, he could go to juvenile detention for five or six years but still have his whole life ahead of him. They told you that too?"

Mick nodded again.

"But you don't want to give them permission for the DNA, is that right?"

Mick just stared.

"So, I've been asked to reason with you and see if I can help convince you to do the right thing. But you know what, Mick? I have no idea what the right thing is. What they say makes sense, but what do I know? I'm just a pastor. I don't know how these things work. If I were you, I wouldn't take advice from me. What you need is a lawyer."

As he said this, he thought he heard an expletive come from behind the glass, or had he imagined it? The room was sound-proof so he must have assumed the angry response, he reasoned.

"Have you thought about getting a lawyer? I really think you need one right now."

Mick seemed to come out of his daze a little and looked up at Brian.

"I can't afford no lawyer," Mick said. "I can't even afford a cup of coffee right now."

"Mick, you're not thinking straight. You've just been devastated by the loss of your wife and now possibly you or your son could be going to prison. You need someone to help you who knows what they're doing. I can't advise you here. Let me find you a lawyer and I will figure out a way to help you pay for them, okay?"

Mick looked at Brian and seemed to be struggling to think.

"Have they arrested you, Mick?"

Mick shook his head.

"Then they can't hold you. You can take your family and leave right now. And then, if they do arrest you, they have to give you a lawyer. Please, Mick, don't do anything without the help of someone who knows what they are doing, okay?"

Just then the door opened and Walters burst in. "Okay, Pastor, that will do, you can go now." He was clearly not happy but it confirmed what Brian had been feeling. The police were trying to do what was best and easiest for them, not necessarily the Vinters. While it was what made the most sense, he was sure a lawyer could improve their situation far more than he ever could.

"Can Mick leave?" Brian asked.

"No, not yet. We have a few more questions for him," Walters said, glaring at Brian. He could almost feel the heat from his anger radiating from his body.

"Is he under arrest?"

"No, he is not."

"Can he leave right now if he wants to?"

"He can leave any time, but it would be in his best interest if he stays and cooperates with our investigation," Walters said without taking his burning eyes off Brian.

Brian found it impossible to maintain eye contact with him, but was not going to be deterred. "Mick, I need to go pick up my son right now. I gave your family a ride down here and I need to take them home now. I've run out of time." Brian turned and leaned toward Mick. "Would you like a ride home with me?"

He didn't know where he was getting the courage for this, but that didn't matter right then.

"Yes," Mick said, "I would like to leave now." He stood up.

"That's okay, Pastor," the detective said, "we can arrange to get them home if you need to leave now."

"I do appreciate that, but it sounds like Mick is ready to go now and I'm pretty sure the kids have had enough," Brian said, moving toward the door, but Walters kept his unyielding and intimidating body in the doorway.

"Didn't you say we could leave, Detective?" Brian said, wondering how he would get by him.

"Yes, you are free to leave," Walters said, but did not budge.

"Will you please excuse us then?"

Slowly, and with great reluctance and annoyance, the detective moved his bulk aside so that Brian and Mick could squeeze by him.

As they passed Detective Walters said, "Thank you very much, Pastor, you've been a great help," with clear sarcasm and bile in his tone.

Brian felt adrenaline suddenly pulsing through his body.

CHAPTER 34

BRIAN AND MICK went out to the waiting area and stood for a few minutes. Brian realized there would be another waiting game if he did not make some noise. He had already caused enough trouble, he thought, but he really had to go. He approached the officer at the window and asked that the children and their grandmother be sent out. She didn't even pretend to listen. He rapped on the glass.   She looked up sharply and said, "Please don't do that!"

Brian said, "I don't mean to be rude, but I have an appointment to get to and you are holding two minor children back there against their parent's will. I need to get them home. Would you please send them out now?"

She stared back at him and without taking her intimidating gaze from him lifted the phone and called to the back. She spoke but Brian couldn't hear her as she had turned off the speaker. She then went back to what she was doing.

Brian stood there incredulous. "Excuse me," he said. "Excuse me!" he said louder now, but she continued to ignore him. He shook his head and stepped away from the glass. He looked at Mick with a look of incredulity. "Can you believe these people?"

Mick returned the look in full agreement. It was the first time Brian felt any meaningful connection with Mick. They stood there waiting, and just as Brian's steam was up again, the door opened and the kids came out along with their grandmother. Hannah ran to her father and they embraced. Kyle was less enthusiastic and something exchanged between father and son. Brian didn't know quite know what it was.

"What happened back there?" Brian asked, looking at Diane.

"Let's just get out of here," she said and they moved to the door and headed out into the biting cold Minnesota sunshine.

Mick had his van in the parking lot and said he would see them later. Hannah asked if she could go with him, but he told her he had work do to and that she should go with Grandma. She was not happy.

Brian asked for a cell phone number, which Mick reluctantly gave him and they parted ways.

Driving back to Diane's, Brian asked them what had happened with the police. Hannah reported they were very nice to her. They gave her a Coke and a candy bar and just asked a lot of questions about their home and how things were at home with everybody.

Kyle, like his father, didn't offer much. "Just asked a million questions," he said. "It was dumb."

However, Brian knew Kyle was not telling them everything. He wondered how Diane and Hannah would react when they learned that the police thought Kyle might be guilty.

Brian still could not imagine how it could be so. Kyle was a moody teenager, but to kill his mother and then cover it up? He knew he misjudged some people sometimes, but he still did not see that possibility in Kyle. He was broken for sure, but if he had done this thing, he would have broken down by now and admitted it. It just didn't fit in Brian's brain. What fourteen-year-old could be that tough?

"Well," Diane began, "I sat alone for a long time and then a woman came in and asked me a lot of questions about Mick and Candy's relationship, how long they dated, how long they were married, about all of Candy's illnesses, about their finances, about how they got along. There were many questions about the kids, what they were like, how everyone got along, and how they were as a family. It was endless questions, and many of them they asked over and over again. I was getting a little annoyed and I kept asking what was going on, but they kept saying that this was all just routine. I think there is something going on, there's something they aren't telling us."

Brian looked in the rearview mirror and could see Kyle's cheeks coloring as he stared out the window. He wondered what was running through his mind right now. He must be terrified. Brian said a silent prayer for him, begging God to help this poor family.

When they got to the house, Kyle jumped out immediately and went inside. Diane looked at the pastor and asked if he was coming in. He looked at his watch and saw it was 5:05.

"I really need to go get my son. I'm already running late," he said. "But I would like a word with you before I go."

They waited for Hannah to get out and she turned to him. "I am going to find you guys a lawyer. There is something going on too and I think Mick and all of you need someone to help you work with the police. They were asking me things that make me very concerned, but I'm not the right person to help with this."

"Like what kinds of things?"

Brian debated what to tell her. He wondered why the police didn't tell her anything and assumed that they didn't want to tip their hand. Is that how they work? He wasn't sure if that was the case, but if it was, no wonder they were pissed at him. They took a chance telling him thinking it would help them, but it backfired. Now he really felt caught in the middle. He wasn't trying to thwart the police. He wasn't on anyone's side, really, he just wanted to do the right thing. If someone was guilty of a crime, he didn't want to help them get away with anything. But he did want to know the truth and he wanted things to be fair. And that's exactly where he felt lost. What was fair in this case? Up against the police without help, the Vinters, even with Brian in their court, were far outmatched. They needed a lawyer, and Brian was going to get them one.

He decided Diane needed to know everything he had been told. He filled her in about what the police suspected. Diane fell into a fit of despair and her tears began again.

"God, this is all my fault," she said when she was able to breathe again.

"Your fault?" Brian said. "How do you figure that?"

"Because I created a monster," she said. "I drove Candy crazy and she drove her family crazy. It's all my fault." She was becoming more hysterical.

Brian tried to hold her hand but she pulled it abruptly away.

He let her cry for a bit, then said, "Listen, I'm really sorry, but I do have to go. I just have to. I hate to leave you like this, but you have to know that we all have things we regret and things we would do differently, but you are not responsible for this. You are not. You are beating yourself up and that won't help anything right now. Those kids need someone right now. They have nobody. Mick is a wreck and he is not able to be there. You have the chance to be there for them now. They need you. Can you do that?"

Wiping her eyes with the backs of her hands, she seemed to find some resolve. "You're right," she said. "I can do that. I have to. It's the least I can do." She looked at him and said, "You think you can find them a lawyer?"

"I will."

"Then I will take care of the kids. Thank you, Pastor," she said, stepping from the car and marching quickly to her front door.

CHAPTER 35

A S BRIAN HURRIED to pick up his son–late once again–he mulled over how to find a lawyer. He thought he would begin with his cousin, who was a big shot corporate lawyer with a firm in Saint Paul. Maybe he could help find a good criminal lawyer.

"I am the bread of life. Whoever comes to me will never go hungry, and whoever believes in me will never be thirsty." These words of Jesus suddenly popped into his head. They were from the Gospel of John, from the text he was preaching on for the coming Sunday. What were these words doing in the forefront of his brain? "I am the bread of life. Whoever comes to me will never go hungry, and whoever believes in me will never be thirsty."

Does this have any bearing on what is happening right now? Brian wondered.

Before he could finish the thought, his car phone began playing a new ringtone, courtesy of his son.

When the pimp's in the crib ma
Drop it like it's hot

Drop it like it's hot
Drop it like it's hot
When the pigs try to get at you
Park it like it's hot
Park it like it's hot
Park it like it's hot . . .

"Hello, this is Pastor Brian," he said after punching the phone icon. He glanced at the caller ID on his phone and saw it was Mike Hemsley. *Uh-oh . . .*

"Holy cow, Pastor, what did you do?"

"Hi, Mike, what do you mean?" he said, knowing exactly what Mike was talking about.

"You've got some detectives pretty pissed off at you here."

"I know, I know, I'm so sorry. I hated doing that, but I had no business advising that family. They shouldn't have asked me to do that."

"Do what?" he asked. "What did they ask you to do?"

"They wanted me to talk Mick into giving his permission to take a DNA sample from Kyle. I don't know if that's a good thing or not. That's not something I should be doing."

"You're right. They shouldn't have put you in that spot. They are just trying to make their case. They didn't know who they were dealing with, I guess," he said and laughed.

"You're not mad at me?"

"No, no, not at all. It was a gutsy move. I'm proud of you."

"Oh, thank God," Brian said. "I was afraid I had burned a bridge."

"Oh, you did do that. I wouldn't expect any of our detectives joining the church anytime in the near future."

"Well, I figured that. I was just worried about making you mad at me," Brian said. "I'm just glad you're not upset."

"Well, if I didn't know this family personally, or you, I might be. But I know those kids and I knew Candy and I think by having a lawyer they will end up with the best possible situation. The detectives just hate when the lawyers get involved, it just makes their lives so much harder. They just like to sew things up quick and easy. You can't blame them."

"Oh, I get that," Brian said. "But I have to live with myself, and if I didn't give Mick the best advice I could it would be on my head."

"And thanks for keeping my name out of things. I really appreciate that. That would not be good."

"Of course, Mike. My word is gold. You know that."

"I know now for sure. Thanks, Pastor. I keep praying. You take care."

Brian said, "Wait, Mike, hang on. Are you still there?" But the connection was gone. He had wanted to ask what was going to happen with this case, what charges might be brought against Kyle, if that happened.

He was late picking up his son, Doug, as usual. His son was forgiving, as usual. He had always been a patient and forgiving boy, Brian thought gratefully. He remembered when little Dougie was four and Brian was scrambling to get out of the house. He was running late for a meeting and had to drop Dougie off at daycare. His son was in the car seat and locked into place. He got in the driver seat and turned the key and nothing happened. His battery was dead. Using a spare battery to jump the car, he was now seriously late. Hustling to make up for time, he backed out in a hurry, and as he wheeled around he saw his giant cup of coffee tip over and fill the passenger footwell with a large caffeinated caramel-colored swimming pool.

He said, "Oh, shoot." Only he didn't say *shoot*. It was the other word.

After a moment, he heard the little voice from the backseat, "Dad, you shouldn't say that word."

So what did Brian do? He lied. You know, like a liar. He said, "I didn't say that word. I said *shoot*. It might have sounded like that word but that's not what I said." He berated himself. *What is wrong with you? Lying to your own son?* He needed to fix this. He recalled the words of the tenth step of AA: "We continued to take personal inventory and when wrong promptly admitted it."

Disregarding his severe tardiness, he pulled the van over to the side of the road, opened the sliding door of the van, and knelt on the edge of the doorwell to be eye level with his boy. Little Dougie looked at him with sweet big blue eyes and a questioning look on his face. His dad had never done anything like this before.

Brian said, "Dougie, I am so sorry. I did say that word. I said it and then I lied to you about saying it. I don't even know why I did that but it was wrong. I never want to lie to you. I don't know what I was thinking, but I hope you will forgive me."

His son's face brightened into a cherubic smile and he said, "That's okay, Dad."

Behind the wheel again, Brian marveled at how quickly he could lie about something so insignificant. It was so automatic. *What is it about us that hates being wrong so much that we forfeit our integrity so quickly and easily?* Brian would never forget that moment. His son's forgiveness was an extraordinary experience.

CHAPTER 36

BEFORE HE WAS awake the following Wednesday morning, Brian's cell phone sounded.

Because you know I'm all about that bass,
'Bout that bass, no treble
I'm all 'bout that bass, 'bout that bass, no treble
I'm all 'bout that bass, 'bout that bass, no treble
I'm all 'bout that bass, 'bout that bass . . .

As he grabbed for it, he tried to clear his brain so he wouldn't sound like he had just awoken. "Good morning, this is Pastor Matterson."

"Oh, I'm sorry, Pastor, I woke you up. I'm sorry to call so early, but I thought you would want to know," Officer Mike Hemsley said.

"Hi, Mike, it's okay. What's going on?" Brian said, sitting up in bed.

"Mick just turned himself in and is confessing to murdering his wife."

"Wow, you're kidding?"

"No, I'm not. They are processing him right now, but frankly we know he's doing it to cover for his son, so I don't think it's going to stick." he said, "All the evidence is pointing to Kyle right now."

"What happens now?"

"Not sure. It depends. They may not even charge him."

"Seriously?"

"Sure. If they think he's covering for his son, or they think he's just trying to get a free lawyer, they won't charge him. It's up to the DA," he said. "But then they might charge him to use as leverage to get Kyle to confess. I'm sure they are weighing all the options."

"Well, keep me posted, will you?"

"I will," Hemsley said and clicked off the phone.

Brian wondered if Hemsley was aware that he hung up on people all the time. *Maybe that's another thing they teach them . . .*

It was Wednesday, the day Brian usually went to the office late as he worked into the evening Wednesday nights teaching confirmation and attending choir practice. Since he was wide awake now at 7:00 a.m., he dressed, ate, and headed to the church thinking he could get a head start on his sermon for once.

He arrived at the dark empty office and looked at the verse for the coming week. The reading was from John's Gospel from the "Bread of Life" discourse, a very lengthy passage of Scripture where Jesus talks about being the bread of life that came down from heaven. Pastors preaching through the Bread of Life discourse have the challenge of coming up with illustrations about bread for five straight weeks. How many different ways can you talk about bread? The topic quickly gets stale. Most pastors can't handle it and will venture away and preach from other passages of Scripture.

Brian had his materials spread around him, the Greek New Testament and lexicon, his interlinear Bible, and several commentaries. He also looked at online commentaries to hear what some more contemporary theologians were saying about this passage. As he surfed through a preaching website, an article caught his attention. It wasn't a commentary, but someone recommending an interview of Stephen Colbert about learning to love the troubles life hands you.

Brian read the interview and it struck a nerve. Stephen had lost his father and brothers in a tragic accident when he was young and told how it was the worst thing that ever happened to him. But even so, it was the thing that made him who he is, all his faith and his success. He said he had to learn to embrace the tragedy as a gift. "You have to learn to love the bomb," Colbert said.

That's good, Brian thought. *I can use that.* He set it aside and moved on.

Before long, a knock came at his door and Brian knew his quiet time was officially over. "Come in," he said. He looked up as Barney came through the door. *What now?* "Barney, you knocked! Thank you!"

"Yep," he said, beaming. "Good morning, Pastor."

"Good morning, Barney."

"Can I sit?"

Brian hated being rude, but he also knew that if Barney sat down it would take a crowbar to remove him and he just didn't have the patience for it at the moment.

"Can I ask what it's about first?"

Barney seemed torn. It was obvious to Brian Barney really wanted to sit. He seemed to struggle for a moment and then went ahead. "Well, it's the youngsters. We really need to do something."

Brian noticed he had some kind of metal box in his hands. "What's the problem?"

"Can I sit and explain it?" Barney asked.

Brian knew what was coming and recognized a broken record was about to be played for him. He had heard it million times before. "If you want to have a long conversation we need to set up a time, Barney. I'm sorry, but right now I am booked. I could meet with you later today," he said, knowing Barney would never make an appointment. He could read the consternation on Barney's face. "Just tell me what the problem is."

"It's this," Barney said, holding up the metal box that Brian could now see was an exit sign housing, green boxy letters showing "EXIT" on one side.

"It's an exit sign."

"Yep."

"So what's the issue?"

"I found this sitting on the window ledge, next to the exit where it goes."

"Did someone get hurt?"

"No."

"So what's the issue?"

"Well, it's supposed to be hanging over the door, in the fixture."

"So it fell down and someone put it on the ledge?" Brian felt like a dentist pulling a stubborn tooth.

"I think the kids were playing a game, jumping up and hitting it, and they knocked it loose."

"You know that's what happened?"

"It's what I think happened."

"What makes you think that?"

"Because it's what they do. They run in the sanctuary. They throw things against the walls, leaving marks. They never clean anything up. How else would it have happened?"

"Well, it could have come loose over time and the door closing or the wind could have knocked it loose. Maybe it just fell and someone found it on the ground, figured out where it went, and put it on the ledge so nobody would trip over it."

"I think it was the youth," Barney said. "That makes more sense to me. Someone needs to talk to them."

"Do you want to talk to them?" Brian asked, knowing the answer. "I can set that up."

"No, Pastor," Barney said, horrified. "They wouldn't listen to me. You need to talk to them."

"Is it broken?"

"No, it just needs to be put back up."

"Well, you put it back up and I'll set up a time for you to address the kids during confirmation class. Will tonight work for you? I like this. You can teach a whole class on respect for the church. What do you think?"

Barney was backing out the door. "That's not funny, Pastor. You know I'm no teacher. I just think the kids need to treat the church better, that's all I'm saying." He was gone before Brian could respond.

That's never happened before. Brian raised his eyebrows and realized he had an effective new weapon to use on Barney.

CHAPTER 37

BARNEY HAD NO sooner left the room than the phone rang. It was a criminal defense attorney. *That was fast.* Brian had called his cousin the night before to see if he knew any attorneys that might consider pro bono work. His cousin said he would make a few calls. Brian didn't expect anything so quickly. He was impressed, and grateful.

"Hello, Pastor Matterson, my name is Daryl Thomas. I'm an attorney with Mackey and Furnham. I spoke with your cousin, Magnus Knudson. He asked me to give you a call."

"Yes, thanks, Daryl. I appreciate the quick response. I have a strange situation here and could definitely use some help. What do you need to know?"

"Give me the basic details, and then we can talk about what kind of help I might be."

Brian explained the suicide of Candy Vinter and the subsequent suspicion of Mick Vinter, the questioning of the kids, the ensuing suspicion of Kyle, and the confession of Mick. He also told him about the detectives asking him to help convince Mick to okay the DNA on Kyle. "That's when I told him he needed an attorney."

"Has anyone been charged at this point?"

"No. Mick just went in this morning to confess, but it may not work. I think they want the DNA on Kyle, but if he won't give it they might just settle for him. But what do I know?"

"Certainly an interesting situation," the attorney said.

"Yes, is it," Brian said. "What do you think? Can you help? They don't have much money. The church might be able to do something to help if we had to." Brian knew that wasn't likely since the church had enough financial problems, but for something like this, he believed they might step up.

"We have our case review in just a few minutes. I will bring this to the team, but I'm sure they will be interested. If we take it, we will need to move quickly. We would want to get Mick out of there as quickly as possible. Will you be available later this morning?" he asked.

Brian gave his cell phone number and felt relieved that he was no longer alone with this and help was on the way, he hoped. He put his sermon materials away. He was too distracted now to concentrate anymore. He began reviewing emails and sorting mail, biding his time until the attorney called back.

As he was making some progress on his correspondence, Beki stopped in with a frowny face. He looked at her and said, "What?"

"The numbers for a refinance are not looking so good. The payments wouldn't be that much higher, but the finance charges would be almost as much as we need for fixing the roof. In the long run, we might make it up with the savings from the lower rate, but all in all it makes little sense financially because they would still want the cash up front to make this work."

Damn . . . That was the most hopeful solution he had in mind. He knew they could do a fundraiser, but those usually only brought in five to ten thousand, not thirty-four. The only way to get the thirty-four-grand from a fundraiser would be through a full-out campaign, and those cost money, and energy, more than Brian had to give.

"What about a short-term line of credit from the bank?" he asked, knowing this was the least best choice of options.

"I asked about that too," she said. "But that's even less likely."

"Really? Why is that?" he asked, surprised. He always thought they could get a small loan any time they needed it.

"Banks don't want to lend to churches right now," she said. "They used to but they can't get any security from a church. If the church defaults, the bank has no recourse. Too many banks have been burned lately, so they just don't do it anymore. Especially churches our size, I guess."

"Why churches our size?" Brian asked puzzled.

"We are the high-risk church. We are not small and we aren't huge. This size church is having the hardest times financially these days, according to the banker."

This was news to Brian, but as he thought about it, it made sense. From his experience and training he knew people wanted either to be in a giant church that offered everything under the sun or a small church where they knew everyone. Brian's church was in the middle, and from other pastors he knew of churches his size, he knew they were struggling to remain viable. They either needed to grow to the next size or give in to the pressure to shrink. Brian felt the stress of it all the time and knew he was not alone.

"Any other ideas? Did the bank have any suggestions?"

"They said we could loan to ourselves?"

"What? What does that mean?"

"They said we should talk to our foundation and see if they will make us a loan."

Brian hadn't thought of that. It made sense. The church could borrow from itself, and instead of paying interest to an outside bank the church would recoup the interest through the foundation. Win-win. However, he also realized this would be a hard sell to the foundation. They were a cautious group and he doubted they would go for it.

"Well, that's an idea. I can run it by them. Thanks, Beki. Let me know if you get any bright ideas or someone walks in and gives us $35,000."

"If that happens, you'll be the first to know, trust me," she said, still wearing her frowny face.

Brian lifted his eyes to the picture of Jesus above his window. "We need a roof that doesn't leak. Could really use some help here," he said. Jesus didn't say anything back, but Brian suddenly felt guilty asking so sincerely for a roof when there were so many other pressing issues in the world.

Maureen's voice suddenly blared through the intercom on his desk phone, "Pastor, there's a Daryl Thomas on the phone for you, says he's an attorney."

"Yes, yes, I want to talk to him."

"I thought you wanted to be left alone. I would love to be left alone for a while," she said, clicking off before he could respond.

Brian picked up the phone and pushed the extension. "Hi, Daryl, that was fast. Did you decide anything?"

"We want to take this case. You said Mick is being held at the Martin Valley Police Station right now?"

"That's what I understand. He went in to make a confession and they are holding him until they decide whether to charge him or not."

"Okay. Can you meet me there in about an hour?"

"Yes, of course. I will be there."

"If you can get there before I do, tell Mick not to say another word or do anything else until I get there," said the attorney.

"I will if they will let me see him. In fact, I can go now."

"I will see you there in an hour," he said and hung up.

"Is that the thing now?" Brian wondered aloud, staring at the phone receiver in his hand. "You just hang up? People don't say goodbye anymore?" Grabbing his coat, he told Maureen he was heading to the police department.

She reminded him he had coffee planned with the quilters that morning.

Brian grimaced. "Please give them my apologies. This is an emergency."

"I will, but they won't like it. They will think you are avoiding them. They are going to think you don't like them."

"Maureen, you know that's not true. Do what you can to smooth the feathers, please?"

"I'll do what I can. They will understand, but I know a couple who won't like you no matter what you do."

He knew who she was talking about. "Why is that?" he asked, shaking his head." Am I really so awful?"

"Just the way some people are," she said. "You just can't win no matter what you do. I've seen it with every pastor we've had here."

"Wow. That is so true, Maureen. It's haunted me my whole career. Drives me crazy."

"Don't let it bother you," she said. "It's them, not you. You go take care of the Vinters. That's what's needed right now."

Brian looked at Maureen with a new appreciation. "You are so smart, Maureen. You know that?" he said and he meant it.

She waved him off, but her cheeks flushed, giving away her delight at the compliment.

CHAPTER 38

WHEN BRIAN GOT to the police station, he saw the same female officer working behind the plate-glass window. He approached with trepidation but resolve and told her he was looking for Mick Vinter. She told him to sit down and she would check for him in a moment. It didn't surprise Brian that she was in no hurry to accommodate him.

He sat on the thinly upholstered green vinyl seats mounted against the wall and felt a strong sense of déjà vu. After yesterday, he assumed they would do as little as they could to accommodate him, less than they already had. He really didn't care, but he was concerned Mick would get too far along without the help of counsel. He sat patiently and prayed for the Vinter family and for guidance, not only on how to help the Vinters but also on how to pay for a new roof.

Thirty minutes had passed when Brian's phone sounded . . .
Because you know I'm all about that bass,
'Bout that bass, no treble
I'm all 'bout that bass, 'bout that bass, no treble

I'm all 'bout that bass, 'bout that bass, no treble
I'm all 'bout that bass, 'bout that bass . . .

It was Sue Solberg, the All Saints parish worker.

"Hi, Sue, what's going on?"

"Hi, Pastor, I hope I am not interrupting you."

"No problem. I know you only call when it's important."

"It is important."

"Okay . . ."

"I was just with women's quilting group this morning and Esther Hanson told me Lilly Braham's mother, Ruth, is in ICU and they are talking about taking her off life support today. I thought you would want to know that as soon as possible."

"I do want to know that. I appreciate it. Is Lilly's mother a member of All Saints?"

"No, she's not. I don't know what church she goes to or if she does."

"Do you have any idea where she is?"

"Esther thinks she's at United Hospital in the ICU."

"Do you have any idea when they may be pulling the plug?"

"I don't. Irene seemed to think it was today."

"Do you have a cell phone number for Lilly?"

She gave him the cell phone number and Brian called. Lilly answered right away.

"Hi, Lilly, this is Pastor Matterson."

"Oh, hi, Pastor. I'm so glad you called."

"I just heard about your mother. She's not doing too well?"

"No, she's not. We are all here at the hospital. We are waiting for her brother to arrive and then we will be taking her off life support. Everybody is so sad. We didn't see this coming, she was doing so well," she said. "I just hope we are doing the right thing."

"Does your mom have a church she goes to, or a pastor?"

"She used to go to Oakwood Lutheran but it's been years since she's been there. She has been attending services at her nursing home for the last many years."

"Is that pastor involved with you?"

"No, I don't think so. She is a chaplain and she's only part-time. I don't think she is in today."

"Would you like me to come over there and be with you when you take her off life support?"

"Oh, pastor, you don't have to do that. I was just hoping to get my mom on the prayer chain."

"It's fine, Lilly, I want to be there. I think it's important."

"I think that would be really great. I think it would mean a lot to Mom, although she probably won't know anyone's there. But I think my family would appreciate it too."

"I will let her nursing home chaplain know and I will also notify Oakwood so they can also be praying. And then I will see you there shortly."

"Thank you, Pastor. I really appreciate it very much."

Brian blessed her and then hung up, just as Daryl Thomas walked in. Daryl was not what Brian was expecting. He was short, small, and very young looking. He carried himself with confidence and was well dressed in a tailored suit and tie, but Brian had a hard time imagining this "kid" trying a court case.

"Are you, Pastor Matterson?" he said as he crossed the room.

"Yes I am. Daryl? Is that right?" Brian said, proffering his hand.

"Daryl Thomas. It's great to meet you."

"Thank you for coming so quickly. I have no idea what I am doing here. I don't think they like me back there, because I'm the one who told Mick to get an attorney."

"That was the right thing to do," Daryl said. "Do they have Mick in the back?"

"Yes, I believe so," he said. "But try getting anything out of her." He nodded to the officer behind the plate-glass window.

"That's normal. I need to get back there as quickly as I can to stop whatever Mick is doing," he said, moving toward the window.

Brian followed the boy attorney over to the window. "Now that you are here, you don't really need me right now, do you?"

"I will have some questions for you, but right now I have to get Mick to let me represent him and stop whatever it is he's trying to do. That's the most important thing right now."

"I have an emergency hospital call. Can we talk later?"

"Of course, you go ahead. I can take care of this," he said, proffering his card, giving one to Brian and then putting another in the metal drawer underneath the plate-glass window. He spoke into the metal speaker, "Attorney for Mick Vinter, I need to see him right now please."

She hit a buzzer and the door to the interrogation hall clicked open. She told him he was in interrogation room three.

Brian was dumbfounded. "How did you do that?"

"They don't mess with attorneys, but everyone else . . . well, they do," he said.

Brian wanted to give the officer a dirty look but she wouldn't give him the chance, turning her eyes immediately back to her computer screen. "I'm not the bad guy here, I'm just trying to help," he said into the speaker. Still no effect or response from the automaton behind the bulletproof glass.

"I can see Mick is in good hands now," Brian said, turning back to the attorney, who was walking through the door to the interrogation rooms beyond. "Let me know if there's any way I can help," he called as the door swung back, and Daryl waved a hand in acknowledgment.

CHAPTER 39

B RIAN WENT OUT to the city hall lobby and found the bench he used before. He used his phone to find the phone numbers of the nursing home and of Oakwood Lutheran. He called both to let them know what was happening with Ruth, then headed to the hospital. He was familiar enough with the hospital to know where the ICU was, but didn't know Ruth's last name. Once there he could easily find the room, as the family would be crowded around nearby.

He soon found Lilly and some extended family gathered outside the room. Lilly saw Brian and rushed toward him with a big hug. Her eyes were red and puffy from crying. "I just so appreciate that you came," she said.

Lilly introduced him around to the family and then explained that her uncle had just arrived and they were getting things in the room ready. They were taking out all her IVs and everything else unnecessary.

"They will wait until we are ready before they stop the respirator. They think she will take a few finals breaths and then just pass away peacefully. She's on a lot of morphine, so she is very comfortable."

"So what happened?" Brian asked.

"She got a cough. They thought it was pneumonia and so they brought her in for x-rays and treatment, but it turned out to be congestive heart failure. They tried a few things, but her lungs just kept filling up with water. She's not even breathing on her own right now. The respirator is keeping her alive," Lilly said, tearing up again.

"It's amazing how sudden these things can be, isn't it?"

Lilly was wiping her eyes, blowing her nose, and nodding in agreement.

"This is happening as soon as they are done?"

"Yes, that's the plan."

"Would you and the family like to take Holy Communion before you let her go? I think that would be meaningful."

"We can do that?"

"Of course. I will go get my communion kit."

When Brian returned, the family was now in the room, gathered around Ruth, a very withered and ancient-looking woman. Her tiny chest lurching up and down from the air pumping mechanically into her lungs. Her wrinkled baggy eyes were tightly shut and probably had not been open in days. The respirator was down her throat and looked extremely uncomfortable. Brian had been told it feels like you are drowning when you have a respirator. Fortunately, most of the people who have one are either in shock or so drugged up they don't care and won't remember.

Brian set up Holy Communion on the rolling hospital cart. He counted nine people in the room including him and set out nine cups. One of the great grandchildren looked to be five or six and Brian asked if she would like to take communion. Everyone looked at each other and then to the parents of the girl.

"Is that okay?" they asked.

"It's up to you. It's certainly okay with me and I believe it's okay with God."

"What about Grandma Ruth?" one of the older kids asked.

"She can take communion too. We will just touch it to her lips. I'm going to let Lilly do that."

Brian saw the nurse anesthetist standing by to turn off the respirator. "Would you like communion too?" he asked him.

He looked surprised and then grateful. "Yes, that would be great."

Once the little wafers and tiny plastic cups of wine were set up on the cart he looked around at all the tearstained faces of this small congregation gathered in that sacred and holy moment. They looked at Brian with sad but ready expectancy.

Brian had learned over the years that even the most militant atheists would become passive and open in moments like these. Standing at the deathbed of someone you love is a rare and awful moment, but also filled with pure spiritual power. Brian opened his Bible to Psalm 121 and looked at each of the mourners in the eyes. They were all listening.

"I am going to read a Psalm to you but I want you to understand what the writer is talking about. These are some very old words and they have stood the test of a very long time. They express the deepest feelings about what our ancient ancestors believed about God. In this Psalm, the writer is making a powerful claim."

Brian looked to see if the young girl was following what he was saying, and she was. Brian had always felt that if he spoke in a way a child could follow, he was doing his job. He had grown up listening to ministers and priests and almost never understood what they were talking about. He never wanted to be that kind of minister, boring and dry, and using words that 90 percent of normal people never use.

"The writer of the Psalm is a Jew and he is living in a place where most people believed in many kinds of local gods. There was a god for everything, for fertility, for rain, for prosperity, for heath, and on and on. The temples for all these local gods sat on the hilltops. The hills were dotted with temples to the gods of Baal.

"When the Jews came along they were the first people to tell the world there is only one God. That's what the writer is talking about in this Psalm. He is saying that we often look to all kinds of places to find what we need, but there is really only one reliable place to look for help.

"A modern version of this Psalm might express how we look to all kinds of things to save us. We look to money, relationships, insurance, and anything we think will give us security in this world. In this situation with Ruth, everything possible had been done to save her life. We've looked to the doctors and specialists and to the hospital. They've done everything they can, but in the end they can't save her. All of our options are gone. Now where can we turn for help? Is there any hope for Ruth now?" He paused and looked at each of their faces listening intently. "I believe there is great hope for Ruth. The best hope of all."

Brian raised his Bible to read Psalm 121.

"I lift my eyes to the hills, from where will my help come? My help comes from the Lord, who made heaven and earth. He will not let your foot be moved; he who keeps you will not slumber. He who keeps Israel will neither slumber nor sleep. The Lord is your keeper; the Lord is your shade at your right hand. The sun shall not strike you by day or the moon by night. The Lord will keep you from all evil; he will keep your life. The Lord will keep your going out and your coming in from this time on and forevermore."

Brian lay down his Bible, picked up a bread wafer from the cart, and held it out for everyone to see. "On the very night when Jesus shared his last meal with his followers he informed them that later that evening he would be arrested. He would be tortured and killed and buried and after three days he would rise again."

He scanned their faces. They were listening, even the little girl.

"After he said this the disciples all became very upset. Even though Jesus is the one about to die, he is the one consoling them. That's when he says these amazing words of hope and promise."

Brian read from the Bible again.

"Do not let your hearts be troubled. Believe in God, believe also in me. In my Father's house, there are many dwelling places. If it were not so, would I have told you that I go to prepare a place for you? And if I go and prepare a place for you, I will come again and will take you to myself, so that where I am, there you may be also."

Brian then leaned down and traced the mark of the cross on Ruth's wrinkled forehead and said, "Did you hear that, Ruth? Jesus has prepared a special place for you. When you take your last breath here, he will be just on the other side. He will meet you and raise you up to be with him and all the saints. It's a wonderful and amazing place. You will be happier than you've ever been before. Please don't worry about us. We will finish our time on earth and we will join you later."

Again, he marked her forehead with a cross and said, "Precious child of God, you've been marked by the cross of Christ and sealed by the Holy Spirit. You have been claimed by God for all eternity."

Brian turned his attention to the bread he had in his hands and said the Words of Institution. "In the night in which he was betrayed, our Lord Jesus took bread, gave thanks for it, then broke it and said, 'Take this and eat it. This is my body given for you. Do this in remembrance of me.' Then he took the cup and after raising it up, blessed it; he gave it to them also and said, 'Drink this all of you. This cup is the new covenant, the new life in my blood given for you and for ALL people for the forgiveness of sin. Do this in remembrance of me.'"

Brian set the cup and bread down and began saying the Lord's Prayer. A few joined in and then a few more, and soon the whole room was saying it together.

When Brian finished, the little great-granddaughter, who was holding her grandma's hand at the time, said excitedly, "She squeezed my hand! While we were praying, she squeezed my hand. She could hear us."

Everyone was moved by this and the presence of the Spirit was powerful and palpable.

Brian distributed the bread and wine to each person present, including the nurse, and had someone give it to him as well. He then took a wafer, dipped it in wine. He gave it to Lilly and said, "Now touch it to her lips and say, 'The body of Christ given for you and the blood of Christ shed for you.'"

She gently touched the red-stained wafer to Ruth's dry, swollen lips and said the words. "The body of Christ given for you and the blood of Christ given for you, Ruth," as her tears fell on Ruth's pillow.

He then laid a hand on Ruth and invited everyone else to put a hand on her. Her extended family surrounded her, most of them weeping silently or fighting back the tears.

Brian said, "Gracious heavenly Father, we commit Ruth to your tender care. Receive her into your kingdom peacefully and set her free from the confines of this mortal body that has done its job. It's now time for her to come home. We know she will open her eyes again and she will see you there waiting for her. You will raise her up. For this great promise, we give you honor, thanks, and praise. Amen."

The room was silent and somber for a moment and then the sniffs and nose blowing filled the sacred silence. Brian dropped back away from the family so they could be closer to Ruth as she took her last breath. He nodded to the nurse, who began the process of turning off the respirator.

Ruth's body seemed to stop breathing when the respirator was turned off, but then suddenly another breath came, shallow and weak. She was quiet again for a long time, and then another convulsive breath. They waited for the next one, but it never came.

Everyone stood, solemn, looking on. Captivated by the power of what they just witnessed, they stood in awe. The only sound was soft weeping and the buzz of electronic devices and distant intercoms.

After several moments, Brian made his way out to the hallway.

The nurse anesthetist came out next and said, "That was special. I've done this a lot but I've never seen anything like that. That was so beautiful. Thank you for including me."

Brian thanked the man and extended his hand, but the nurse grabbed Brian and gave him a bear hug. There were no words after that.

The family came out one by one and several of them hugged him. When Lilly came out, he hugged her and she thanked him profusely. He asked about funeral arrangements and if there was anything the church could do for her and her family. Ruth's funeral would be at Oakwood Lutheran. Brian would attend if he could.

CHAPTER 40

ON HIS WAY back to the church, Brian called Diane and told her about the attorney. She had not heard that Mick was confessing to killing Candy and that was too much for her.

"I just can't believe that," she said, "I . . . I just can't believe that, I can't talk right now," and she hung up the phone.

Brian pulled to the side of the road and sent Diane a text message: "So sorry about the news. Attorney needs to meet with the family later today, four or so. Let me know. God bless you."

As he pulled into his regular parking space at the church, his phone buzzed instead of playing "It's All About the Bass" because he had turned off his ringer for the service at the hospital, mortified at the thought of that song blaring out while giving communion at a deathbed.

"Hello, this is Pastor Matterson."

"Hello, Pastor, it's Daryl Thomas."

"Hi, Daryl. How did it go with Mick?"

"Well, it's a little confusing. I'm still not sure what's going on. Mick allowed me to represent him. He seemed grateful for that. He didn't want the help at first, but he finally relented. He is a man of few words. It's hard to know what he's thinking."

"Tell me about it."

"He made a full written confession and they are planning to charge him with the crime, but I don't think cops think he did it. They want him to give permission to take a DNA sample from Kyle. Mick knows they want Kyle for this, but he's not willing to let them have Kyle if he can help it, only I don't think he will be able to do that."

"What do you mean?"

"Mick's story is full of holes. Several things don't line up."

"Like what?"

"Like he and Candy had a fight around 8:30 p.m. and he left the house after she threatened to kill him. Mick drove around for about an hour and then ended up at a bar. He was at the bar until 2:00 a.m. The bartender vouches for that. He never left. The autopsy says the bruising on her neck may have occurred before she allegedly hung herself, which raises many interesting questions. It isn't clear yet, but the initial guess is the bruising on the neck might even be several hours old before death. We are waiting for further tests to confirm."

"If she wasn't strangled, then it's possible she was choked enough to disable her so someone could later hang her without a struggle?"

"I suppose," Daryl said. "Mick has changed his story several times to match the timeline the cops put together. Mick is now claiming he strangled her before leaving the house and then came back later after the bar closed and then put her in the closet to make it look like a suicide. He then went downstairs and slept on the couch and told the kids he had spent the night there on the couch."

"But didn't the kids hear Candy yelling at Mick as he was leaving the house? How could he have strangled her?"

"That's one of the big holes in his story. He's claiming the kids are confused. He said she was dead when he left. Mick is scared and he's determined to save his son from these charges. He thinks if he just says he did it, the details shouldn't matter. I tried explaining to him having Kyle charged is much better for the whole family, but he doesn't want to hear that. He wants to confess, take the blame, and be done with it. I can at least help him with sentencing, get him a better deal, but I don't think the cops are taking him seriously. He gave me permission to speak to you about his case, by the way. I would not ordinarily divulge this much. This is all highly confidential."

"Yes, of course it is. So what happens now?"

"Well, I need to meet with the family and see what they know. I think they will charge Mick with this and use it to leverage a confession from Kyle. They did meet with Kyle, and I think they think they can get him to break. They're certain he's the guilty one. So I need to meet with him and see what I think," he said. "It would be better in the long run for everyone involved for Kyle to be the one charged. He would get off a lot easier than Mick will."

"Yes, I think I agree with that too, but I would sure like to know what really happened."

"I agree with that too. The cops have a working theory. They think Kyle confronted his mother after Mick left. The situation was already heated to boiling. Kyle lost his temper, grabbed his mother's throat, and maybe didn't intend to kill her but it went too far and left her unconscious or near dead. Then after stewing on it a while, he came up with a plan to cover it up. He got a rope and tried to make it look like she did it herself."

"That's pretty much what I was thinking too."

"So, you have an appointment set up with the family?"

"I'm working on it."

"Okay, let me know."

They said goodbye and Brian was relieved someone didn't hang up on him for once. "Whatever happened to the long Minnesota goodbyes?" he wondered. "Is that another victim of modernity?"

He learned about the long Minnesota goodbyes after marrying Donna and moving to Minnesota. In Minnesota, saying goodbye is an important ritual. You first announce you are leaving and then you stay for another half hour. You announce your departure several times during that time. When you do make it to the door, a final announcement goes out that you are actually leaving. Everyone in the home comes to gather there and talk some more. After shoes and coats are on you move out to the porch. Most of the household follows you out to the car. You meander out to the car, perhaps talking about the car itself, its condition, number miles it has, problems you've encountered. The men might even raise the hood and talk about the engine a little. Once in the car, the windows come down and you stand and chat for a time about what fun it was to get together and when it might happen again. When you do finally leave, the host family follows you down the drive as you back out and they continue waving until your vehicle is out of sight. Just after visual contact is lost, the driver honks the horn to let you know they are still there and still waving.

The most important part of the ritual comes next. The departing guest must call when they get where they are going. Failing to report a safe arrival is a terrible *faux pas* as it causes the host family tremendous anxiety. This is because their responsibility for your safety does not end until you make that call and conclude the visit. If something were to happen to you on the drive home, they would be responsible for it for the rest of their lives. The call is required to conclude the visit. That concluding call will usually become a longer conversation, with an extensive review of the visit.

Brian had to learn this ritual since he grew up in a home where you were lucky if someone looked up from the television when you left. Maybe a hand might go up to wave goodbye. There might be a: "Okay, thanks for coming" or "See you later, man," but eyes would not leave the television screen unless it was a special occasion.

CHAPTER 41

BRIAN REALLY NEEDED to get to his emails and prepare to teach confirmation that night. Emails continued to pile up and he knew people would start to grumble when they didn't hear back from him in a timely manner. He longed for a world without email. Oh, and the sermon. Always the sermon. He needed to proofread the newsletter, write a letter of commendation for an Eagle Scout, put together the agenda for the council, and come up with a plan to raise $35,000 for the roof. Those were the most pressing needs of the day . . . so far.

Diane had texted saying 4:00 p.m. was fine and included an apology for cutting him off. He texted back and asked if she needed to talk. She said she was okay and that they could talk at four. Brian texted the attorney to let him know they could meet with the family at four. He sent him the address as well.

* * *

Brian arrived early at Diane's to see how she was coping with the news of Mick's confession. She welcomed him in and then led him to the narrow galley kitchen, which was cramped but tidy and appeared mostly unused. They sat at the table for two that stood along the wall, next to a window looking out on a snow-scraped cement patio.

As she poured them coffee, Brian said, "It was pretty surprising news about Mick. How are you doing?"

"I can't even think about it," she said. "And I just don't think it's true. I can't see Mick doing that to Candy, ever. He has never even raised his voice to her or any of the children. I'm just so afraid of what this will do to the children. They've already been through so much."

"It is shocking and hard to believe," Brian agreed, and wondered how she would deal with the news about Kyle's involvement. After a moment, he continued, "Tell me what you know about their relationship and the family. I can't quite get a sense of what is going on with this family."

"You and me both," she said. "They didn't let me get very close, but from what I could tell it was not good. When they got married, I remember feeling sorry for Mickey, because I knew what a handful Candy was. She was high maintenance her whole life and I don't think Mickey had any idea what he was in for. She was able to put on a good front and make people believe she was this sweet and helpful girl, but it was all an act. Behind the scenes, she was mess. I hate to say this about her now, but it's true. She wasn't well, and I expected there would eventually be some kind of scene or blow-up, but never anything like this."

"So how did it last as long as it did?"

"I always wondered that too. It was all Mickey. He's just so patient. He just put up with it and put up with it. I guess he just finally snapped. That's all I can think of," she said. "But if he is guilty of this then I can't say I can blame him much. I know how that feels."

"When you say put up with it, what exactly did he put up with?"

"You name it. Her constant illnesses, one right after another. I never knew when to believe her. Mickey did everything. He worked and then came home and took care of the kids. He cleaned, cooked, did the laundry, everything. And all she did was yell at him, make him serve her, and make him feel small. I think she even resented the kids because they took Mickey away from her and her selfish needs." She paused and took a sip of coffee. "And those poor kids had to grow up in the middle of all that. Thank God for Mickey or they wouldn't have had a chance."

She looked out the window and whispered, "I can't believe I'm talking this way about my own daughter just days after her funeral. This is all really my fault. I was a terrible mother and I made her this way. It's all my fault . . ." Her voice wavered to silence.

Before Brian could console her, the doorbell intruded. She gave Brian a pitiful look and asked, "Could you get that, please? I need to clean myself up."

Brian greeted Daryl Thomas, invited him in, and led him into the kitchen, where he poured him some coffee. Diane came out and Brian introduced them.

"Hello, Diane, I am so sorry for your loss and now this situation. My heart goes out to you," Daryl said.

"Thank you. And thank you for coming. We can really use the help. I feel so lost," she said.

"That's totally understandable. That's why I'm here. I'm going to guide you through this and help you understand what's going on every step of the way, okay?"

"I really appreciate it, but I am also concerned. I don't know if we can afford an attorney, I'm certain Mickey cannot. I can help a little, but I don't have much either."

"Please don't worry about that. Our firm believes in helping people who cannot help themselves. We will keep the costs to a minimum and the church has offered to help as well," he said, as Brian winced inwardly.

We would, but can we? What happened to pro bono?

Diane turned to the pastor and thanked him.

"What I need to do now," Daryl began, "is to try to make sense of what's happening. I don't think we have the whole story and so I need you to tell me everything you know so I can try to fit all the pieces together, okay?"

"Yes, of course," she said. "Let's go sit in the living room and I will tell you what I know. I don't think I have much to give you that you don't already know."

"That's okay, it's important to hear from as many people as possible. I would like to have the children involved, especially Kyle. Are they here and can they join us?"

"Yes, they are both here, but I don't think Hannah should be here for this. Is it okay if we leave her out?"

"That would be fine. But I will have to visit with her separately at some point, however."

Diane got up from the table to fetch Kyle. They moved to the living room and settled around the coffee table. Brian could hear the knock and verbal exchange between Diane and Kyle. Kyle was resisting, but Diane was being firm. She came out, sat down again, and said, "He will be out in just a moment. He's really having a hard time."

"Undoubtedly," Daryl said.

After a moment they heard Kyle's door open and he presented himself in the living room.

"Hello, Kyle. Please have a seat," Daryl said.

Kyle was beginning to look as bad as his father now. Darkness under his eyes, rumpled clothing, hair uncombed for what looked like days. Kyle moved as though on death row. He would not look at anyone.

"Kyle, this is Daryl. Daryl is an attorney who is working with your family to help you."

Kyle, not looking up from the hands in his lap, said, "Why do we need an attorney when it's obvious my mom killed herself?"

Brian could see the leading edge of a scratch mark on Kyle's wrist that the police indicated. There were at least two of them on his hand that disappeared up into his sleeve.

"Whenever there is any kind of death the police get involved and their job is to make sure things are just like they seem. In this case, however, there are some things they don't understand and it makes them think they don't have the whole story. So they have been pushing for more answers," Daryl said. "I am here to make sure they get the right answers, because we don't want anyone getting into trouble for something they didn't do."

"I don't understand," Kyle said.

"I will tell you what I know and then you can tell me if there is anything missing. This may be hard for you, so we'll go nice and slow, okay, Kyle?"

Kyle nodded reluctantly, still staring down at his hands.

Daryl began, "It all started when you found your mother in the closet and you called 911. It was obvious that she had hung herself. Can you think of any reasons she would want to do that?"

Kyle just shrugged.

Daryl said, "Kyle, I know this is hard, but the more you tell me, the better I can help you and your family. Can you try to think of any reason your mother would want to kill herself?"

"I don't know," Kyle said. "Maybe because of her cancer and how it was making her feel."

"You say maybe. Could there be other reasons?"

Kyle was clearly uncomfortable and struggling with his answers. "She was never happy. She was always mad at us and at dad, so maybe she was just very depressed."

"What was she mad about?"

"Everything. She was always screaming at us no matter what we did. The only time she was nice was when we were in front of other people. Then she would act like this perfect person."

"I see . . . so tell me what happened that night, the night she killed herself."

Kyle squirmed in his seat, agonizing. Diane encouraged him to keep going. "Well, they got into a big fight."

"Do you know what they were fighting about?"

"I don't know. They were always fighting. Or she was always yelling. But this time was different because we could hear Dad fighting back. He never did that."

"But you don't know what the fight was about?"

"No. But it was the first time Dad got so mad he left the house"

"Your father never left like that before?"

"No, never," Kyle said. "He would never leave us alone with her."

"Did she say anything to you two after your dad left?" Daryl asked.

"She yelled at us and told us we should be in bed. Then she went into her bedroom and slammed the door hard. It was only 9:00 but we went anyway because we were afraid."

"Were you more afraid than any other time she was mad?"

Kyle nodded.

"Tell me why you were more afraid this time."

Kyle squirmed some more. "Because Dad had never left the house before." He paused, and then added, "And because of what she yelled at him when he left the house."

"What did she yell at him?"

"She said, 'If you do I will kill you.'"

"Do you know what she was talking about?"

Kyle shook his head.

"If you had to guess what she meant, what do you think it was?"

"I guess she was saying if he leaves, she would kill him."

"Do you think she meant it?"

Kyle didn't want to answer.

Daryl pressed him. "Do you think she meant it, Kyle?"

"Yeah, I guess so. I don't know."

"So then what happened?"

"We went right to bed. I laid there for a long time because I couldn't sleep. I was waiting for Dad to come home but he never did. But in morning he was there helping us get ready for school. He had slept on the couch."

"You didn't fight with your mom?"

Kyle paused as Daryl looked at him closely. He finally shook his head.

Daryl pressed him again. "You and your mother didn't fight, too?"

Kyle just shook his head again. Brian realized Kyle was holding his breath.

"Kyle, it's important you understand I need to know everything you can tell me, every detail. I am on your side. I am working to help you and your family. I need to know what you said to your mother at that time. It's important."

Kyle exhaled loudly, his eyebrows furrowed. The veins in this neck were raised and his jaw was clenched. "I said we just went to bed," Kyle said a little too tersely.

"Okay, Kyle. If you say that's the way it was then I believe you. You have no idea when your dad came home?"

He shook his head.

"Okay, then what happened?"

"We went to school in the morning. When I came home, Mom's car was in the garage. I called for her when I came in the house but she didn't answer. I put on some video games and then I thought maybe she was sick in bed, so after a while I went to check on her. I knocked but there was no answer. I opened the door a little to look in and I could see her bed was empty. I said, 'Mom? Are you home?' but there was no answer. I pushed the door more open and I could see her closet across the bed, and there she was, hanging with a rope around her neck."

"Wow, Kyle, that must have been a terrible shock."

Kyle nodded staring down at his hands.

"Now I have to ask you something hard. Do you think you can handle it?"

"I guess so."

"Do you think your father had anything to do with her being dead?"

Kyle looked up at the lawyer for the first time. "No. I don't. My father would never do that. He would never hurt anyone, ever." He spoke with conviction.

"Now, Kyle, I have to tell you something even harder. I'm sorry to be the one to tell you this, but you are going to hear about it anyway, so it's better you know now." Daryl paused for a moment and then said. "Your father is at the police station right now and he has confessed to killing your mother."

At this, Kyle jumped to his feet. "That's bullshit!" he roared, "There is no way!" He stomped out of the living room and a moment later his bedroom door closed with a slam that shook the house.

The three of them sat there staring after him and nobody said a word for several moments.

"He'll be okay," Diane said. "We should just let him cool off for a bit." She then turned to Daryl. "So what's going to happen to Mickey?"

"Well, that depends. The police and the DA have many questions they still don't have answers to. I spoke with the DA and they are sympathetic to this situation but they are clear that this was not a suicide. They think somebody killed Candy and they don't think it was Mick."

"I don't understand," Diane said. "Who else could have done this? Mickey is the only one that could have."

"So now," Daryl said, looking pointedly at Diane, "I need you to brace yourself. I have something hard to tell you too."

Diane's eyes grew wide. "What?"

"The police think Mick is giving himself up to cover for Kyle."

Diane's eyes grew even wider with horror. "What?" she said. "They think Kyle did this?" Her hands flew up to cover her face. "This can't be happening," she said and her anguish flowed from deep within her. "So that's why they wanted to talk to the kids," she said through her tears. "I told you I didn't think Mickey could do this, but I know Kyle couldn't have either. That's just ludicrous.

She killed herself, I know she did. Why can't they just leave this poor family alone? They've been through so much already."

"It does seem unlikely that Kyle could do such a thing, but from what the police are saying it is more plausible," Daryl said. "All the evidence points more to Kyle than it does to Mick."

"What evidence?" she asked.

"Well, first there is the DNA. It doesn't match Mick. Mick has no wounds to account for the DNA found under Candy's fingernails. Kyle does have some scratch wounds that would fit, but they can't examine him more carefully or take a DNA sample without parental or guardian approval. They are fairly certain Kyle is the DNA match because Mick was a very close match. Then there is the alibi. Mick's story has been changed several times and each time to fit the evidence. He's not very believable. First he said he came home and strangled her after the bar he was at closed. Then he made it look like a suicide. However, the bruises from the strangulation came several hours before the rope around her neck took her life. So then Mick says he choked her to death before he left the house, then came back after the bar closed. Nevertheless, we have the statement from both the kids that she was alive, well, and screaming at him when he left. When asked for specific details about how he staged her suicide, he fails miserably. He couldn't say what kind of rope it was, how he tied the knots, and other important details. I'm a trial lawyer and I can tell you his story does not add up."

"So what makes them think Kyle did it?" she asked and then said, "I can't believe we are having this conversation. This is all just a bad dream." She began to cry again.

When she had settled, Daryl continued. "They think Kyle heard her threaten to kill his father, and to defend him he attacked her and choked her to death, probably accidently. Then, in a panic, he found some rope in the garage and made it look like a suicide."

"This can't really be happening."

Both men nodded in sympathy and agreement.

"What happens now?" she said.

"Well, they have arrested Mick and can hold him as long as they want. They will arraign him fairly quickly, but before that happens I think they want to use him as a bargaining chip to get at Kyle. Mick is refusing to give permission for a DNA sample from Kyle, and it's clear to everyone that he is just trying to cover for Kyle. And I have to say it looks that way to me too."

"Oh my god," Diane said. "I can't believe this, I just can't believe this. Kyle, what's going to happen to Kyle?"

"That depends," Daryl said. "If he gives himself up they will go a lot easier on him. Right now, if they do put this on Mick I can negotiate a lighter sentence, but I don't think they have any intention of putting this on him when they don't think he did it. The harder they have to work to put this on Kyle, the tougher the sentence will be. I can negotiate that too, but cooperation is always better in the end. When they factor all that was happening in the family and the pressures they were under, I think any judge would be sympathetic. Worst-case scenario he goes to a hard-core juvenile facility and serves five to ten years. However, I don't see any judge sending him there. He would more likely do five years in a facility that will do more to help him get well. He's not a bad kid; he's a good kid in a terrible situation. That's clear to anyone who looks at this."

"I don't even know what to say. I just can't believe they think Kyle could have done something like this. Are they sure she didn't just hang herself?"

"Yes, they are sure. They don't have the full forensic study yet, but they think at this point the cause of death was strangulation by human hands several hours before she was hung."

"This is crazy," she said. "What are we supposed to do now?"

"Well, if we could talk to Kyle some more and feel him out on this, I am hoping I can convince him to turn himself in and from there we can negotiate some kind of agreement with the DA. I think if I can make Kyle understand how it's better for everyone if he turns himself in, we can settle this quietly and easily, but that is up to Kyle now," he said. "Do you think he would talk to us some more?"

"I can see if he will come back out here," she said.

Diane steeled herself, got up, and went down the hall to Kyle's room. They could hear her knock and call his name. She called and knocked some more, but there was no response. She came back to the living room.

"He's not answering and his door is locked."

Brian offered to try and went down the hall. He too knocked, yelled, and cajoled to no avail. He returned to the other two and asked Diane, "Is there a window in the room he can open and get out?"

Diane nodded.

Daryl got up at that point and he moved with Brian back to Kyle's door. They banged on the door and threatened to break it down.

Diane came up behind them with a coat hanger. "You just need to push an end in that little hole and it will unlock."

They popped the lock, flung open the door, and were immediately relieved to see that Kyle had not hurt himself. But he wasn't in the room. The window was open, the room was chilled, freezing air blowing back the curtains.

CHAPTER 42

DIANE HURRIED TO shut the window and saw fresh footprints in the snow leading away toward the back of the house.

"I don't know where he might go," she said. "He doesn't know this neighborhood. He is probably just walking off some steam. He was pretty upset."

"Can you imagine?" Brian said. "Losing your mom to suicide and then hearing your father is confessing to killing her? Plus, he was the one who found her. That's a lot for a fourteen-year-old."

"And don't forget, it's possible he may be the one who actually did this," Daryl said.

The three of them were standing in the boy's chilled room with their thoughts, when Diane suddenly said, "He's not wearing his coat! You don't think he's planning to do anything to himself, do you?"

"I was just wondering the same thing," Brian said.

"We need to find him!" Daryl said, leaning out the window. "There are footprints in the snow, heading toward the alley." He turned to Diane. "You know this area; which way might he have gone? We'll split up to look for him."

They all hurried to put on coats while Daryl laid out a game plan.

"Diane, you take Hannah and try to follow his footsteps, see if you can track him. Make sure you all have your phones," Daryl said. "Pastor, you take your car and circle west and south, and I will go east and north. Go out as far as you think he could have gone by now and circle your way back toward the house."

They went out to examine the footprints, but they ended at the alley, which had been recently plowed. They guessed he went toward the nearest street and assumed, dressed as he was, he would be moving quickly, but where?

The frantic search for Kyle began.

Several minutes into the search Brian's phone buzzed. Diane was concerned. "What if he is headed toward the river? If he was going to hurt himself that's where he might go," she said with an edge of panic in her voice.

Realizing she could be right about this worst-case scenario, Brian said, "I will go to the river and make my way back to you. You go that way. We will catch him. There is no way he could already be that far on foot."

Brian called Daryl to let him know what they were doing as he raced toward the river, all the way praying. He drove recklessly back and forth, up and down streets, looking hard for an underdressed boy moving fast.

Again, his phone buzzed. "It just occurred to me that Kyle might be heading to the police station to turn himself in. He's going to try and save his father's life again," Daryl said.

Brian considered this a moment and agreed. "I think you're right. Can you drive in that direction and see if you can find him?"

"I already am," Daryl said and clicked off.

Again the phone buzzed and Brian answered, "Tell me you found him!"

"I'm sorry, what? Is this Pastor Matterson?" the voice said.

Brian recognized the voice and was surprised. "Mick, I thought you had been arrested!"

"I'm still being held but they gave me a phone call and said I could call someone. You were the only person I could think of."

Brian wondered why he didn't call Daryl, his attorney!

"What's happening, Mick?"

There was a long pause on the phone and Brian could sense that Mick was trying to compose himself. "It's Kyle," he finally managed choke out. Brian had a sick feeling.

"What do you mean Kyle? We are looking for him right now. What do you know about him?"

A long pause and the clearly distraught voice of Mick finally said, "He's here. He's turned himself in. Says he did it. He says he killed Candy and I think they believe him."

"Oh my God," Brian said. "How much more can one family take? Mick, I'm so sorry for you. You must be a wreck. I can't believe you guys are going through all this."

"I know," was all Mick could choke out.

"What do you know so far?"

"That's all I know. They are asking him questions. They keep asking me for permission to test his DNA, but I'm never going to do that."

"Listen, Mick, you know the lawyer that was there today?"

"Yeah."

"He's here with us helping to find your son."

"Why are you looking for Kyle?"

"We were talking about the case and Kyle got upset when he heard that you had turned yourself in and went to his room. Before we knew it, he had climbed through his window. We thought he was out wandering around, but now we know he was going to save you. I need to get that attorney down there as quickly as possible. Kyle shouldn't be talking to anyone without someone there. Is that okay with you?"

"I would really appreciate that."

"Don't worry. This is a terrible situation, but we'll get through it. There are a lot of people praying for you and trying to help."

"Okay. Thank you," he said, choking on the last word, straining to hold his emotions in check.

After he hung up with Mick, Brian quickly dialed Daryl and told him the situation.

"I thought's that's what he would do," Daryl said. "I'm almost there now."

"Keep me posted, please, as soon as you can," Brian said, knowing his presence on the scene would not be helpful.

"Will do, Pastor," Daryl said and clicked off.

Brian called Diane and told her the situation and to call off the search. He met them at the house, consoling Diane and praying with them, for Kyle, and for whatever this might mean for him and this poor family before heading back to the church to get ready for confirmation class.

CHAPTER 43

S HORTLY BEFORE THE council meeting was to convene at 6:00 p.m. the next day, Brian got a call from Daryl.

"Hello, Pastor Matterson, it's me, Daryl Thomas."

"Hi, Daryl. I've been dying to know what's happening."

"Well, Kyle did go to the police and turn himself in. He confessed to killing his mother. They were taking his statement and had almost completed it by the time I got there," he said. "They aren't wasting any time with this. They want a full statement before anyone like me can stop them."

"Can they do that? Don't they have to advise him of his rights or at least have an adult there?"

"Not until they arrest him. They don't need anyone's permission to question a child until he is arrested, so that's what they did."

"What has Kyle told them?"

"He says his parents were having a huge fight, but could not say what about. He heard his mother threatening to kill his father when he left the house. She said, quote, 'If you do I will kill you, Mick. I am serious.' He then left the home. They have regular fights, but his dad had never left the house before and she had never threatened to kill him. Kyle got angry seeing his father leaving and his mother threatening his life and went to her room to confront her. Their conversation elevated and she struck him. He grabbed her by the neck, pushing her down on the bed and began choking her as hard as he could. She struggled and scratched but he kept choking her until she died. He then says he went to his room and was freaking out about what to do. He decided to make it look like a suicide. He got rope from the garage and staged her suicide in the closet."

"Wow," Brian said. "What do you think, Daryl? Did they believe him? Are they going to charge him?"

"Yes, I believe they will. It's the only thing that makes sense. They will probably charge him but there are still some problems with his statement."

"Like what?"

"A few minor things and a few major ones. First, he says he hung her shortly after strangling her. That doesn't line up with what the injuries show. It's been confirmed that the bruising from the strangulation was there at least two hours before the contusions from the rope around her neck. Cause of death was hanging, not strangulation."

"Okay, that's definitely a major discrepancy. Didn't they originally say it was strangulation?"

"Yes, but the forensics are back and they clearly indicate the strangulation bruises are hours old, before the hanging took her life. And then when Kyle was pressed on what kind of rope he used, where he found it, what kind of knots did he tie, all those kinds of details, well, Kyle isn't even close. His testimony about the strangulation is very clear, but the details of the hanging are way off."

"So what do you make of that? They think he strangled her but didn't hang her?"

"They believe he did it, or is the most likely suspect, but there are still some big holes in the story and they don't think they have the whole truth yet. Father and son seem to be covering for each other, and the police think there is something important they aren't telling them. The working theory that began to develop after Kyle's statement is that perhaps he did strangle her nearly to death and left her on the bed. Then, Mick came home much later, saw her there and then he staged the hanging to look like a suicide to protect his son."

"But Mick is such a protective, caring parent. Why would he take any chance that one of the kids would find her like that?"

"I don't know. That's a good question. Probably just didn't think it through," Daryl said. "So now, armed with this new theory of a father and son conspiracy, the police questioned Mick again about his alleged part in this cover-up. However, when he was asked to describe the rope, the knots, where and how she was hanged, he was clearly lying and making things up. His version does not match the facts at the crime scene."

"What a mess," Brian said. "What's going to happen now?"

"Well, the DA has to look at all this and make a determination. Somebody is going to be charged, but they don't know who and for what. I would bet they will charge Kyle, but they don't know yet what the charge will be. Possible second-degree murder, but I can get that down to manslaughter with the hazy facts we have so far," Daryl said. "I'm not sure if they will charge Mick with anything, perhaps obstruction of justice but probably not. No jury is going to blame him for what he did."

Having to get to his council meeting, Brian cut off his conversation with Daryl and went to the meeting with his head spinning.

The meeting went pretty much as Brian predicted. They talked extensively about the budget, the lack of money, and how they were going to pay for things. This time, however, with the roof expense presented, the anxiety and conversation were excessive. First, Brian presented the information provided by Aksel Erickson. Aksel was standing by, looking like a deer in headlights through his part of the meeting. They discussed the roof situation extensively with solutions bandied about for nearly an hour. Finally, nothing was decided. They were frozen with fear and could not take action. As was often the case, the council and the congregation would need some time to absorb this gut shot before they could face the inevitable decision. Aksel was visibly relieved when finally invited to depart.

Next, the financial report. The income was behind the expenses as usual. They spent forty-five minutes on what the problem was and what some of the solutions might be, even though this was the financial pattern for the entire life of the congregation and had been for years and years since the beginning of time. Spending was within budget, but giving was behind budget. The council, without fail, would debate about lowering expenses to match the income.

Brian would let the conversation run its course because it had to and then he would kindly remind everyone this was all normal. It was normal for this church and for every church. Furthermore, he reminded them that when the budget spending is in line with the proposed and approved annual budget, then the only thing wrong with the budget was giving. They should not be looking to troubleshoot spending, but rather focus on the real problem, which was always the giving.

"We don't have a spending problem, we have a giving problem," Brian said.

Everyone agreed and they approved the report with the understanding that the pastor would encourage the congregation to give more.

Brian gave his report, telling about his pastoral calls and the coffee machine repair and answered questions. There were many questions about Candy Vinter, but Brian was not able to tell them much. He told them it was the biggest mess he had ever dealt with and implored them to pray fervently.

Under new business, someone brought up church damage caused by the youth. Brian knew before hearing any more that Barney had gotten someone's ear and convinced them the kids were tearing the church apart. Sure enough, the complaint was about the broken exit sign and they spent another thirty minutes talking about all other things the youth are doing wrong and what could be done about it. Brian listened and waited. When the conversation had run its course, he told the council he had already talked to Barney about the situation with the sign. They concluded there was no way to know if this was even something the youth had done. Barney had fixed the sign and it was working fine. No action was taken against the youth.

CHAPTER 44

AS USUAL, THE meeting ran long and Brian was late getting home. Before walking across to the parsonage, he decided to try calling Mick and was surprised when he answered.

"Mick, are you out of jail?"

"Yes, but they are holding Kyle. I don't know what to do about it. He's gotta be terrified."

"No kidding. That must be awful for you. I'm so sorry. But why have you been released? I thought you gave a confession?"

"They said they could only hold me so long without charging me, so they let me go."

"Does this mean they aren't going to charge you?"

"No. I mean they said they still might. They just haven't decided who to charge with what. They think maybe me and Kyle were both involved."

"Were you involved?" Brian asked. "You can tell me, Mick. I'm your pastor and I won't tell anyone. I can't even be forced to testify against you."

Mick was silent for a long time.

"Mick?" Brian prompted.

"I was involved. I killed her. Kyle had nothing to do with this."

"Mick, I know that's what you are saying, but as I understand things that is not the way it's looking."

"But that's the way it is," Mick snapped.

Brian decided not to press him. "Wow, Mick, this is all so crazy."

"I know."

"What can I do to help you right now, Mick? What do you need?"

"I don't know."

"Have you eaten anything lately?"

"They gave me some food in jail but I didn't eat much of it. It was pretty bad."

"I'm taking you for a decent meal. Meet me at the Perkins in fifteen minutes," Brian said, saying it more as a command than an invitation. He was testing out his recently acquired Jedi mind trick.

"Okay," Mick said.

Brian told Donna what was going on before heading to Perkins. He asked her to make up the guest room just in case and not to wait up for him. Mick needed a friend right now more than anything else in the world.

Mick was already there when he arrived and was in the waiting area. They asked for the booth in the back corner of the restaurant and sat across from each other.

"You must be in some kind of hell," Brian said, looking across at the haggard face of Mick Vinter, whose face was drawn, eyes dark-ringed with grief and lack of sleep. He was in his mid-thirties but looked like he'd aged twenty years since Brian last saw him. He was wearing a plaid button-down wool shirt that had sleeves that reached his mid forearms. It was wrinkled, well worn, and dirty. He could have easily been mistaken as a homeless person.

"It is hell, I think."

"Well, let's get something to eat and maybe you'll feel a little better," he said.

They ordered from the menu. Mick got the turkey dinner with all the trimmings and Brian had the banana cream pie and decaf coffee. "Where have you been lately? I drive by your house and you are never there."

"I try to avoid that place if I can."

"I can imagine. But where do you sleep?"

"I stayed in a motel a few nights, but can't afford that anymore. I have a friend who let me stay with him a couple nights, but I don't like being there. I don't think he really wants me there either. Sometimes I sleep in my van. I have been at the house a couple times, on the couch, but I can't sleep very good when I'm there."

"What about your kids, are you worried about them?"

Mick's face lifted sharply, a flash of anger in his eyes. "What do you mean, do I worry about them? What do you think? That's all I do!"

"I didn't mean to suggest you didn't care about them," Brian said, both hands held out in a gesture of forgiveness. "I just meant they need their dad right now . . . and you aren't there."

"It's because I care about them I'm not there. They are way better off with their grandmother than me right now. She can care for them. I can't even care for myself. They deserve better."

"Well, they are going to need you, so we need you to get stronger. Will you let me help you do that?"

Mick pondered the question for a while, then looked Brian in the eye. "Why would you want to help me?"

"Why wouldn't I?" Brian countered.

"After all we did?"

"After all you did? What does that mean? I don't know what you are talking about."

Mick stopped pushing mashed potatoes around with his fork, his hand slowly curling into a fist around the utensil.

Brian stayed still and then quietly said, "Mick, I sense there is something unhealthy going on in your family, some big secret, but I have no idea what it is."

Mick still didn't move for several moments and just before Brian was about to speak again, Mick asked, "Did you know she was never sick?"

"Yes . . . I had heard that . . ."

Mick glanced up, seemingly surprised that Brian knew. "All them fundraisers you did for us and you knew?"

"No . . . no, I didn't learn until recently. Candy's mother . . . it doesn't matter. It's not your fault."

"It was all bullshit. It was all a part of Candy's game. She used it to get attention and money and to get out of working. I knew all about it and I didn't do nothing. Just stood by and let her get away with it," he said. "And the kids knew it was happening too, and that's what I hated the most," he said, his expression and tone filled with bitter self-loathing

"Is that what you were fighting about the night she killed herself?"

"Sort of," Mick said, tucking back into his potatoes.

"What do you mean?"

Again, the long pause as Mick seemed to contemplate. "Yeah, that's what we were fighting about."

"I understand that night when you left the house she threatened to kill you. She said something like, 'you better not.' What was that about?" Brian asked. "You better not what?"

Mick chewed carefully and slowly as he thought about the question. He finally said, "If I tell you something you have to keep it to yourself, right?"

"Of course," Brian said. "I'm your pastor. The law protects everything we talk about, unless you threaten to kill someone or hurt yourself. Then the law requires I tell someone. But everything else is completely private. I can't even be compelled to divulge what you say in court. Everything you tell me is between you and me."

Mick set his fork down and looked Brian in the eye, more so than he had ever done before. "You knew she worked for the police department in accounting? Right?"

Brian nodded.

"Well, that night she told me at home they were doing an audit of her department and she warned me that her name might come up."

"What does that mean?"

"That's what I asked her," Mick replied. "She said that maybe she had been skimming a little here and there. I couldn't believe it. I told her she had to give it all back. She said it was too late for that. All she had to do was keep denying it and the worst thing that could happen is she might lose her job. She said the police department wouldn't want to make a big deal out of it because it would make them look bad. They would just let her go quietly."

"She was embezzling?" Brian asked. "Any idea how much?"

"I don't know, but I found out after she died that she has her own little savings account in her name with more than $30,000 in it. Who knows there might be more somewhere else."

"So that's what the fight was about?" Brian asked.

"Yeah," Mick said, picking up his fork again. After a bite he said, "I told her if she didn't turn herself in I would tell on her. She said if I did she would kill me and I really think she might have tried."

"Is that when you grabbed her by the throat?"

"No, I swear I never touched her. I never did. She hit me all the time, but I would never hit a woman. That's how I was raised."

"So how did those bruises get on her neck?"

The question stopped his chewing. He stared into the middle distance and seemed to be fighting back heavy emotions. "Best I can figure is that Kyle hears the argument and her threats to kill me and he attacks her. She and the kids never got along. She was awful hard on them."

"But I saw her all the time at church with her kids. She seemed like a perfectly good mother."

Mick scoffed in disgust. "That was all for show. Soon as they were in the car or back home she was all over them all the time. I felt like a referee. I always got in between. I would rather she take it out on me than them."

"So do you think Kyle killed her and made it look like an accident?"

"I don't know what to think. I don't want to think that. I don't want to think that, but it's the only thing that makes sense," Mick said, again seeming to struggle with his emotions.

"That would be my fault too for letting it get that far," Mick said. "Kyle shouldn't have to suffer for this, he's already suffered enough. I should be paying the price for this. It's my fault."

They sat in silence for several moments, Brian eating his pie, Mick picking at his dinner.

Brian finally spoke, "Well, Mick, you and your family have been through hell and you are still in the middle of it. I do think the worst is over and no matter what happens next some healing can begin. I want you to know that I will walk with you through this and do everything I can to help you get your lives back, okay?"

Mick suddenly put his face in his hands and wept. Brian wanted to move over and console him, but they were in public and he knew Mick would not be comfortable with him making a scene. So he just said, "Let it go, Mick. You got a lot to cry about."

Mick sat there with his head in his hands, his shoulders shaking and tears falling into his mashed potatoes and gravy. The only sound he made was an occasional sniffle. Brian also felt tears welling in him. All that grief was too much.

Without looking up from his hands, Mick said, "There's no more life for us. Our lives are over."

"What are you talking about, Mick? Your lives are not over, not by a long shot. God always has a way of bringing something good out of something awful, always," Brian said sincerely.

"The worst is not over yet, not when people find out all that she did. When they find out she stole from the police department and faked all her illnesses and we took money from them fundraisers.

We won't be able to show our faces anywhere again. Those poor kids are going to be treated like lepers. I won't be able to look anyone in the eye ever after this. And if Kyle gets charged . . ." He choked on the last word and couldn't continue as his silent tears came again.

Brian leaned forward, voice lowered and urgent. "Mick, you're not thinking straight. People have an amazing ability to forgive and forget. Besides, people are not going to hear about all those things. And even if they do they are going to understand, and if anything, they will be supportive, realizing what you were dealing with and how hard it must have been for you. People will be very sympathetic, you'll see. Let's just take this one day at a time and not worry about the rest of your lives right now, okay? Right now, things aren't great, but we can get through today. We'll just do that one day at a time and trust God and you will be surprised by what can happen. Can you do that? Can you do that, Mick, just try to trust God?"

Mick shrugged his shoulders, took a napkin, blew his nose, and wiped his eyes with his sleeves. "I don't know. I haven't been very good at trusting God. I've been kind of mad at God. Look what good he did us. I'm sorry, I don't mean offend to you. I just don't know about God right now."

"Well, I don't either, Mick. I just know I've been in some pretty shitty places myself, places I never should have gotten out of, but somehow I did. I look back at the things I've done and what I deserved to have happen but instead things have worked out. I've seen it happen to me and to lots of other people. I believe God will get you through this, I really do, Mick. Just say you'll try and that's all you have to do."

Mick stared down at his plate of food, now growing cold along with his appetite, and said nothing.

"All you need to do, Mick, is say you will try."

After a moment of uneasy silence Brian asked, "Mick, would it be okay if we prayed?"

Mick looked up, then looked around the restaurant to see who was watching. "You want us to pray here?"

"Sure. I'm not going to be loud or draw a scene. I'm just going to nicely ask God for help. It's what you need right now more than anything else, more than anything else I can do for you."

Mick was uneasy, but he relented. "Okay, I guess so. Go ahead."

Brian folded his hands on the table around his empty pie plate and bowed his head. Mick folded his hands beneath the table, bowed his head slightly, and closed his eyes. The pastor began to pray.

"Gracious and loving God. Mick needs your help right now, right this very moment. As you already well know, this situation is far too great a burden for him to bear. He can't take it anymore, he can't fix it and he can't see any good way through this mess. He can't do this alone. The weight of it all is threating to crush his life and further destroy his family. Father, this is a human mess that needs a miracle. Please give your help and bring healing and life."

Brian was silent for a moment. Then with his head still bowed and eyes still closed, he spoke to Mick. "Mick, what do you want to say to God?"

Brian knew Mick wasn't expecting this and would struggle with it. As he suspected, Mick did not say anything.

Brian prompted him. "Mick, just imagine God is sitting here with us. What would you tell him? What would you ask him? Go ahead, he is listening."

Mick started slowly. "Um . . . I guess I would tell him . . ."

"Don't talk to me," Brian said, "talk to God,"

Again silence. Then, "Dear God, I don't know what to say to you. I don't have a right to talk to you. I've ignored you my whole life, so I don't know why you would ever listen to me . . ."

Silence again. Brian waited.

"But if you are there and you could help me I would really appreciate it. I have made a big mess of things. I've totally let my family down. I don't deserve to be a father and I don't deserve to even ask for help. But right now, I don't know what else I can do. I don't want to live, but I don't want to leave my kids. My son might be going to jail because I am such a stupid fool. Please help me. Please, God. I'm so sorry and I'm so scared. Just please help me. Just help me to know what to do, how to fix this."

Again silence.

"Dear Jesus," Brian took over, "You came to earth because you wanted us to know we are loved unconditionally. You wanted us to know that no matter how bad life gets or how bad we've been, if we call on you and try to learn to trust you, you would always be with us. Please carry Mick now through this mess. Come to his rescue. Save Mick and his family. Don't do it because we deserve it, but do it because you love us and because you said you would if we ask. Amen."

Brian opened his eyes and looked across the table. Mick's hands were still under the table. His head still bowed, and he saw another tear fall.

CHAPTER 45

I T WAS NOW past 11:00 p.m.
Mick refused to stay the night
at Brian's house no matter how hard Brian insisted. Minnesota
public radio was playing as he made his way home, but Brian
wasn't listing. He was reflecting on all that had been happening
and wondering what would happen next to the Vinter family.
He thought about poor Kyle and what is life would be like now,
knowing that he had killed his own mother and would be spending
the most formative years of his life in juvenile detention with all
manner of wild children. What could become of him?

The Spice Girls suddenly began singing through his sound
system.

So tell me what you want, what you really, really want
I'll tell you what I want, what I really, really want
So tell me what you want, what you really, really want
I wanna, (ha) I wanna, (ha) I wanna, (ha) I wanna, (ha)
I wanna really, really, really wanna zigazig ah . . .

Brian was baffled how his son could have gotten to his phone and changed the ringtone since the last time it rang. He pressed the steering wheel phone icon. "Hi, this is Pastor Matterson,"

"Hello, Pastor. You probably don't know me. My name is Darla Johnson. I'm a member of your church, but I haven't been there for a long time."

"No, I'm not sure I remember you, although your name seems familiar. I've seen it before, but no, I'm not sure who you are."

"You probably know my parents, Orville and Mirna Johnson? I was confirmed at All Saints many years ago, long before you came. I've been there a couple of times since, you know, Christmas and Easter, but not much else. I hate to admit that."

"That's okay, Darla, I understand. I do know your parents," he said. "What's going on with you? Is everything okay?"

"Well, it's the strangest thing," she said. "I should be calling the police, but I just wanted to talk with you first because I figure you are involved with this."

"Okay, you have my attention," he said. "What's going on?"

"Well, I'm not sure. That's just it. It has to do with Candy Vinter."

"Okay . . ."

"I ran into Candy about two weeks ago at the mall. We only talked for a few minutes. I told her I was housesitting for my snowbird parents and was buying a bathing suit, getting ready to go down to see them. Tonight, I just got back from being gone for ten days, about an hour ago. I had heard on Facebook that Candy had killed herself, so I knew about it, which is why I was so surprised when I got home and listened to my phone messages. There was a message for me from Candy."

"Really!" Brian said. "A message from Candy?

"It's so strange, I just don't know what to do . . . that's why I wanted to talk to you first before calling the police."

"What was the message?"

"Well, it just doesn't make sense why she would call me at my parents' house. I really hardly know her. We were the same age and I knew her from school and she was in my confirmation class there at church. We were in some things together but we never became friends or anything. I just don't understand why she would call me. It doesn't make any sense," she said, sounding agitated.

"Darla, what was the message, what did Candy say?" Brian urged.

"Well, she sounds very upset in the message. She says, 'Darla, it's Candy Vinter. I didn't know who else to call.' She tells me she is at home and that Mick, her husband, had just attacked her and choked her and was threatening to kill her. She said he left the room but she could hear him downstairs banging things around . . . then she screams, 'Oh my god, he's coming back. He's coming up the stairs. He's going to kill me. Call 911 please . . . call the police, my husband is going to kill me . . .' And then the call just ends there, she just clicks off."

"Wow," Brian said. "That's a terrible call to get when you just arrived home. I'm sorry you had to get that. I can understand why you're upset. I would be too. Are you okay?"

"Well, I'm a little shaken. I just don't know what I'm supposed to do with this," she said. "I feel terrible I wasn't here to help her. But I'm mostly very confused. This just doesn't make any sense. Why didn't she just call 911?"

"No kidding, it is weird. I think I would feel the same way, Darla."

"I had heard she committed suicide. But was she murdered? Do they think Mick did this to her?"

"Well, there are some questions and it's not exactly clear what happened yet, but that recording will add more confusion, I'm afraid," Brian said. "Can you hang on a moment, Darla? I'm in my car and I just want to pull off the road for minute to talk about this."

"Sure."

Brian pulled off the highway and into the parking lot of a closed muffler repair shop. His brain was spinning at this new information. *What did it mean?* He was trying to put the pieces together and not sure what to tell Darla. He thought about Daryl Thomas.

"Darla, can you hold on a minute. This is very important information. Would you be okay if I get the attorney on the phone and get his advice? Would you mind holding?"

"No, that would be fine."

Brian put Darla on hold and quickly pulled up the number of Daryl Thomas and hit the dial icon. Daryl answered on the second ring. "Pastor Matterson."

"Hi, Daryl, this is . . . you already know. I was driving home and just got a very interesting phone call. I have someone on the other line I think you should hear. She is an acquaintance of Candy Vinter who just returned home from a trip and found a message on her parents' phone machine. It's from Candy Vinter the night she died."

"Really," Daryl said. "That is an interesting phone call, very interesting. What does she say?"

"I still have her on the other line. Can I conference you in and let her tell you?"

"Yes, of course."

Brian pushed the conference call button on his smart phone and introduced Daryl and Darla. Darla conveyed to Daryl everything she had told Brian.

"Well, that's just bizarre," Daryl said. "It makes very little sense."

Both Brian and Darla spoke simultaneously, agreeing with Daryl's assessment.

"So she's been attacked, she's about to be murdered, and she calls a distant acquaintance and leaves a phone message on her friend's parents' home phone? That's inexplicable," Daryl says. "Why didn't she just dial 911?"

"What do you think it means? What was she thinking?" Brian asks.

"God knows what she was thinking," Daryl says. "I would really like to hear that recording, Darla. Could I come by in the morning and pick it up? That is a key piece of evidence and it will need to be turned over to the police first thing in the morning. I could take it in for you, but the police are going to want to talk to you. I can be with you for that if you like."

"Would I need to have you there? Do I need an attorney?" Darla said, alarm in her voice.

"No, no, of course not. You don't need an attorney. I am just offering for moral support. We will both have to answer questions about how we got this evidence. Pastor, you too. And I just thought it would make it easier for you if we were with you, that's all."

"Yes, I think I would like that," she said. "But tomorrow? I have to work tomorrow. That's why I came back today. I've been gone for two weeks. I really can't be gone tomorrow."

There was silence on the line for a moment.

"Could we come over now and get the tape, Darla? The police can question you later and I can commit to being there with you when they do. Would that be okay?"

"Um . . . yeah, I guess so," she said, "If you can come right away. It's getting late."

It was now close to 11:30 p.m. Brian called home, explained the situation to Donna, and then pointed his car toward the home of Darla's parents.

The two men arrived simultaneously and Darla was waiting for them. Darla's parents lived in one of the nicer parts of Martin Valley in a large two-story custom craftsman-style home on a street with many other homes of the similar upscale design. They were in Darla's father's den, gathered around a large mahogany desk, listening to the phone recording with Candy Vinter's voice speaking from beyond the grave.

"It sounds scripted to me," Daryl said when the recording ended. "I think she is clearly trying to set Mick up for murdering her."

"That's what I was thinking too."

Darla looked at the two men and seemed confused. "I don't understand," she said. "Why would she do that?"

The two men looked at each other, considering what they could tell Darla.

Pastor Matterson took over. "We are learning that Candy was a broken person who was very lost and confused, and things in her life got way out of control and she found the only way out she could."

"There are many details about this case that we aren't at liberty to tell you right now, Darla," Daryl cut in, "but with all that we know, it appears that Candy did take her own life and this tape helps make that clear. You have helped solve this."

Looking perplexed, Darla shot looks back and forth between the two men. "But . . . this tape means it was murder, doesn't it?"

Daryl continued, "I know it looks that way, Darla. That's what Candy wanted us to think, but with all the other information we have, we know this can't possibly be what happened. Candy found herself cornered by many circumstances beyond her control. She decided she needed to take her own life, but for some reason we will never understand, she wanted to hurt her husband in the process. This tape is a poor attempt at framing him. I don't think anyone will disagree with that."

Brian nodded his head in agreement.

On the way out of the house, Brian, following Daryl, carried the phone recorder to his car. They stood by Daryl's car at the curb in the cold dark silence for several moments. Daryl opened his door and the interior lights from his grey Lexus dispelled some of the darkness.

"I think it's starting to warm up out here," Daryl said.

"About time," Brian said. "So, what happens now?"

"First thing tomorrow I set up a meeting with the DA. I play the tape and see what they want to do. I'm pretty sure this will be the end of it."

"Just like that?"

"They have no choice. They have to let this go."

"So, Mick and Kyle walk?"

"Yep," Daryl said.

Brian drove home that night, marveling. This was the most dramatic and quickest answer to prayer he had ever experienced. Mick and his family had been through enough already.

"Thank you, dear Lord," he said aloud.

CHAPTER 46

THE NEXT MORNING at 10 a.m., Brian met Daryl at the police department where they met with Detective Walters and the district attorney. Seated across from each other at a large wooden table in the conference room at the police headquarters, Detective Walters was effectively burning holes through Brian with his stony dark eyes. His expression and demeanor were intimidating and seemed particularly menacing toward Brian. Brian wondered why this man would seem to be so bothered by what turns out to be the truth. Did his case and his need for someone to pay a price really outweigh the truth? Did he even care about the innocence of a traumatized young boy?

Daryl pushed the play button on the recorder and they listened as Candy's voice filled the room. Brian, having heard it several times now, was able to hear just how scripted it did sound.

Did she really think this would work?

"…my husband is going to kill me," Candy's voice cries out and the phone goes dead. Daryl punches the off button on the recorder and looks at the faces of the DA and detective.

"Gentlemen, there are so many problems with this case I don't know where to begin," he said. "You need to let that young boy go now and let this family get on with their lives."

"What I heard," Detective Walters said, "was clear evidence of guilt, open and shut."

The DA looked over at the detective as if to say: "That's enough."

"Okay, what are you thinking?" the DA asked Daryl.

"What do you mean what am I thinking? Are you kidding?" Daryl responded. "You need to drop all charges right now."

"How do you figure? There are still a lot of unanswered questions here."

Daryl laughed in the DA's face. "You have nothing. Here's what we have. We have an angry exchange between a husband and wife where she threatens to kill him. We have a wife who has been embezzling–embezzling!–money from the police department! And has been doing so for *years*. We have a wife who has been abusing her husband and children. We have a wife who has been falsifying illness to gain sympathy and money from her church and coworkers. Was her husband about to expose her and that's why she was threating to kill him? Makes perfect sense to me. That's what my client will say. We have a son who hears the exchange, comes to the defense of a father he has watched being abused for too long, loses his temper, and in a heated exchange chokes his mother but not enough to kill her. What is she to do? Her world is falling apart. She is brutally attacked by her own son. She is about to be caught in all her schemes. She is running out of options. She does the only thing she can do–take her own life. However, that's not enough for her. She can't just take her own life, she has to get revenge. If she is going out, she is going to take her husband with her. She has to cause as much hurt as she can to the husband she has used and abused for years. She can't kill him, but she can ruin him by framing him for murder. Only she does a terrible job of it. In her panic and distraught thinking she doesn't think it through. A normal person would call 911, but who does she call? She calls someone she hardly knows, someone she knows won't be there to respond and come to her rescue too soon." Daryl paused in his rapid-fire discourse, then gave a hard look at the DA and detective. "I'm just getting warmed up. I have a lot more than this. So, do you think we have any reasonable doubt here? You think there is any jury in the world that won't take pity on this family? You think the police department will appreciate the publicity of being ripped off by one of their own? How can they protect the public from crime when they cannot even protect themselves from it? The police department will be humiliated." He leaned back in his chair with a grim smile. "This is going to be fun."

Brian watched the boy-faced attorney with a new respect. He knew what he was doing.

The DA sat staring at Daryl.

"So tell me," Daryl pressed him. "What have you got?"

"I'll tell you what we've got," Detective Walters cut in. "We have the defensive wounds on the boy. We have choking bruises on the victim consistent with the defensive wounds. We will have a DNA match. We have a signed confession from the boy. That's plenty. She may have been trying to frame her husband to protect her son, but how do we know the person coming back up those stairs to take her life wasn't the boy in that audio tape? That tape doesn't prove anything."

Daryl scoffed at the detective. "None of that will hold up and you know it."

The DA stared some more, and then finally turned to the detective. "Cut the kid loose . . ." The detective began to object, but the DA cut him off. "Just do it," he snapped angrily.

CHAPTER 47

PASTOR BRIAN'S HEART filled with gratitude as he got up to preach his Easter message and saw the Vinter family sitting seven pews from the back, Mick, Kyle, Hannah, and Diane. This was the third week in a row, sitting in the same place as if they had been there all their lives. As he preached he would look their way often and see they were listening closely, all of them engaged with his message. He could always tell when people were really listening, and these four were clearly soaking it in, every one of them, every time they came. He especially enjoyed looking in their eyes as they came forward during communion, seeing the gratitude and new life that filled their faces. They had been set free from a terrible ongoing nightmare and were healing now, all of them.

Following the service that morning, as parishioners filed out of the sanctuary shaking the pastor's hand, a few actually making eye contact, Mick shook Pastor Brian's hand and said, "I need to talk to you."

"Sure," Brian said, "When?"

"Do you have any time right now?"

"Well, I will in a little bit here . . . I just need to mingle until everyone is gone, if you don't mind waiting."

"I don't mind."

"There's coffee and hot cross buns for Easter in the fellowship hall. I will come in there when I can."

Mick took his family into the fellowship hall for refreshments while Pastor Brian circulated among his sheep in the narthex until the herd thinned considerably. He changed out of his vestments and made his way into the fellowship hall, where he found Mick and his family waiting patiently with coffee, juice, and rolls. Mick had wanted to speak in private, so Diane watched the kids as Mick and Brian excused themselves and made their way to Brian's office. Brian shut the door and they sat across from each other at Brian's desk, looking at each other. Mick's gaze was flitting nervously around the room. It brought to Brian's mind the image of a little boy in the principal's office. He realized, as he had in the past, this could be an intimidating place for some people to be.

"So where are things at now?" Brian asked.

"You mean with the police?" Mick replied.

"With everything, the police, you, and the kids. How are you all doing?"

"We are doing really good, actually. That's kind of what I wanted to talk to you about."

"I can't tell you how glad I am to hear that. You seem like you are doing great and it makes me so happy. I was so worried about all of you."

"The police have dropped the investigation and they are sure that Candy killed herself, because that's the only thing that makes sense now."

"Do you think that's what happened?"

"Yeah, I'm sure it was. I wasn't sure at first. I thought maybe Kyle did do it. After I left the house that night, she fought with Kyle and he grabbed her by the throat and left the bruises. She must've been pretty upset after that. She must've thought that with everything about to be exposed, all she could do was to kill herself and make it look like I did it."

"My gosh, she must have really hated you to do that. What was that all about? Why was she so angry with you?"

"I don't know," Mick said, a choke in his voice. "I never understood that. I always just tried to make things easy for her. I just tried so hard but it was never enough. The more I tried the worse it got, she just seemed to hate me more and more."

"That must have been horrible for you."

"It was . . . it was," Mick said in a low voice, wiping a tear from one eye. "I think I started hating myself just as much as she hated me. My counselor said she was broken and hated herself, so she took it out on me and made me feel worthless. It worked pretty well."

"That doesn't surprise me," Brian said. "That's what hate does, it just makes more hate. It tears everything down around it and spreads like a disease. Nothing good comes from it."

Mick nodded, staring down at the desktop in front of him, his anxious hands holding the edges of it as though for support.

"Well, I'm glad you are seeing a counselor. That's helping then?"

"Yeah. We all are. We are seeing that lady you told us about."

"And it's helping?"

"It's helping a lot. Really a lot."

"We will keep paying for that for as long as you need it, okay? So you go as long as you want to."

"You don't need to do that. Diane's insurance covers some of it and we can handle it. There is no way I can let the church pay for it. The church has done enough for us."

"The important thing is that you keep going. You have a lot of years of pain to work through. Don't let money be the reason to stop."

Mick nodded and they were quiet for a moment. Mick reached into his back pocket and produced an envelope. He placed it on the table and slid it across to the pastor. "This is what I wanted to give you. It's a thank you for all you did. For saving me and my family . . ."

"Mick, I didn't do that. God did that. I was just one piece of a puzzle. I couldn't have done anything without God's help. It was my honor and it makes me feel pretty special that I got to be a part of helping. So thank you too."

"Well, I know that without that attorney you got us and the way you kept pushing they were going to get us for something. So you did save us."

"I only do what God tells me do to, so make sure most of your thanks goes where it belongs."

Mick smiled and nodded. "I will," he said. "You also made me say I would try and trust God, so you did that too."

"You guys have a lot of healing to do, but the worst part is over now. You can all start to rebuild your lives. It's just too bad we couldn't have saved Candy's life, too."

"I've thought about that a lot," Mick said. "I wish we could have saved her too, because I know somewhere deep in there was the Candy I once knew . . . but after so much bad stuff grew up around her, she couldn't find her way out and I don't think anyone could get in either. Diane told me some of the things you said at her memorial service and I think I am okay now knowing she's not suffering anymore. I think she was in hell here already, but now she is not. And I think that's okay."

"Wow, Mick, that's pretty good," Brian said. "If you got that from me I'm glad to hear it. That's what I believe."

Mick nodded and stood up ready to leave. "There is more in the letter, but you can read that after I leave. We are moving to a new house and Diane is going to live with us for a while and help with the kids until they are older and we get better. I never liked her before, but she's been really great and I'm really glad to have her help, even though she still won't stop calling me Mickey."

"I'm glad," Brian said. "It's part of her healing too, I think. I thank God."

"I do too," Mick said as he stood, shook Brian's hand, and walked out, shutting the door behind him.

Pastor Brian spun his chair around facing the window. He leaned back and put his feet on the desk. He slipped his finger into the envelope and tore it open along the seam. There was a handwritten letter inside, and when Brian unfolded it a check dropped out and landed on his chest. He read the letter:

Dear Pastor Matterson,

From me and Diane and the kids I want to say thank you for all you did for us. We will never forget how hard you worked to get us out of trouble. Thank you very, very much. We will never forget you for that.

Inside this letter is a check for $35,000. This is money that Candy had in an account. I don't know where all this money came from, but I'm pretty sure some of it was from them fundraisers you did at the church for her when she got sick and you helped us. As it turns out, she really wasn't sick all those times. She had a problem with faking sickness and we mostly knew about it but were too ashamed to say anything. Please don't tell anyone because we would rather keep this quiet. We all feel so bad about it, but we feel giving this money to the church helps us feel better. Also, Candy had stolen some money from the police department, but when we tried to give it back, they told us that insurance had taken care of it and they would rather us just keep the money and that we should let this go quietly and not drag Candy's name through the mud. We don't feel good about keeping it, so we want the church to have it. I hope that's okay.

Anyway, we are very glad for your help and we are all glad to be in church again. It feels really good. And thanks for helping me believe in God again.

Sincerely, Mick Vinter

Brian plucked the check from his chest and stared. It was signed by Mick, and sure enough, the amount was for an even $35,000. Brian then reached over and grabbed a sheet of paper from his desk and held it up next to the check. It was the official estimate for the repair of the roof to begin that week. It was for $34,355. He next thought of the coffeemaker repair of $645. Added to the roof estimate, it came to an even $35,000.

He looked up to the picture of the contemplating Jesus above his window, and smiled. *Is this fun for you?*

Taking a deep breath, he felt a sense of awe deep in his soul. With his heart full of gratitude, he let his gaze fall on the scene outside the window. The trees were starting to bud. He looked for the bag in the tree across the street, but it was gone. He grinned and stretched his arms overhead, ready to . . .

Suddenly, his door burst open.

It was Barney.

"Pastor! You are not going to *believe* what them kids did down in the youth room . . ."